Bark to the Future

Susan C. Daffron

An Alpine Grove Romantic Comedy

Book 5

Published by Magic Fur Press
An imprint of Logical Expressions, Inc.
P.O. Box 383
Ponderay, ID 83852

Bark to the Future

ISBN: 978-1-61038-031-7 (paperback)
       978-1-61038-032-4 (EPUB)

Like all of my books, *Bark to the Future* is dedicated to
my husband James Byrd,
my best friend and biggest supporter.
Thanks for everything!

<u>Books by Susan C. Daffron</u>
The Alpine Grove Romantic Comedies
Chez Stinky

Fuzzy Logic

The Art of Wag

Snow Furries

Bark to the Future

Howl at the Loon

The Good, the Bad, and the Pugly

The Treasure of the Hairy Cadre

The Luck of the Paw

Daydream Retriever

The Hound of Music

The Jennings & O'Shea Mysteries
Sensing Trouble

Sensing Secrets

Sensing Truth

Chapter 1

Now What?

"Everyone knows that high-school reunions are just a panoply of artifice, Mom." Elizabeth Connolly twisted the phone cord in her hand, trying to contain her exasperation. "Maybe I haven't explained my position clearly to you, but I have no intention of ever seeing those people again. And it's absurd to have a ten-year reunion in the wrong year. It's 1996 now. My esteemed classmates need to abandon the idea that a decade has passed. It has been eleven years since 1985. At this point, it's time to move on. Maybe they can be a bit more organized about the fifteen-year celebration."

"Please don't get agitated, dear." Her mother sighed. "You don't have to start using words from the unabridged dictionary. I'm just letting you know that a couple of your classmates stopped by the store and asked me about it."

"I don't want to talk to anyone I went to high school with. Ever." Beth clenched the receiver in her fist. Her habit of selecting precise words was better than the alternative. Unintelligible stuttering mumbles were a turn-off to just about everyone. Mom had to know that even the idea of the inevitable social interactions of a reunion struck terror into her introverted soul.

"Beth, be reasonable. You were the valedictorian and they want you to be there because you made that wonderful speech at graduation. And it's not fair to blame them for the timing.

You know that because of the big Thanksgiving blizzard, the reunion had to be rescheduled."

"But to February? What are they thinking? No one wants to go to Alpine Grove in February."

"That's not true, dear. There are skiers clomping about everywhere in those huge furry boots. They love it here and book sales are finally starting to inch back up again, which is a relief. It was a great holiday season at the store, but then there's always the inevitable slow period afterward."

"You know I detest winter. All the snow, cold, and gray. It's dreadful." Beth pulled the elastic out of her hair and ran her fingers through the long mahogany strands, tugging at an errant tangle.

"Oh, you should see it! Right now, it's so pretty. After all the storms in November and December, the weather seems to have calmed down. It has been sunny and the skiers tell me that the conditions are fantastic."

"I don't relish skiing-related activities. You know that."

"Maybe you could try it again? I'd love to see you for my birthday too. It's been so long since you've been home, and I know you've been working too hard. I'm worried about you."

"I'm fine." Beth took off her glasses and rubbed her eyes. It had been a long day at work with countless petty co-worker disputes. The pounding in her temples was finally starting to subside. It had been such a relief to take her contact lenses out. "We have a big product launch coming up. I'm ensuring that the solution is viable and managing a lot of people and processes that affect the critical path." Oops. Mom hated it when she degenerated into corporate geek-speak. But after so many hours of being immersed in the lingo, relaxing was a struggle.

Her mother paused and finally replied evenly, "I know your job is important, dear, but this is a big birthday for me. Sixty is an important milestone. I'm officially going to be old."

"I know you're just being facetious, but please don't say that. You're not old. Unless you've been withholding significant health information from me, it's unlikely you're going to transform into a decrepit senior citizen overnight." Beth's mother was her best friend in the whole world. Mom was going to have to defy all odds and live to be at least 120 years old.

"I just miss you, dear. Please think about a visit. Bea Sullivan is throwing a big birthday party for me and I'd love it if you were there. Bea knows everyone, and it sounds like she has invited half the town."

"You know I miss you too. I'll try, but please don't assume I can attend. Getting to Alpine Grove in the winter months can be problematic. Maybe I could visit in the spring after the snow and mud are gone. I know it's a bit premature, but I hope you have a happy birthday."

There was a thump and Beth could hear her mother say, "Oh Arlo, what have you done?" She came back on the line and said, "Beth, I have to go now. Arlo has made a mess and I need to clean it up before the stain sets into the poor old dining-room rug."

"Okay. I'll call you on your birthday." Beth hung up the phone and rested her arms on the table. Her mother's insistence on a visit was unusual and decidedly worrisome. Maybe she *should* visit, since it had been a while. But going back to her hometown always brought back memories Beth preferred to forget.

She leaned her head down on her arms. Sometimes her mother was not forthcoming with information, preferring to dwell in the realm of idle chitchat. Margaret Connelly's ability to engage in small talk helped her sell more books, but it could be frustrating to Beth sometimes.

Maybe there was something important Mom wasn't disclosing. That would be typical. To be fair, Beth hadn't been exaggerating about her work responsibilities. She had so much to do at work before the launch at the end of the month. Weeks of long hours were taking a toll, and she was exhausted. But right now, it was probably freezing in Alpine Grove. The average February temperature in Tucson was 70.5 degrees. This was the time of year when everyone *wanted* to be here in the desert. Certainly not when it was 102 in July.

It was never a good idea to dwell on high-school memories. Beth knew better, but talking to her mother brought it all back. Realistically, Beth had spent most of high school just wanting it to be over so she could get out of Alpine Grove. But there was a lot her mother didn't know, particularly about what happened the summer after senior year. Because Beth had been the "super brain" of the class and painfully shy, most people just ignored her and left her alone. The feeling was mutual. Most of the students in the Cedar County High School class of 1985 didn't matter one way or another to her. But there was one person in particular Beth didn't want to see ever again.

Beth leaned her head back on the sofa and put her arm over her eyes, as if blocking the light could block her thoughts as well. That summer after graduation was unlike any other time in her life. A decade later, she still dreamed about it all the time. It had been a magical summer and so many things had changed for her. But by the time fall rolled around, Beth knew she had to leave Alpine Grove and get on with her life. She had to be a grown up. Maybe what she'd done was cowardly. But in the end, she had made the right choice, even if the way she had gone about it hadn't been ideal. Back then, she had huge opportunities ahead of her with the full scholarship to the University of Arizona and everything that followed it.

Intellectually, Beth had no doubts about the decisions she'd made ten years ago because they all led to where she was now. Being a manager at Research Technology Processing or "RTP," one of the largest technology companies in the United States, was intellectually challenging and financially rewarding. She had her own house, a brilliant boyfriend who was a professor at the University of Arizona, and a fantastic job with limitless potential for advancement. Plus, thanks to generous employment benefits that included tuition reimbursement, she was finally getting close to finishing her PhD. All of her youthful dreams had come true. What more could any woman want? And yet, even with all her accomplishments, she still found herself wondering 'what if' more often than she cared to admit.

Of course, the quixotic side of herself that she endeavored to suppress at work secretly thought it might be fun to go back to Alpine Grove just to show everyone that the odd bookish girl who never talked to anyone actually had made something of herself.

Beth pushed herself up off the couch and smiled. It would be even more satisfying if all the cheerleaders had gotten fat.

The next morning, Beth drove south from her house on the east side of Tucson to the science and technology park. The road trailed through the desert, and saguaros zipped by her windows. As the Santa Catalina Mountains receded behind her, it seemed the desert was especially colorful and bright in the crisp early morning sunshine. She was looking forward to seeing Graham after work. She actually was going to leave work on time because they planned to go out to dinner at a new restaurant. The last time they'd scheduled a date, he'd had to cancel at the last minute. Because of their busy work schedules, it seemed like it had been a long time since she'd seen him.

After another long day of herding cats, as the programmers liked to say at RTP, Beth returned to worrying about her conversation with her mother as she drove to meet Graham at the Mexican restaurant. Sitting at interminable traffic lights gave her lots of time for more pointless rumination. Finally, she'd had enough of her own thoughts. It was time to stop dwelling on high school and Alpine Grove. What was wrong with her?

At the restaurant, Beth walked through the huge wooden doors and waved to Graham as she crossed the room toward the table. He stood up and pulled out a chair for her. Beth always felt a little twinge of pride that she was dining with such a handsome and brilliant man. When she had met Graham, the intellectually stimulating conversations they'd had were so refreshing. At the time, it had felt like she was finally dating a grown-up.

Beth loved the color of his deep dark-brown eyes and the way his wavy brown hair flowed back from his forehead. There were a few gray hairs at his temples that she knew distressed him, but she thought it was dashing, in a young Sean Connery or Harrison Ford way. It was clear that he would be one of those men who would segue nicely from good-looking to distinguished as he got older.

Graham put his hand on her shoulder and bent to kiss her cheek as she sat down. "Hello Beth. You look lovely this evening."

"Thank you. It's so good to see you again. I enjoy talking on the phone with you, but it's not the same as seeing you in person." She leaned across the table to put her hand on his. "Shall we go to my house after dinner? From here, it's probably closer than yours."

He interlaced his fingers with hers. "I'm afraid I can't tonight, darling. I have a meeting bright and early tomorrow morning and it wouldn't look good if I don't attend."

"I thought faculty meetings were on Thursdays."

Graham smiled. "Never question the vagaries of the academic environment. It's ephemeral and sometimes even a bit whimsical, given to flights of fancy."

"You mean Gerald got the bright idea to call a staff meeting on a different day?"

"Yes, but he's the head of the department and he made a special point to me about being there." He squeezed her hand. "So how was your day?"

Beth shook her head. "Busy. Stressful because of the launch. But I think there's something more going on. I was glad not to work late tonight for a change. There's an undercurrent of anxiety that's perplexing to me. Of course, I'm not privy to the activities in the higher echelons of the company, but many employees seem to be huddled and whispering more than usual. I don't think it's my imagination."

He let go of her hand and gestured dismissively. "Beth, we've talked about this before. You know how you fret about being socially awkward. That makes you overly sensitive to the reactions of other people. You always think people are talking about you, and they're not. I'm sure it's nothing but idle water-cooler chitchat."

"I hope you're right. I know there are always rumors of RAs at a big company like RTP. And it's certainly not like the employee counts haven't dropped during my tenure there."

Graham waved to attract the attention of a waiter and turned back to Beth. "It's ridiculous that they can't call a layoff what it really is: a firing. A euphemism like 'resource action' or 'RA' is just insulting to people whose lives are affected by big-company politics and stock machinations."

The waiter arrived and Graham ordered for both of them. Beth enjoyed the fact that he always knew just what she wanted. Nothing too hot, since too much jalapeno could lead to digestive discomfort for her. He could be so thoughtful about little details like that.

Graham caught Beth up on the latest university gossip until their meal arrived. After the waiter set down the enchiladas on the table, Beth said, "Oh, you'll find this amusing. My mother wants me to go to my high-school reunion. I guess some of my classmates have stopped by the bookstore asking after me."

Graham knit his brows. "Good heavens Beth, why does your mother care?"

"Alpine Grove is like that. Everyone knows everyone. Because I was the valedictorian, I guess they think it's important for me to be at the ten-year reunion."

"But you graduated in 1985."

"Yes, I did. They had to postpone it."

"Well, that's a bit odd."

Beth gripped her necklace, her fingertips fiddling with the pendant at the end of the chain. "My hometown is a little odd in some ways, I suppose."

"So you've told me. I can't imagine you wanting to go back there. You've moved well beyond small-town life."

"I was thinking it could actually be enjoyable if you went with me. In all the time you've known me, you've still never been to Alpine Grove."

Graham raised his eyebrows. "I think I'll pass on a trip to sleepy rural America, thank you."

"It's not that bad. You make Alpine Grove sound like some uncivilized wasteland, but many of the people who live there are very pleasant."

"You certainly haven't made it sound like it is redolent with excitement. More like a bastion of dive bars."

"Well no one will mistake the Mystic Moon Saloan for a cultural way station, particularly since the owner can't spell saloon correctly." Beth speared a piece of her enchilada with her fork. "But Alpine Grove is where I grew up. It's part of my history. And I've always wanted you to meet my mother. I'm sure you'd be enjoy conversing with her—your literary interests are quite compatible. She's extremely well-read."

"I would certainly assume so, after so many years of owning a bookstore."

Beth looked down at her half-eaten meal. Yes, she was from a little town in the middle of nowhere, and she wasn't as sophisticated as most people Graham knew. But not only had he not met her mother, she hadn't met any member of his family, either. It had been more than six years now. Yes, they'd had problems, but also some good times, particularly when they first met.

Most of the time, Beth had no clue what Graham was thinking or how he felt. Although she tried to be honest and minimize misunderstandings, her efforts often failed. She was so bad at relationships. It was probably her fault he had never wanted to commit to anything. So they just kept seeing each other informally, taking the opportunity to enjoy evenings together when their busy schedules permitted it.

Every once in a while, it seemed like he wanted to move their relationship to the next level, but every time she thought he was going to tell her how he felt, he gave her jewelry instead. Other times, after they'd had an awful fight, she had been convinced he never wanted to see her again. Then he'd call as if nothing had happened.

She twisted the chain of her necklace in her fingers. Men were so confusing. Today was one of those days when it felt like she didn't understand Graham at all. Realistically, Beth wasn't known for her keen social skills. Most of the time she didn't understand most *people*, male or female. A social butterfly she was not. More like a social cockroach, doomed to be shunned even after successfully outlasting dinosaurs.

Graham pointed at her with his fork. "Beth, aren't you enjoying your enchilada? The spicing is quite traditional. It reminds me of the food I had on that trip I took to Mazatlan. Very authentic."

Beth looked up. Graham hadn't invited her on that vacation. "It's fine. I'm just not very hungry. I'm a little concerned about what my mother said when I talked to her."

"About the reunion? That's just not smart, Beth. You told me what high school was like for you. I'm sure the small-town social dynamics will move on to other topics and your mother will get over it. You're not a teenager anymore. You don't have to do everything your mother suggests."

"I know." Beth put down her fork and put her hands in her lap. "You're right. That's what I told her. But her birthday is coming up, and she asked if I would come visit. Even though I live far away, we've stayed close and I feel bad to be missing the celebration. She rarely asks me to do anything like that, so I'm worried there's something else going on."

"Oh Beth, you always concern yourself with trivial worries about nothing. You know you have a lot of work to do for the launch."

"I know." Even the thought of going back to work the next day was exhausting.

"You should focus on your responsibilities. I'm sure your mother understands that."

"You're right. I know. I'm just being silly." But Beth couldn't shake the feeling that something bad was going to happen, and that she should go to Alpine Grove.

～

The next morning, Beth settled into work at her desk and logged into the company intranet. They were using a new system that connected all employees and gave them unprecedented access to communication and collaboration tools. She could see who else was working on the intranet at any time as well. This was such an exciting time to be in technology, and RTP was launching a new line of systems that were specifically designed to help employees work together in new ways. Beth found she was actually looking forward to the launch so she could talk more freely about the new technology with other people.

She typed her password into the screen and went through her e-mail. There was a missive marked "high importance" that she opened first. It was a list of names and a draft of a letter that needed to be reviewed. She noticed that her name was on the list in the e-mail and then saved the attachment so she could provide her comments on the letter.

As she read through the letter, her stomach clenched. It was a draft of an employee resource action notification. After the deep cuts in 1993, Beth had thought things were better. Back then RTP had slashed 50,000 workers. And that was only a few years after the devastating layoffs in Tucson, when they shuttered the storage-manufacturing facility. After those two major restructuring events, Beth had thought her job was safe.

The letter was quite detailed and to the point. A portion of her division was being moved offshore. Unless she wanted to re-apply for her job and move to Bangalore, she would receive two week's pay for each six months of service. The cuts were necessary to ensure shareholder value and keep earnings per share at the desired level.

Beth stared at her monitor, not quite believing what she was reading. This couldn't be happening. Her whole career and life revolved around RTP. She loved the company. They'd recruited her right out of college, and being an RTPer and a member of the Blue Wave was part of her professional identity.

What was she going to do?

One thing she definitely was *not* going to do was write comments on a draft letter telling her that her own job had been eliminated. They had to be kidding. Obviously somebody had made a rather serious addressing error on this e-mail. Beth looked at the addressee list and noticed the mistake. It was likely that after this major gaffe, Rachel would probably be getting her own resource action letter too.

Beth stood up in a daze. She needed to talk to her manager and see if this was all some terrible mistake. Picking up the phone, she dialed Joan's extension. When her boss picked up, Beth said simply, "Joan, I need to see you. I'll be in your office momentarily," and hung up.

As she walked down the long carpeted hallway, it was as if the photographs of the products, CEOs, and distinguished engineers were mocking her. Maybe this was all some type of terrible joke. Or maybe her name had been a misprint. An accident. It had to be.

She got to the door marked "Joan Bailey" and tapped lightly before walking inside, closing the door, and standing in front of the desk. Joan looked up at her. "Beth, what has gotten into you? You know my schedule is jammed. I have a call in ten minutes with the guys in China."

"Joan, I just got an e-mail that I need to discuss with you."

"Can't it wait?"

"No. It really can't. I need to know if I'm being RA-ed."

Joan's eyebrows shot up and a look of horror flashed in her eyes. "How do you know about that?"

"Rachel sent an e-mail asking managers to review the draft RA letter. However, it appears I'm on the RA list. Needless to say, I'm not going to review a letter telling me my job has been sent overseas. Is this actually true?"

There was a pounding on the door. Beth looked over her shoulder and saw the silhouettes of several of her co-workers, who were standing beyond the glass panel next to the door frame. Joan nodded at Beth. "I'm afraid so. I'm really sorry, Beth."

"I think you should reschedule that call." Beth waved toward the door. "My name was not the only one on that misdirected e-mail. It looks like you have quite a few people to talk to now. I'm going to go pack my things."

"Wait, you can't just leave. What about the launch?"

Beth paused and placed her hands on her hips. "Joan, you can't seriously believe that I'm going to invest energy into the launch at this point. Perhaps you can ask my replacement in India to do it. Right now, I need to go home and update my resume." What resume? She barely even *had* a resume.

Joan stood up. "But we haven't hired anyone yet! Come on Beth, we've been friends for a long time. I need you."

"I'm sorry Joan. There's no way. I was putting off a trip until after the launch, but now that things have changed so… so *dramatically*, I'm going to go to my hometown. My mother wants me to visit her. I also need to talk to my professors about my classes at the university. You know how hard it is to find a job in Tucson. I'll have to find a new job and probably move, so I need to drop my classes before the cut-off."

"Beth, you can't do that. We have to do a knowledge transfer!"

"I'll take my laptop with me. You can e-mail me if you have a question you believe I can answer. I should be back in Tucson in approximately a week. I'll let you know when I return." Beth paused at the door and looked back at Joan. Her shoulders slumped as she locked her gaze with her now-former boss. "Joan, I've invested my entire working life into this company. I'm sorry, but I just can't be here right now. I need to go home and process this development. Otherwise,

I'll start to cry right here in your office. And frankly, I'd prefer not to be found weeping at work. It's not professional."

She sniffed hurriedly, ducked her head, and left, weaving her way through the crowd outside Joan's office. She walked briskly down the hallway, but it was difficult not to break into a run to get to her own cubbyhole more quickly.

After she got to her space, she grabbed a few things and her purse and scurried out of the building. As she opened her car door, the first tears started streaming down her face. She dug into her purse and grabbed a fistful of tissues out of the little travel pack before letting herself start to sob. She squeezed her eyes shut and covered them with her palms, hoping her contact lenses wouldn't float out of place or pop out.

What was she going to do now?

After crying in the parking lot for a while, desperately hoping no one saw her, Beth collected herself enough to drive home. She felt slightly nauseated and headachy after all the sobbing. Taking out her contacts and putting on her glasses and ugly sweatpants would feel so good. All she wanted to do was curl up on the sofa and escape into a novel for a while.

Working at RTP hadn't been just a job for her. Most of her life had revolved around the company. She had started work at RTP right after college and never considered working anywhere else. When was the last time she'd even considered updating her resume? She'd never had to look for a job before. With the exception of Graham and a few other people at the university, all of the people she knew worked at RTP. Beth had intended to work for RTP for the rest of her professional life. Countless people she worked with had been there for decades and she'd had no reason to believe her career there would be any different.

At least the unemployment rate wasn't terrible at the moment. Economic indicators were better than they'd been in some time. But to find work, she'd probably have to leave Tucson, since RTP was virtually the only high-tech employer in the area. Where would she go? She'd have to sell her house. The whole concept of uprooting her life and starting over was terrifying. It had taken her years to become comfortable with her colleagues at RTP. Now she'd have to completely start over at a new company that was filled with people she didn't know.

But first, she needed to talk to Mom. That was the extraordinary thing about mothers—they were always there to console you when the chips were down. And right now the chips had reached a new low point. Mom had comforted her countless times when she was growing up. Usually it involved some dreadful social situation that Beth had botched.

Of course, there was also the humiliation of those horrible presidential fitness tests when she could only do one pull-up. And the incident when she had killed the terrarium that was supposed to be her sixth-grade science project. Mom was so supportive and assured her it wouldn't be the end of her academic career. It hadn't been, although it was notable that Mom never asked Beth to care for any of her plants.

After Beth's father left Alpine Grove when she was eight, it had been just Beth and her mom against the world. She rarely saw her father, who had a whole new family in Vermont. Growing up, most of the hours she wasn't in school, Beth was busy helping her mother at the bookstore. All that reading time probably contributed to the perfect score she'd gotten on the verbal portion of the SATs. Getting lost in fictional worlds also helped Beth forget about her social inadequacies and the general stupidity of school. The day-to-day life of a brainy, uncool loser was depressing. Anne of Green Gables never had those problems.

Beth smiled at the idea of spending time in the bookstore again. When she walked in, the unique aroma of old paper that pervaded the store was always comforting, somehow. Although Twice Told Tales mostly focused on used books, her mother had a small collection of new best-sellers and greeting cards, along with a few gift items. Margaret Connolly was brilliant at setting up creative displays of books and local crafts so they looked enticing. Mom had an amazing ability to take something pedestrian like an ugly quilted tea cozy and make it look adorable. Her mother also had a knack for finding the best lines of greeting cards. Customers would stand in front of the card display for hours just chuckling at the most entertaining ones. The store was a fixture in Alpine Grove, thanks to her mother's many years of dedication.

Beth opened the door to her house and spent more time than usual observing the nuances of the little brick bungalow. What if she had to move? Although the house wasn't really any different from countless other desert homes built in the seventies, it was hers. She'd had the flooring re-done in dark rich hardwood and a landscaper had come in and installed a pergola for her backyard. Although most of the plants were southwest natives that didn't need much water, her one indulgence had been a set of water misters installed on the pergola. During the scorching depths of summer, she'd sit outside in the shade, turn on the misters, and enjoy the little cool oasis she'd created in her backyard.

Beth washed her face, removed her contacts, and tried to pull herself together a bit more before calling her mother. She dialed the number and smiled when she heard her mother's voice. "Hi Mom."

"Beth! I'm so glad to hear from you so soon. I know you're busy. How is the launch going?"

She cleared her throat. "Um...well...I'm...I'm not quite as busy as one might imagine."

"Bethie, are you all right? What's wrong? What happened?"

"I was RA-ed. I haven't even fully comprehended what that means yet!" Beth sniffed and grabbed a tissue from the box. "Laid off, I mean. F...F...Fired! RTP calls a layoff a resource action. An RA. Whatever. I was *terminated*. They are shipping my job off to someone in India."

"Oh honey, I'm so sorry. Is there anything I can do?"

"No. But I want to get away from here. Is your invitation still open? I'd love to see you. I could come for your birthday, now that I don't have to worry about work responsibilities. It would be nice to see Bea again too. She's always been such a kind person, even when I was little. I promise I'll try to cope with the cold and the snow without too much complaint."

Her mother chuckled. "Well that would be a first. Of course you can visit. And I know you don't like the cold, but it really has been lovely here. I wasn't just saying that. It will be so wonderful to see you, dear. We'll relax and have a good time. I just got a great new shipment of books at the store. Don't worry, everything will be okay. You'll find a new job."

Beth pulled off her glasses and wiped her eyes with a tissue. "I know. Thanks. It's just right now it doesn't feel like it. I've never looked for a job before. I don't even have a decent resume. But I'm looking forward to spending some time there, clearing my head. I'll take some walks with Arlo too. That always helps."

"He is a sympathetic little fellow. Walking him gives you lots of time to think, because he doesn't go very fast."

"I don't suppose his digestion has improved, has it?"

"No. The vet says he has an irritable bowel."

"I'm afraid it might be time to concede defeat on the rug, Mom."

Her mother laughed. "I know. Maybe we can shop for a new one while you're here."

"I'd enjoy that. I'll get my flights set up and let you know the details. I'm looking forward to seeing you."

"You too, Bethie. I love you."

Beth hung up the phone and started planning her trip. After traumatic events, talking to her mother always made her feel better. Now she needed to get plane reservations and a rental car. Unfortunately, at this time of year she really should rent a four-wheel drive in case it snowed. That would be an expensive proposition. Good thing RTP was giving her that severance package. She was going to need it.

Beth shook her head in wonder. How could everything change so much in just one day? At least her mother hadn't mentioned the reunion. Just because she was going to Alpine Grove did not mean she had to go compare notes with her former classmates. The thought made her shudder, particularly now that she wasn't gainfully employed anymore. All the disapproving looks and critical comments would be just too humiliating.

Of course, if people came back for the event, they might be wandering around town too. What if she ran into them?

Certain people from her past really needed to stay in the past. It was all too easy to imagine herself ducking behind a giant snow bank to avoid someone. She'd done it before, after all. Fortunately, she'd heard almost nothing about her classmates since 1985, so odds were good that most of them wouldn't show up. People had probably moved on. Maybe Graham was right. She shouldn't give in to unfounded fears and feelings that had no basis in fact.

Beth's intuition had been appallingly accurate about the layoff though. She sighed. That was not a concept she wanted to ponder right now. Enough! It was time to get organized for her trip.

Chapter 2

Adjustments

For Beth, the next few days were filled with tasks related to her new status as a member of the unemployed. She dropped her university classes for the semester and attempted to set up a meeting with her adviser to explain her situation. Maybe she should just settle for a master's degree and give up on the PhD and her dissertation. It all seemed pointless now.

Although Beth loved school, now that she didn't work at RTP, getting an advanced degree was unlikely to help her career in the future. RTP was one of the only companies doing the type of advanced research that justified having a PhD. She had always quietly hoped that she might receive one of the coveted RTP honorary designations or receive an award from the Women in Technology group, like one of the general managers had. What an honor that would be. But all that was over. She needed to stop dwelling on what might have been.

Beth called Graham and told him that she needed to cancel their Valentine's Day date because of her trip to Alpine Grove. She apologized and explained about the resource action. He was initially surprised that RTP had "canned her so egregiously," but then he went on a long tirade about corporate greed, the lack of ethics among the RTP leadership team, and the decline and fall of capitalism in America. Thank goodness Graham couldn't see her face over the phone, because it was hard to hide her annoyance. Sometimes a girl needed a little sympathy, not a big philosophical rant.

He wasn't the greatest listener on a good day, but she'd just lost her job, for heaven's sake. Couldn't he be at least slightly interested in how she felt? It was also more than a bit irritating that he seemed to care so little about their Valentine's Day plans. She had agonized about the best way to break the news to him. Perhaps she shouldn't have been so circumspect.

The flight from Tucson to Los Angeles was mercifully short. Thanks to her last-minute reservation, Beth managed to get the worst seat on the plane. There was a reason no one wanted the last row with the non-reclining seats next to the lavatories. Beth hid behind her book and pretended not to notice people. But by the end of the flight, she knew far more about the toilet habits of her fellow passengers than she ever wanted to know. It was a relief to walk into the LAX terminal and merge into the crowd of anonymous travelers.

After signing paperwork and giving the rental agency what seemed like an exorbitant amount of money for a shiny new Ford Explorer, she headed away from the city. Driving up the mountain toward Alpine Grove, Beth was overwhelmed with memories. She had named various turns along the winding road when she was little. She passed by 'Deer Meadow,' where large ungulates tended to gather and 'Skippy Corner,' where she'd once seen a peanut-butter-colored young bear. Everything was covered with snow now, but it was easy to imagine the familiar areas in every season. As she drove down the main street of town, she was struck again by how little things seemed to change. It appeared that the old Frederickson's building was being restored, but other than that, Alpine Grove seemed untouched by the passage of time. A number of staple businesses like Bea Haven Gifts and her mom's bookstore, Twice Told Tales, looked exactly the same as they had ten or twenty years ago.

She turned down a side street and drove to her mother's house, where she'd grown up. The old house had been built in 1909 and its gray clapboard siding and white trim looked as neat and tidy as ever. Underneath the snow, Beth knew her mother had tended to all the plants, carefully shutting down the garden so her favorite perennial flowers would live to bloom another year.

The house had a gambrel roof and white columns that held up a little overhang above the front door. After reading *Gone With the Wind* when she was twelve years old, Beth thought the columns were "the coolest" because Tara had columns too. Although it certainly wasn't plantation size, the unusual entry did set the house apart from the other houses in the old neighborhood. Grabbing her luggage from the backseat, Beth got out and went up the walkway and the three steps to the front door. As she entered the home, she was greeted by the sounds of her mother's Shetland sheepdog Arlo, barking indignantly from the kitchen where he'd been confined behind a tall wooden baby gate.

"Hi Arlo. It's just me."

The dog started bounding around happily behind the gate. Beth clicked the latch and let it swing open so he could run out into the living room. "Do you want to walk down to the store and say hi to Mom?"

Arlo expressed his agreement loudly and ran around in a circle, clearly thrilled at the prospect of an unscheduled walk. Beth grabbed an old heavy winter coat from the hall closet and the dog's leash from the hook next to the door.

Snapping the leash onto his collar, she said, "Okay, buddy, are you ready to embark?" Beth giggled at his single bark in response. Arlo was up for any excuse to be vocal. It was such a sheltie thing.

Locking the door behind her, Beth stepped back outside into the sunny, cold afternoon. It obviously hadn't snowed lately, because all the sidewalks and roads were completely clear. The temperature was in the low thirties, which was warm for Alpine Grove in February, but it didn't exactly feel balmy to Beth. Too many years of enjoying the desert sunshine had 'thinned her blood,' as people liked to say. Now she was the type of serious cold wimp who used to get teased back when she lived here. Fortunately, her mother had a vast collection of outerwear, and every coat had at least two pairs of gloves rammed in the pockets, so Beth was ready for anything.

The house was five blocks away from the main street of town where the bookstore was located. As Beth and Arlo meandered along the familiar tree-lined sidewalks, she recalled all the times she'd walked this way before. Arlo was not exactly a speed walker, so Beth had lots of time to survey the neighborhood. Nothing much had changed. When she was growing up, every day after school she went to the bookstore, did her homework, read, and sometimes helped out with store-related tasks, depending on what her mother was doing. After the store closed, she and her mother would stroll through the neighborhood and discuss the events of the day.

Even though she'd visited her mother in Alpine Grove a number of times since she'd moved away, everything seemed different now. Maybe it was because Beth's life was at such a crossroads. For the first time ever, Beth had no idea what was going to happen next. Most of the time she'd been in school, she was thinking about graduating and getting a scholarship so she could go to college. And then during college, she focused on doing well, so she could get a good job afterward. She'd worked hard for years and everything had just fallen naturally into place. Until it all fell apart. Being laid off had nothing to do with how well you did. No one cared if you got straight As or fantastic performance reviews when someone in India was willing to do the same job for vastly less money.

As she grieved the loss of her job and the life she'd created in Tucson, it was hard not to feel bitter and angry at RTP. Intellectually, she knew the company had been good to her for years, and now she had a great severance package, so she had plenty of time to figure out what she was going to do. But she was at loose ends. There were no deadlines. No one was depending on her insights and intimate knowledge of specialized technology. Suddenly, there was just nothing.

Sighing at her spiraling depressing thoughts, Beth turned onto the main street of town with Arlo leading the way. He was obviously excited that they were heading toward the bookstore. In front of the old Frederickson's building, a woman who looked somewhat familiar was walking toward Beth. Of course, for anyone who had grown up in Alpine Grove, it seemed like you half-recognized just about everyone. At least the sense of knowing every single person in town was no longer quite as oppressive since Beth had been away for ten years. But odds were good that if she went to the grocery store, she'd be able to identify dozens of people and their reading habits.

Beth nodded at the pretty blonde woman, who smiled politely in return before opening the door to the stairs that went up to the second-floor offices. Beth noticed that the first floor now housed an advertising agency. That was new. The real-estate office that had been there before must have finally closed. Beth stopped and said to Arlo, "Oh, I know! That was Bea Sullivan's daughter. What was her name? Tracy?"

Arlo looked up at Beth, but didn't provide any insights. It was starting to come back. Tracy was a year younger than Beth. A member of the class of 1986 and a cheerleader. Ugh. No wonder Beth had trouble remembering who she was. Tracy didn't seem to have recognized her, either. No great surprise there. The cheerleaders traveled in a completely different social strata than Beth had. Yet another reason she was hoping Mom would not bring up the whole reunion idea again. Reliving bygone high-school days was definitely not Beth's idea of a good time.

~

Beth walked into the bookstore and smiled at the familiar scene. Her mother was sitting behind the antique writing desk she used as a counter, reading a thick hardback book. She looked up at the sound of the jangling of the bells on the door and leaped out of the chair. After deftly dodging a tall book display, she held out her arms. "Bethie! You made it!"

Beth ran into her mother's embrace, dragging Arlo behind her as he yipped in protest. Releasing the hug with a final squeeze, she said. "It was an easy trip. Arlo was exhilarated by my arrival and the unexpected stroll through the neighborhood." She bent down to stroke his head. "Right buddy?" Arlo wagged, enjoying the attention.

"I'm sure he missed you. He likes any excuse to get outside and visit with his favorite neighborhood squirrel friends."

"They seem to have a rather antagonistic relationship."

Margaret Connolly laughed heartily, her short gray curly hair bobbing around her head and swishing against her chin "I can't argue with that. I'm so glad you're here."

"Me too. I missed you." Beth looked at the book display. "New mysteries?"

"Yes. I just got in the latest Sue Grafton. She's up to L now. I think M is coming out later this year."

"Ooh, and the new Harry Bosch novel! By Michael Connolly, my favorite twin-surnamed author."

Margaret smiled. "Yes. I had a feeling you'd be excited about that. Immersing yourself in a little Michael Connolly will make you feel better. No matter what has happened in your life, it's probably better than what's going on with poor Harry these days."

Beth grinned. "Oh, don't reveal anything, Mom. I want to be surprised." She picked up another book. "E.L. Jakes?"

"Oh, you'd hate her stuff. It's just awful, but people buy it anyway."

"Okay." Beth picked up another book. "Here's another new one."

"Not really. It's probably only new to you, dear. He's written five mysteries so far. I am completely addicted to them. In fact, I've got the paperbacks of a couple at home; I'll find them for you. The main character has an unusual personality. He starts out as a cop and ends up going into detective work. There's an interesting woman and several other characters that reappear too. They're great reads."

Beth read the back flap of the book. "Hmm. A.J. Emerson. I've never heard of this person, but it certainly seems initials are in vogue for authors. Sure, I'll try them if you think they're good. It feels a little odd having no responsibilities, so a big pile of new reading material would be welcome. I'll probably need to do a lot of reading to distract myself." She looked up from the book. "I can also help out here if you want. Maybe sort and price some books? Since Janice quit, I know you've had trouble finding someone."

Margaret waved her hand toward the front window. "Oh, it's just the time of year. Everyone wants to ski. They don't want to work. I'm sure I'll find someone in the next month or so. It's just the slow season. You know we go through this every year. But the Chamber of Commerce has an idea for a Mardi Gras celebration to help stir up a little tourist activity and maybe even get locals to come out of hibernation and shop. That's not until next year though. It would be nice if it works, since the last few weeks have been slow."

"I can sympathize with the idea of hibernation. It's cold."

"Beth, you promised not to whine."

"I'm sorry. That slipped out. I'll try to curtail my weather-related grousing."

Margaret pushed a wayward curl behind her ear. "After I close the store, I'm going to take a few books down to Mrs. Oliphant. Her gout is bothering her so she hasn't been able to come in, but she called and wanted a few of these new books after I mentioned them. She was so excited, she paid for them over the phone. I told her I'd drop them by her house on my way home."

"Okay. Arlo and I will be waiting for you. I'll see what I can come up with for dinner."

"Thanks, dear. I'll see you later."

Beth walked back to the house and set to work chopping vegetables for a soup. While it was simmering, she looked around and found an old paperback that she may or may not have already read. She was settling into a nice bout of power-reading when Arlo began barking hysterically at a siren outside. "Arlo, be quiet!" The dog began to howl and race around the room. "Good grief, Arlo. Stop it!"

Beth got up as the siren wailed by. The neighborhood and Alpine Grove in general was normally so quiet, it was odd to have emergency vehicles so close. She peered out the window, but it was gone. Arlo settled back down and laid in front of the sofa looking offended. Beth sat down and stroked his back. "Sorry, buddy. I didn't realize sirens were such an issue for you."

Later, the phone rang and Beth had an awkward moment of confusion. This wasn't her home anymore. Should she answer it? Pretend no one was home and let the answering machine pick up? Shrugging, she figured she'd ask her mother about the phone protocol later. The sound of her mother's voice encouraged the caller to leave a message. Oops, it could be personal and now she was going to hear whatever the caller might say. *Sorry, Mom.*

Her mother's voice came sharply from the machine, "Beth, I know you're there. Pick up!"

Beth scrambled off the couch, grabbed the phone, and shut off the machine. "I'm sorry, Mom. I wasn't sure if I should answer."

"I need you to pick me up later."

"Okay. Are you still at Mrs. Oliphant's house?"

"No, I'm at the hospital. I fell. They are going to do x-rays, and I'm waiting now."

"What happened? Are you hurt?" Beth gripped her necklace.

Margaret cleared her throat. "This is embarrassing. I walked down there and I didn't see an ice patch and I fell on my…well…my butt. They think I may have possibly broken my tailbone."

"Your coccyx?"

"Yes. It was painful, but I'm on some rather lovely medication now, so I'm very relaxed."

"I'll be right there, Mom!" Beth ran to the kitchen and turned the heat off for the soup on the stove, gathered up her purse, stowed Arlo in the kitchen behind his gate, and ran out the door. *Please be okay, Mom!*

Beth brought her mother home from the hospital and helped her into bed. She set the bottles of pills and instructions from the doctors on the dresser. "Are you sure you feel all right? Do you want anything to eat? The soup is still sitting on the stove, and I can heat it up for you."

"No dear, I'm just tired. But we need to talk about the store. Are you sure you can handle it? I know dealing with customers isn't fun for you. Most things are the same, although I did get a new computer."

"I'll be okay." Beth pushed some books aside on a settee near the bed and sat down. "The computer won't be a problem. Is there a password I should know?"

"My initials and then Arlo. All lower case."

"I hate leaving you by yourself. Will you be okay here with Arlo?"

"Yes, I'll be fine. My dog-walker Cindy will be by for his walk, so it will be just like any other day for him, except he'll have me around to keep him company. And Jill is going to stop by on her lunch hour to check on me. It's such a relief that you're here to take care of the store."

Beth moved a book that was digging into her back and looked at it. "I'm glad you feel that way." She'd do pretty much anything to help her mother. Even subject herself to the world of retail again.

"Beth, there is one thing. I know we've talked about this before, but you need to make an effort to make customers feel comfortable."

Beth tried not to roll her eyes. "Really, Mom? Do we have to have this conversation *again*?"

"Yes, dear. You need to try to relax. Take deep breaths. You know when you are upset, nervous, or self-conscious, you start to sound like a robot."

"That's an unflattering way to describe my use of language. I prefer to think of it as being precise and taking advantage of my comprehensive vocabulary, instead of blubbering like an idiot."

"Maybe. But using ten-dollar words can confuse people and make them feel uncomfortable. People who are uncomfortable don't buy books. I know you don't like social situations and dealing with people you don't know, but please just try to use smaller words, okay?"

"I'm not in high school anymore. I deal—or I dealt—with people every day at work."

"I know, but many of them are engineers and PhDs who use lots of technical jargon and acronyms."

Beth waved the paperback in her hand toward the window. "I think you may have just insulted your customers' intelligence."

"I don't mean it like that. My customers are wonderful. Just *try* to be friendly, dear. Sometimes I know you still feel like a painfully shy little girl inside, but just do what you can to make customers feel welcome. They really aren't staring at you or judging you. I promise. They just want something good to read."

"Fine. I'll talk like a Valley Girl and you know, tell them that all the books at the store are all just like totally awesome."

"Don't be snotty, dear. I'm sure working at the store will all come back to you. Just be nice to people, and you'll do fine."

"Gag me." Beth thumped the book back onto the pile next to her. Dealing with customers again was going to be nerve-wracking. At least it was the slow season. Maybe they'd all stay home.

~

The next morning, Beth got ready to go to the store. She gave her mom her pills and helped her get set up on the sofa downstairs with lots of magazines and books to read.

"Stop hovering, Beth. You'll be late opening the store."

Beth handed her a throw pillow. "Are you sure you're okay?"

"Yes." Margaret reached over to pet Arlo, who had settled in next to her. "Please go away."

"All right, but call me if you need anything."

"I will. Good luck. Sell lots of books."

Beth left the house and walked down to the store, her mom's gigantic key ring jangling in her coat pocket. It was a pretty, sunny day and the snow along the sidewalk glistened in the morning light.

All this good weather might bring out lots of voracious readers and then she'd have to make small talk. What could she talk about? One: the weather. Two: books. Three? Was she really out of material after two topics? Beth fiddled with the keys in her pocket to give her trembling fingers something else to do. She'd done this before. It would be okay. Mom always said customers were just people. Of course, that was exactly the problem.

At least Beth could get her hands on those new books her mother had mentioned. She had years of experience in surreptitiously reading new books and making sure they stayed pristine, so they could still be sold as new. That new Michael Connolly novel looked excellent.

According to Margaret, the back room was still full of used-book inventory that needed to be sorted, priced, and shelved. Mom's forays out to the inevitable end-of-season garage sales last fall had been productive, so the storage room was bursting with books. Mom would be thrilled if Beth could help her get caught up with the sorting project. Beth might be a terrible salesperson, but at least she could try to be useful.

Beth unlocked the back door, entered the storage room, and locked the door behind her. She turned her head to look around the room. Wow. Mom wasn't kidding. Stacks of boxes filled with books were everywhere. A narrow pathway meandered through the boxes toward the front of the store. There was no way Mom could fit even one-tenth of these books into the shelves. Sorting through this mess could take most of the rest of her life.

Beth bent to open a box and peek inside. She sighed at the contents. *Mom, why do you always do this?* The box was filled with old textbooks and reference materials no one would ever want again. A complete set of the 1953 *Encyclopedia Britannica* suffering from water damage not only smelled bad, but the information was so out of date that no one would consider opening the pages ever again. Ugh.

Beth continued to the front of the store and turned to look at the clock on the wall. Five minutes until the store opened. Taking a deep breath, she pressed the power button on the computer and typed the password. The icons on the desktop included an inventory program that Beth had never seen before and spreadsheets with names that indicated they probably contained accounting information. There also was a point-of-sale program. Was Mom really using that? She had always preferred writing out receipts by hand and using the old-fashioned cash register that still sat on the writing desk. Beth pulled a notepad out of the desk drawer and began listing questions to ask her mother that evening.

Beth unlocked the front door and settled in behind the writing desk with the Michael Connolly novel she'd been eyeing the day before. She reluctantly looked away from the pages as the front-door bells jingled. She gripped the cover more tightly as a somewhat portly man with gray hair and a long overcoat walked in. Beth smiled as politely as she could. "May I help you?"

The man looked startled. "Who are you? Where is Margaret?"

Beth stood up and tried to look attentive and friendly instead of uncomfortable and panicky. "I'm Elizabeth Connolly, Margaret's daughter."

His expression was downcast. "Oh, I was hoping to see Margaret. I guess I'll just be going then."

"Did you want to look at any of our books?"

"No. 'Bye."

Beth sat back down in the chair with a thump. Even when she tried to be friendly and not behave like a mutant geek, she still seemed to repel people. You would think that after years of working on her shyness, it wouldn't still be so hard. Why couldn't she just be a normal person?

Later, the bells jangled again and Beth looked up from her reading. She had been absently spinning a pencil around in her hand and she stopped and put it down on the desk. "May I help you?"

The woman walked across the store to Beth and pointed at her. "I know you!"

Beth shook her head. "I'm sorry, have we met?"

"Beth! It's me! Danielle! We were in history class together. I'm back for the reunion."

The short woman had blonde curly hair and a face that resembled no one Beth had ever seen before. Who was this person? Beth managed a feeble smile. "Hi Danielle. It's great to see you again."

"How have you been? Do you still live here? Wasn't this your mom's store? Did you take it over?"

"Uh, no. I live in Tucson…Tucson, Arizona. I'm just visiting for my mother's birthday. It's coming up soon."

Danielle flipped back a curl from her face. "Aren't you going to come to the reunion? You *have* to come! It's this weekend, and I'm on the committee. We're going to have *such* a good time. There is going to be an eighties trivia contest and an open bar!"

"I don't think so." Beth looked down at her hands in her lap. They weren't shaking too badly. "My mother is incapacitated at the moment, so I need to help out here at the store."

"The reunion is at night." Danielle turned her head to look out the plate glass window. "Unless things have radically changed, nothing in Alpine Grove is open past five, except the dive bars."

"Oh. Well, that's true. But I should assist her at home too."

Danielle's eyes widened. "Wow, is your mom really sick? Like, is she going to *die*? It's fatal isn't it? Oh Beth, I'm so sorry! I'll tell everyone on the reunion committee. We'll send her flowers!"

Beth's jaw dropped. "No! Puh…please, *please* don't do that." In twenty minutes, word would spread throughout town and all of Alpine Grove was going to think her mother was at death's door. "My mother is okay. Really! She just slipped on the ice and bruised her…I mean…she bruised a bone in her back. And pulled some muscles. She just needs to rest for a few days."

Danielle gave Beth a knowing look. "Well then, that means you can come to the reunion, doesn't it?"

"I suppose so." Her shoulders slumped. *Noooo!*

"Great! I'll tell everybody. And remember, you *promised*. I'll make up a name badge for you today. We're putting everyone's yearbook picture on the badges so we can tell who is who."

Beth tried not to cringe. "That sounds like a good idea." Maybe she'd figure out who Danielle actually was at this execrable event. She cleared her throat, hoping it would indicate a change of subject. "So are you interested in finding a particular book?"

"No, I'm just going to look around. I sort of forgot that there's nothing to do here and my husband ditched me for the afternoon."

Beth pointed at the display of mysteries. "The new Michael Connelly novel is out. It's one of the ones with the character of Harry Bosch. I'm reading it and it's quite good."

Danielle's curls bobbed back and forth. "Never heard of him. Oh, but here's one from A.J. Emerson. His stuff is totally awesome!" She picked up a book and handed it to Beth. "Check out the photo on the back cover too. Isn't he a hottie?"

Beth flipped the book over. "Well, that's certainly an artificial-looking studio shot. It's clearly a spurious representation of an idealized novelist."

"What?"

Beth held the photo up in front of her. "Don't you think that photo looks fake?"

"No!" Danielle shook her head vigorously. "I know A.J. Emerson is totally real. That's him. I'm positive! I read an interview in *People* magazine with him, and he even sounds hot. There's sexy stuff in the books too, so he's just got to be scorching. I'm sure of it."

"Would you like a receipt?" Beth held up the little book, flapping the carbonless pages back and forth.

"No. I don't need a bag either. I'm just going to walk back to the hotel and start reading. My husband is watching the game at the 311. Ten minutes in town and he's already at the scuzziest bar with the cheapest beer."

"I guess you don't like sports?"

"Beth! I was a cheerleader, remember? Of *course*, I like sports. But I don't like the 311. It's still disgusting. Even more disgusting than the H12 motel. I can't believe Glenn wouldn't spring for a room at the Enchanted Moose. That's where the reunion is and I'm on the committee! Now I have to drive all the way out there, back and forth."

"I'm sorry." The drive had to be at least fifteen whole minutes with all that bumper-to-bumper Alpine Grove rush-hour traffic. Sheesh.

Danielle looked up at the clock on the wall. "It's getting late—I should go! I am not going to have time to read Mr. Dreamy's book, after all. I need to go drag Glenn out of the bar and get to The Moose. There's a meeting of the decorating committee."

A flash of memory hit Beth. "Wait, you're married to Glenn *Eisenhower*?"

"Of course. Don't you remember? He was my high school sweetheart. We have three kids now, but fortunately they're back in Tulsa with their grandma. So we're gonna par-teee! I can't wait! I'll see you on Saturday."

Beth sat back down heavily. This was unbelievable. That manipulative cheerleader had actually talked her into going to the reunion. Mom had better appreciate the fact that she'd agreed to go to this idiotic event for her, because if she hadn't, Danielle would have busied herself planning Margaret's funeral.

~

At the end of the day, Beth gleefully locked the door of the bookstore and walked back home. One day over with! After the skittish man and the cheerleader, a few of Beth's retail coping mechanisms returned and she had sold some books without feeling like an awkward, deviant refugee from high-tech Corporate America. Mom would be pleased.

Beth opened the door and Arlo came rushing over, barking himself into a frenzy of furry sheltie madness. "Stop it Arlo! It's just me."

Margaret called from the sofa, "Did you sell lots of books today, dear?"

After completing the removal of her copious quantities of outerwear, Beth walked into the living room. "Yes, I did. It was hard at first, but it got better. And the new display you set up is great. Everyone seems drawn to it. You might need to order some more of those Sue Grafton books."

"That's wonderful, Beth. Good for you! Please call the distributor tomorrow about those mysteries. The number is in the Rolodex."

"I will." Beth moved a book and sat on the edge of the sofa. "There was a sort of odd guy who came in right after I opened the store though. He wanted to see you. An older man with gray hair?"

Margaret nodded. "That's Ralph."

"Ralph?"

"I don't know his last name."

"Oh, do you mean he's from a meeting?"

"Yes. If he needs to talk, he sometimes stops by right after I open because usually no one is there yet."

"Oops." Beth gripped her necklace and made a face. "No wonder he was so disenchanted with me."

"It's not a big deal, Beth. He can go to a meeting. There's lots of support out there for him."

Beth gave her mother a half-smile. "So, does he have the hots for you or something?"

"Oh please, Beth. It's supposed to be anonymous. I prefer not to get involved with people in the program. I know people do, but it just feels too incestuous to me."

"I don't even understand how AA works in a place like Alpine Grove. *Nothing* is anonymous here."

"I suppose there are a few challenges. But I have a wonderful community of friends. Jill came over today and we had a great talk. She's feeling much better about the other librarian there now. They had a bit of a spat I think, but it's all blown over."

Arlo put his paws on Beth's knees, indicating he wanted to get into her lap. Beth hoisted him up. "Oh, and one more thing. I have to go to this horrid reunion after all. A cheerleader named Danielle came in and twisted my words around. I promised her I'd go."

Margaret clapped her hands together. "Oh that's wonderful! You can take the daffodils over for them too."

"You mean plants? Really?" Mom knew better than to trust her with plants.

"Yes, dear. The daffodil bulbs I forced are so pretty. Didn't you see them in the sunroom? I told Jill that I can't see them from here and those lovely blooms were just going to waste. We were talking and she said one of your classmates went to the library and was complaining about how they weren't going to have any pretty flowers because the cost of arrangements from the florist was beyond their budget."

"So I have to take plants to the reunion?"

"No, silly. Beforehand." Margaret pushed herself up so she could reach over and pet Arlo. "On Friday. Just drive out to the Enchanted Moose after you close the store. You'll get to meet everyone on the decorating committee."

"Great." As if the reunion itself weren't bad enough.

"Oh and honey, we have a little problem with Arlo. Cindy came by to walk him, but she said she is going to have to go out of town and she needs a day or so to get everything organized with her son too. She suggested that I board Arlo for a few days at some boarding kennel north of town. I guess she spent Thanksgiving there with her brother. It was a somewhat confusing story and I had just taken some painkillers." Margaret ruffled the dog's ear playfully. "Anyway, the story doesn't matter. You need to work at the store and I just can't take care of him here until I feel better. This afternoon I called the woman who owns the place—Kat Stevens—and she's delightful."

"So you want me to take Arlo out to this kennel?" Beth stroked the dog's head. "Sorry, buddy."

"Well you know what will happen if he doesn't get his walk. As it was, he had a little accident today. I think he's stressed because he knows I'm not feeling well. Cindy helped me clean it up, but you might want to look around for other spots."

"When do you want me to take him there?"

"Well, Cindy said she can walk him tomorrow, but it was obviously a problem. I think she's only doing it because I begged. If you could take him out there tomorrow after you close the store that would be wonderful. Kat will be expecting you."

Beth sighed. Driving Arlo out to the sticks was not how she'd envisioned spending her Valentine's Day. Graham was undoubtedly going to be having far more fun than she was.

She held up her hand, counting off the tasks. "So I need to take Arlo on Wednesday and the daffodils on Friday. Is there anything else?"

"Well, I think I might be well enough to go to a meeting on Thursday. I'd really like to go."

"Are they still out at the nondenominational church on the highway?"

"Yes. The Thursday meetings are at seven thirty."

"Okay." Arlo bumped into Beth as he turned around on the sofa trying to curl his head around toward his tail. Beth knew what the butt sniff meant. She inhaled and wrinkled her nose. "Eww, Arlo, gross!"

Margaret waved toward the dining room. "I know. He's a little gassy. And I'm not sure if that's all it is. The smell, well, it's consistent."

Beth put Arlo back on the floor, got up, and began walking around looking for Arlo deposits. She stopped in the dining room. "Um Mom, I hope you're stocked up on that enzymatic cleaner. I'm going to need the big bottle in here."

Margaret sighed and slumped down on the sofa. "Oh dear. That poor rug."

As Beth crawled around on her hands and knees scrubbing at the dining room rug, she started to feel better about boarding Arlo for a while. Maybe all that fresh country air would help his digestion.

~

The next day at the bookstore was easier as Beth returned to the old routines of helping customers and sorting books. She had gone through only two boxes so far. The slow pace was particularly discouraging because most of the books she'd examined were essentially trash like the old damaged encyclopedias. Inevitably, she was going to have to make a run out to the recycling bins at the dump. Throwing away books—even damaged books—made her feel a little sick inside.

Clearly, Mom had been going to estate auctions again and being a little too liberal in her bidding activities. Just because there was a lot of three hundred books at the sale didn't mean those three hundred books were ones anyone would actually want to read. Beth suspected that Mom viewed the whole auction scene like a game show. When it came to books, Mom just wanted to know what was behind door number one. Sadly, the answer was often more fodder for the recycle bins.

At five, Beth locked the door and walked back to the house, so she could collect Arlo for his journey to doggie camp, as her mother was now calling it. Beth had a feeling that no matter how positively her mother tried to spin it, Arlo was going to be less than enthusiastic about being away from the cushy comforts of home.

Beth gathered Arlo's things and loaded the dog into the backseat of the Explorer. She turned to look at him. "Okay buddy, are you ready for doggie camp?" Arlo glared back at her in stony silence. Margaret had warned Beth that the dog was not a fan of car travel, since rides in automobiles usually meant a trip to the vet or worse.

Beth wound her way out of town and headed north on the back roads. It had been years since she'd been in this area. One of her elementary school friends had lived north of town out in the boonies somewhere and Beth had attended a big birthday bash in second or third grade. The whole class had been invited. Amy had moved away though, and Beth had been crushed. Making friends had always been difficult for her, even in elementary school.

Beth held the note with the directions up against the steering wheel as she bumped down the driveway. The place certainly didn't lack for privacy. Given the number on the mailbox out on the road, she'd found the right driveway, but it seemed to go on forever. The right front wheel of the Explorer slammed into a hole, jarring Arlo off the backseat. He barked in protest, clambered back up and glared at Beth in the rearview mirror. It was like he knew she could see him. "Sorry Arlo. I'll be more careful."

Finally, a log house came into view. There was an old green truck outside, parked under a huge tree near a tired-looking wooden outbuilding. Beth pulled in next to the truck in a space that had been cleared of snow. She got out and hugged herself against the cold. Looking up at the huge cedar trees that surrounded the clearing, she had to admit it was beautiful. The whole place looked like it should be on a Christmas card. Beth turned as the front door opened and a short woman bundled up in a large coat started down the front steps. Beth waved in greeting.

The woman walked up to the Explorer. "Hi, I'm Kat. You must be Beth?"

"Yes, it is a pleasure to meet you."

Kat bent to peer into the Explorer. "Hi Arlo." She turned to Beth. "He looks pissed-off."

"He fell off the backseat when I hit a hole. Now he's a bit annoyed, I think. Let me get him out." Beth opened the door and snapped on Arlo's leash. "Hey buddy, time to go."

Arlo stood on the seat and Beth wrapped her arms around his stout body, lifting him out and placing him on the ground next to her. "He's not much of an athlete."

Kat looked down at the stocky sheltie. "I can see that."

The front door opened and a man with sandy blonde hair looked out. "Kat, are you out here?"

Kat waved, "Yes. Come meet Arlo."

The man ducked back into the house and then reappeared wearing a heavy winter coat. As he started down the stairs, Beth bit her lip. It was Joel Ross. What was *he* doing here? He looked totally different with long hair and a beard. How odd and out of context. As he walked up to them Beth tried to smile, "Hi, Joel."

Joel stopped in front of them. If Beth had to guess, she'd say the look on his face was something akin to dismay coupled with extreme discomfort. He said, "Wow. Hi, Beth. It's been a long time."

"Yes. How have you been?" Beth tried not to take his horrified look too personally. How unspeakably awkward was this?

Kat looked back and forth. "Do you two know each other?"

Joel nodded.

Beth said, "I grew up here. As you can imagine, it's not inconceivable that you might meet other residents over the years."

Kat raised her eyebrows and glanced at Joel. "I see."

Joel said, "Beth was home from college." Beth could feel the heat on her cheeks as he glanced at her with those amazing green eyes. "It was back when I was just up here on weekends."

As a thought flashed through her mind, Beth exhaled loudly and giggled. "Wait! You mean my mother's dog-walker Cindy is your bratty sister?"

The tense expression on Joel's face relaxed. "Yes." He grinned. "And now she has her own bratty kid. It's payback time."

"Karma always gets you in the end," Kat said.

Beth gestured toward the forest. "What happened to your house? It was out here somewhere, right? Did you ever finish it?"

"Yes. I finished it. And it's still there," Joel said. "It's rented now though, since I'm living here."

Beth fiddled with her necklace. "So, ah, I guess you got married."

Joel arched an eyebrow. "No."

"According to my mother, we're living in sin," Kat said. "So about Arlo? Do you have all his records and food? Your mom made it sound like he has a special diet."

"Oh…ah…yes! Yes, I do." Beth reached into the backseat for the bag. "There are cans of pumpkin in here. It's supposed to help with his digestive issues. And his veterinary information is in the manila envelope."

Kat took the bag and handed it to Joel. "Maybe you could take that into the house?"

Joel nodded and said to Beth, "It was nice to see you again. Say 'hi' to your mom for me."

"I will."

Kat took the leash from her and looked down at Arlo, who was standing quietly sniffing the air. "Okay, I think I've got everything. Feel free to call and check in."

"Thank you."

Kat turned toward the forest behind the house. "We're going to take a little walk now, so Arlo can meet the other dogs."

Beth let go of her necklace. She was such a social clod. This was her cue to leave. "Okay. Well, I'll just be going now."

"We'll see you in a few days. I hope your mother feels better soon."

Beth crawled back into the Explorer. What were the odds of seeing Joel Ross again? He *used* to work in Los Angeles, for heaven's sake. What was he doing here? Was she doomed to meet every person she wanted to forget in Alpine Grove on this trip?

Chapter 3

Daffodils & Deloreans

K at walked with Arlo around to the back of the house. She looked down at the dog, who had a definite waddle to his stride. What a pudgy sheltie. Sheep would probably laugh in his face if he tried to herd them. She opened the back door partway and called into the house. "Could you bring everyone outside?"

Joel emerged from his office. "All right. Be right there."

Kat slowly walked Arlo toward the forest trail she usually took with her dogs. Arlo poked along, stopping to sniff at every piece of forest debris they passed. The door opened and Linus the huge brown dog galloped out with Tessa the golden retriever in tow. They were harnessed together so Linus could use his substantial weight to keep Tessa from disappearing off into the woods forever. Linus skidded to a stop when he saw Arlo, who started barking at the canine intruders. Kat bent down. "Arlo, meet Linus and Tessa. Consider establishing a friendship with them. It's much better for you if you do."

Arlo stopped barking long enough to sniff the dogs to determine if they met with his approval. Tessa lost interest quickly and started indicating she wanted to continue her walk. After his social obligations were over, Linus obliged and the two dogs ran ahead down the trail.

The door opened again and the border collie Lori, and Lady, Joel's collie mix, ran outside followed by Joel, who was walking Chelsey, the Australian shepherd mix, on a leash.

Arlo started barking again and Lori leaped around him for a few seconds before getting bored and running off into the forest. Lady stopped and Arlo glared at her. Lady put up her hackles and straightened her tail, apparently not appreciating the smaller dog's uppity stance. Kat glanced at Joel. "Bad news. I think your dog is having an attitude problem."

He waved his hand toward the forest and said in a stern tone, "Lady! Be nice or go away."

Lady looked up at him and ran off after Lori. Joel turned to Kat. "They don't seem to appreciate one another. Shelties are basically just short collies. Maybe it's an inter-collie dispute."

"I don't know. But it's not good." Kat looked down at Arlo. "I hate to break it to you, but this means you're staying outside in the Tessa Hut. Only those who play nice in the sandbox get to stay inside the house." The Tessa Hut was the nickname for the outbuilding in front of the house, which was where Tessa had been confined when Kat inherited the house. The outbuilding had been substantially rehabilitated and had a chain-link enclosure and a heater inside. Although it worked as a kennel, Kat was pretty sure Arlo was used to far more plush accommodations.

Chelsey and Arlo seemed to have no problems with one another and they all began walking slowly through the forest. Joel took Kat's free hand. "This could take a while. Arlo has to be the most lethargic sheltie I've ever seen."

"I think he isn't getting much exercise at home. Hopefully he won't have a stroke while he's here." Kat looked up into Joel's face. "So that was fun. Our first Valentine's Day together and I get to meet one of your ex-girlfriends."

"It's not my fault. I had no idea she was in town. She moved away years ago."

Still annoyed, Kat let go of his hand and stopped to wait for Arlo to finish a complex sniffing maneuver. "I suppose not. I guess this was before the super-model girlfriend?"

"Yes."

"Care to elaborate?"

"No."

Kat raised her gloved hands, palms up. "You know I'll just invent something and probably get mad at you."

"Fine. Yes, I went out with her. She was home from college. We met at her mom's bookstore and started talking. It was a long time ago. And if it makes you feel better, although we went out a couple times, neither of us really had much fun. She's incredibly smart and we talked about geeky stuff, since that's what she was studying in college. I'll spare you."

"Thank you." Kat followed Arlo as he began lumbering back along the path. "I suppose it might have been like my date with the lawyer when I first got here. Worst date ever."

He grinned. "It wasn't *that* bad. Beth is kind of shy, but she's a nice person. We just didn't hit it off. In retrospect, it was sort of odd, since we do have a lot in common."

Kat took a deep breath, trying to let go of the anxious ache that had settled in the pit of her stomach. Talking to Joel about prior girlfriends was a sure way to trigger a bout of extreme insecurity. "Come on Arlo. Let's get a move on. We could die of exposure out here."

"The other dogs are probably waiting at the back door wanting to be let inside."

"Yeah, let's turn around before Arlo completely grinds to a halt. It could take the rest of our lives to get this dog through the whole loop trail. I think he may be even slower than Roxy the dachshund. And that's saying something, since she had really short legs." Kat spun on her heel, with Arlo trailing after her. "C'mon Arlo. I think you're getting walked separately from now on."

Joel took her hand again. "You're still mad, aren't you?"

"Maybe a little. But I'll get over it."

He stopped and pulled her around to face him. "You're sure?"

"Yes. I need to get back and get Arlo settled in so I can work on my article."

"How's it going?"

"It's not." She glanced up at him. "Sometimes I think I'm not cut out for the whole writing thing. And then I have problems with a dog and wonder if the whole boarding kennel idea is just stupid too."

"Wow. You're not in a good mood."

"No."

Joel squeezed her hand. "I'm sorry."

"Thanks. I'm sorry I'm surly." She looked down at Arlo and sighed. "It doesn't help that this is the most slug-like animal I've ever seen. I'm getting cold."

They stopped again as Arlo began another complex sniffing and pacing production that seemed to indicate something momentous might happen. Joel enveloped Kat in his embrace. "Happy Valentine's Day."

"Happy is a stretch. Maybe next year."

He kissed her and whispered. "I love you."

She smiled. "Okay, I changed my mind. I love you back, so that makes it the best Valentine's Day, ever."

After getting Arlo ensconced in the Tessa Hut, Kat spent most of the rest of the afternoon listening to the distant sound of his barking. It was a good thing that her office was in the daylight basement. The house was a log home with a concrete foundation that was set into a hillside, so the downstairs was partially underground, which did a lot to muffle the sound of angry sheltie.

Kat felt bad that the dog was taking his confinement so poorly. Didn't the dog ever sleep? She took him out for some extra walks throughout the day in an effort to tire him out. Eventually, every dog had to nap—it was the canine way. At least with umpteen opportunities to relieve himself, he shouldn't have any accidents.

By the time evening rolled around, Kat was ready to curl up in bed with her novel and forget about the day and all her writing frustrations. It was late and tomorrow she was going to regret staying up reading, but she just had to find out how the story ended. Joel rolled over in bed and laid flat on his back staring at the ceiling. "Okay, that was bizarre."

Kat looked up from her novel. "Care to share?"

"Not really. I just had some weird dreams, that's all."

"When I was so sick over Thanksgiving, I was the queen of weird dreams. Did you have fun wandering along the Yellow Brick Road like I did?"

"No. But you were zapping people with a stun gun. You zapped that guy Rob and his hair stood straight up. It was disturbing."

"Maybe I was embracing my inner tough chick. I have had a pretty crummy day, after all. But Rob's hair used to look like that anyway. So it wasn't my fault. Tracy said the barber fixed it."

Joel groaned, rolled over, and draped his arm across Kat's waist. "Maybe you told me that."

"At least I'm giving your subconscious something to do."

"I have too much on my mind, I guess."

Kat put her hand on his arm. "Like what? And if you say 'old girlfriends' I'm not going to be pleased." One super-brilliant ex was hard enough on her ego for one day.

"No, nothing like that."

"I'm thinking it's definitely time for you to share now."

"You aren't going to like it."

Kat squeezed his forearm. "Tell me anyway. I've been in a bad mood all day. Might as well keep the streak going." Sometimes encouraging Joel to communicate could be challenging, but it was worth it. Fortunately, she could be persistent when necessary.

"I have been trying to find a good time to tell you about this."

"Well there's a bad lead-in to a conversation. I think you found the right time. You know if you don't talk to me, I'll just start worrying about it, whatever it is."

Joel sat up and looked into her face. "I have to go away for a while."

"What do you mean go away? Where?"

"Out East. I have to pick up the airline ticket at the travel agent tomorrow."

She gripped his arm more tightly. "Are you kidding? You're telling me this *now*." This was taking reticence to a new level.

"I've only known for a couple of days."

"I rescind my comment about Valentine's Day. Good holidays don't include ex-girlfriends or sudden travel plans that don't include me."

"Sorry."

"I don't understand." Kat clutched at her novel. "Didn't we just have this conversation a few weeks ago when you were thinking about renting your cabin? You didn't want to go anywhere. And I didn't want you to go anywhere either."

"Yes, but this is different. I don't want to go. I *have* to go." Joel took the book out of Kat's hands and set it aside. "Shredding paper isn't going to help. My aunt Eileen is having surgery. So I *have* to go. You know why."

"Surgery?" Kat slumped down on the pillows. He was right. She did know, since not too long ago he'd told her more about his family. "Okay, I do understand why, but I don't have to like it. How long will you be gone?"

"I'm not sure. The ticket doesn't have a return date. I'm the only one who has the flexibility to help Eileen because I can work from anywhere. Have laptop; can travel. Cindy and Johnny are going to fly out for a couple days too, but Cindy has to get back, since she has to work walking dogs and Johnny has school."

"Wow." Kat sighed. "An open-ended ticket? That implies a long time. This is serious, isn't it?"

"Yes. Eileen wants to be at home. She doesn't want to recuperate in a hospital."

Kat put her head down on Joel's chest and hugged him. "I'm so sorry. I know it's not something you want to do. But you wouldn't be you if you didn't go and help out."

"Eileen did the same thing for me after the accident when I was seventeen. She dropped everything and came out to care for me and Cindy after our parents died. It's my turn."

"I know. But I'm going to miss you." They'd barely been apart since he'd moved in. The idea of not having his calm, reassuring presence here with her was beyond depressing.

"I'll miss you too. But she doesn't have any kids or much family left. Just me and Cindy. We're the closest thing."

Kat stroked his arm. "The idea of you and your sister trapped in a plane together is more than a little alarming." Small hostile countries got along better than Joel and his sister did.

"I know. At least we aren't sitting together."

"Good thing. I'm sure the rest of the passengers will appreciate that. Can I offer a word of advice?"

"Okay."

"Don't fight with Cindy in front of your aunt. The poor woman is already sick."

"I'll keep that in mind. Maybe you could drop me off at Cindy's place. Then we can drive to the airport in her car. If it snows, you have the truck so you can plow."

"There's a happy thought. Your truck and I have some issues with one another. We're still working on it." Kat's plowing experiences with the old green Ford had not been a highlight of her winter.

"You'll be fine."

"I'll be lonely and your dog is going to miss you too. Lady is not what you would call responsive to my requests for obedience. She only listens to you."

"I'm sure she'll behave."

"Yeah, right."

~

Over the next two days at the bookstore, Beth spent a lot of time sorting books and dreading the idea of dropping off flowers and meeting the reunion decorating committee. Carting twenty-five daffodils around and then attempting to be nice to people she didn't like in 1985 was destined to be even more demoralizing than encountering Joel Ross, who years ago had made it clear he wasn't interested in her, even though she'd had a terrible crush on him at the time.

Beth picked a well-worn paperback out of a box and flipped through the pages. It appeared someone had ripped out the last chapter. She threw it into the growing recycle pile. She might not be a titan of retail, but even Beth knew that selling a book with no ending was a sure way to lose customers.

She picked up another book, which practically disintegrated in her hands. Sheets of thin, aged paper fluttered to the floor. *Recycle pile.*

The fact she hadn't been able to reach Graham last night was also bothering her. It was Valentine's Day and she'd left a couple of messages on his answering machine to say 'hi.' They hadn't talked even once since she'd arrived in Alpine Grove. Then he hadn't returned her messages yesterday. Sometimes he got busy and didn't return calls. In fact, every once in a while Beth teased him about being an absent-minded professor, which he rarely found amusing. Sure, some people said *she* had no sense of humor, but Graham made Beth look like a laugh riot. What was he doing? It felt like it had been ages since she'd heard his scholarly deep voice.

After a long day of sorting books, Beth closed the store and returned to her mother's house. Loading all twenty-five daffodil pots into the Explorer took thirteen trips from the house to the car. She stood in front of the sofa facing her mother. "Okay, Mom, that's all of them."

"Jill talked to Vanessa and she knows you're dropping them off tonight. She's excited about the flowers and said to go to the meeting area and let them know. She'll round up some people to help bring them inside."

Beth was pretty sure she remembered who Vanessa was, which was reassuring. Vanessa was a heavyset girl who had been in a number of the same advanced-placement classes Beth had taken senior year. Maybe AP chemistry? Even though Vanessa had been brainy, unlike Beth, she seemed to embrace her geek factor. In high school, Beth had never felt comfortable like that. Mostly she wanted to be somewhere—anywhere—else. Putting her hand on her mother's shoulder, she said, "Will you be okay here? It shouldn't really take long."

"Beth, I'm fine. I can walk, you know. Just not very far or for very long."

"If you get hungry, you can heat up the leftovers."

"You're dawdling Beth. Go."

Reluctantly, Beth left the house and got into the Explorer. She drove out of town and down the highway to the Enchanted Moose. Because the high school drew students from the entire county, the reunion was located at "The Moose," which was more centrally located than any place in the town of Alpine Grove itself. It was an older motel and convention center that also had an associated RV park.

There was a mediocre restaurant on-site, which Beth hoped wasn't catering anything for the reunion. Objectively speaking, the Moose was sort of a dump. No one was going to confuse their high-school reunion with a formal opulent affair. Beth considered her mother's comments about the reunion committee budget. Maybe the daffodils would help. At least they were colorful.

She parked out front, walked to the entrance, and yanked at the glass door to enter the old building. An elderly woman was sitting behind the long wooden check-in counter. She was wearing a calico-print dress and appeared to be fast asleep, the gray bun on her head nodding up and down as she snored quietly. Was it considered rude to wake someone up in a situation like this? Beth clutched at her necklace for a moment. What was she supposed to do? She straightened her shoulders. This was stupid. Time to be a grown-up. What if she were a high-powered executive checking in? The woman would *have* to help her.

Beth stood in front of the counter and leaned toward the woman. "Excuse me."

The woman snorted, but didn't wake up. Beth tried arching her body over the counter as far as she could, and said more loudly, "*Excuse me!*"

Starting awake, the woman waved her arms in circles and fell off the chair and onto the floor with an indelicate thud. Beth ran around the end of the counter and tried to help her up. "I'm so sorry. Are you all right?"

The woman stood up, pushed Beth away, and brushed at her knobby knees. "Who are you?"

"I'm Beth Connolly. I need to drop off some stuff for the high-school reunion tomorrow. Maybe someone told you? The flowers? I just wanted to know where I should take them."

"Oh, you reunion people." She waved toward the back of the building. "You need to go around the side. There's a service entrance. It gets you to all the meeting areas. Those people are all back there chattering away, doing who knows what."

"Okay." Why did she feel like she'd just been given a dressing-down by her grandmother?

After driving around the Enchanted Moose parking lot a few times, Beth finally found the service entrance. She opened the door and walked into a hallway. One of the meeting rooms had a table out front next to a sign that said, "Welcome Cedar County High School Class of 1985." Beth tried not to cringe. Somehow seeing it in print made the whole idea of attending the event tomorrow all the more dreadful.

She peeked into the room, which was filled with women setting up something on a partially assembled stage. A couple of chunky men were attempting to hang lights while other men stood around holding beers in their hands. Beth recognized Glenn Eisenhower as one of the onlookers. He certainly had not aged well. Kat was right. Karma could be a bummer.

A woman with short red hair bustled by her and Beth said, "Excuse me. I'm looking for Vanessa. Is she here?"

The woman stopped and turned around. "Beth, hi! It's me."

"Vanessa?" The Vanessa she knew was *not* a svelte redhead.

"Yup. It's me. In the flesh."

"You look…in…incredible."

"You can say it Beth. I lost 35 pounds and I dyed my hair. You know my hair isn't really this color. I got into aerobics in college. I still teach classes for fun, and I'm going to start training for a marathon this summer."

"That's wonderful, Vanessa." Beth jammed her trembling hands in her coat pockets so no one could see them. Did everyone except her have their life together?

"So did you bring your mom's daffodils?" Vanessa waved toward the room. "We need all the help we can get. I mean, let's face it. This is The Moose. There's only so much we can do."

Beth turned her head and looked around the room. "Yes, it looks the same, doesn't it? My mother gave me twenty-five pots of daffodils. Do you think you could recruit some people to help me bring them inside?"

"Twenty-five? Wow, that's fantastic! You betcha. Let's get those losers off their butts." Vanessa stopped, put her fingers in her mouth and whistled. She pointed at the beer drinkers. "You guys, over there. Time to help unload. There are plants in the car. Be careful with them. One plant on each table. Got it?"

They nodded mutely and scattered to set down their beers. Beth turned to Vanessa. "I wish I'd had you at some of my meetings at work."

"Teaching aerobics not only helps get you in shape—you also learn to shout and motivate people who may or may not want to be motivated."

"I suppose that's true. I've never been very good at that type of thing."

Vanessa supervised the unloading and placement of the daffodils, which actually did brighten up the space. Each daffodil was like a festive little glimpse of spring.

As Beth was preparing to leave, Danielle, the cheerleader she'd met at bookstore, ran up to her and grabbed her arm. "Please say thank you to your mom. All of us on the committee were so upset that we couldn't afford flowers!"

"I'll be sure to tell her. She loves daffodils, and every year she forces more bulbs than she knows what to do with. She'll be happy they'll be appreciated."

"See you tomorrow night. It's going to be so much fun!"

Beth smiled weakly. "Can't wait."

~

After another long day of sorting books at the bookstore, Beth returned to her mother's house. She could no longer put off the looming and formidable question that had plagued her all day. What was she going to wear to the reunion?

She went into the house, hung up her coat, and walked into the living room. Margaret was not curled up in her nest of afghans on the sofa. Should she be up so soon? Beth walked into the kitchen. "I can do that if you want."

"Hi Beth. I'm starting to get a little squirrelly just lying around." She pointed at an eight-quart stockpot on the stove. "I made a batch of soup."

Beth peered into the pot. "It looks good. Wasn't all that standing hard on your back?"

"I paced myself. I hope it's good, because I got out of hand with the chopping and used the rest of that bag of potatoes. There's enough here to feed an army. Maybe I'll freeze some and save it."

"Good idea. Just be sure to mark the containers this time."

Margaret stirred the soup. "Are you getting excited about the reunion tonight?"

"No. I still can't believe I agreed to this. And all day I have been in a quandary about what to wear."

"Did you look in the closet? You never bring enough warm clothing when you visit, so I'm afraid to give anything away. I think there are some pretty dresses. I know there's a nice green one."

"That is my prom dress. And, before you say anything, *no*. Absolutely not."

"Okay. Let's look through my closet too. Maybe we can come up with a combination that will work."

Beth put her arm around Margaret's shoulders. "Thanks. That would be great."

Later, after many involved wardrobe debates with her mother, Beth finally was dressed acceptably in a pretty floral skirt of her mother's that matched one of the blouses she'd brought from Tucson. At last, she was ready to leave. Standing in the entryway, she hugged her mother. "Even though I vetoed the dress, I feel like I'm going to the prom again."

"Well the young man you went with was very nice. What was his name?"

"Drew."

"Maybe you'll see him tonight."

"Please don't say that! He's the *last* person I want to see. This is going to be bad enough as it is."

"Didn't you date him for a while?"

"I don't want to discuss that right now. I've got to go, but I'm sure I'll be home early."

"All right, dear." Margaret patted her shoulder and turned to return to the living room. "I'll see you later."

As Beth drove out to the Enchanted Moose, she thought about where Drew Emery might be now. After high school, he probably relocated to North Carolina, since his family was all out East. The odds of him attending the reunion had to be low. It was too far. There was no way he would even consider showing up. He only attended Cedar County High for the last half of senior year, anyway. He wasn't like the rest of them, who had been stuck with each other since first grade.

Seeing Drew again would be onerous for multiple reasons. Best not to think about it. She'd just say hello to anyone she actually recognized, suffer through some small talk without mentioning her little unemployment problem, and then leave early. Her obligation to attend would be fulfilled and she could forget this whole thing ever happened.

She parked the Explorer and went back to the meeting rooms. True to her word, Danielle was sitting at a table that was covered with name tags. Beth was surprised at the quantity. Her graduating class had been about 150 people and this looked to be a respectable number of them—perhaps 25 to 50 percent of the graduates. The committee must have engaged in a serious reunion-recruitment campaign.

Danielle waved eagerly at Beth and then handed her a name tag. "Here you go!"

Beth looked down at her gruesome senior picture and tried not to grimace. "Thank you."

"I'll see you inside! My shift is almost up."

Beth squinted at the little black-and-white photo on Danielle's name tag. Her face had looked completely different then. Different nose, eyes, lips and chin. Danielle had certainly had a lot of work done. And in high school, everyone had called her Dani. No wonder she didn't recognize the woman. Everything made more sense now. Beth attached the name tag to her blouse and turned toward the door. "See you later."

As she moved, suddenly everything became blurry. Beth blinked quickly and stepped back away from the table and over to a corner near the doorway. Not now! She touched her left eye with her finger, trying to move her contact lens back into position. At least it hadn't popped out. The last thing she needed was a contact lens debacle in the middle of the reunion. She blinked a few more times and could see again. Okay. One disaster averted. Time to get this over with. At least Danielle had witnessed her arrival, and she'd undoubtedly report to everyone that Beth had fulfilled her promise.

Turning, she entered the large meeting area. The lighting had been dimmed, probably to disguise some of the less attractive elements of the Enchanted Moose decor. Tiny white lights glimmered everywhere. Someone must have found a post-Christmas lighting closeout at the KMart down the road. The little twinkly lights were everywhere, giving the room a festive, sparkly feel. Each daffodil was surrounded by evergreen boughs and a circle of lights that lit up the citron-colored blooms, making them seem even more bright and cheerful.

Beth smiled as she looked around the room. The decorating committee had done a remarkable job, given what they had to work with. People were bustling around the room and Beth realized that she recognized many of them, which was astounding. Memories came rushing back. Not all of them were good, but it was remarkable how many people she saw that she had forgotten about entirely.

Of course, the typical high-school social stereotypes were represented—cheerleaders like Danielle and jocks like Glenn. But there were also people Beth had actually liked. Some she'd eaten lunch with a few times when she hadn't opted to hide out in the school library. The girl she'd done that extra-credit project with in AP English was standing near the stage. What was her name?

Beth waved at Vanessa, who grinned at her in reply. As she walked toward the side of the room where the refreshments were, she felt a glimmer of hope. Maybe this evening wouldn't be as horrible as she'd feared. She paused again near the wall to remove her coat and smiled at a tall, smartly dressed woman who looked vaguely familiar. The woman was also removing her long coat. Looking at Beth, she flashed a smile in return, revealing perfect, straight teeth. "Beth! How are you?"

"I'm fine." This woman must have had an amazing orthodontist. No one had teeth that flawless. Who was she? This was absurd. Did she remember no one in her class at all? It was going to be a long evening if she had to ask everyone she met who they were.

The woman moved closer to Beth and waved both hands up and down. She grinned. "Wow, look at you! You look fantastic, Beth. Your mom told me that you live in Tucson now."

Beth could feel the heat on her cheeks. Why wasn't this person wearing her name tag? Wait. There was a family resemblance—this woman had to be Carl's sister. But his sister wasn't in their class. "I'm sorry. I'm having trouble placing you. Are you related to Carl Johnson?"

The woman looked down at herself. "No. I am Carl. Or I was. Now I'm Carla. I guess your mom didn't mention seeing me at the bookstore the other day."

"No...no she didn't. Wow. I love your outfit. That blue looks great on you."

Carla looked down and ran her palm along the front of the sapphire-blue sheath dress. "I know. It was a fabulous deal too. I got it at The Broadway and I just adore the feel of the fabric." She looked back up at Beth. "It feels sort of funny talking to you about dresses after all those tutoring sessions at the end of senior year."

"At least you passed English and didn't lose your football scholarship." Carl had been Mr. Popularity. And now Carla was even more gorgeous than he'd been in high school.

Carla put her hand on Beth's arm. "I'm really grateful for your help."

"It didn't seem like it at the time."

"I know. I was a jerk."

Beth looked up. "Well...yes. I didn't think you knew that. It was a long time ago. I like to think I've changed a bit too."

Carla readjusted her coat in her arms. "I love your mom's store. And she's exactly the same—always excited about reading some new novel."

"Yes, Mom loves her books. I guess you changed your mind about reading for pleasure. It's not just a thing boring losers do."

"I changed my mind about a lot of things. I shouldn't have called you that."

"It's okay. People said worse." Beth knew her cheeks had to be twelve shades of red by now. Thank goodness for the dim lighting. Could she possibly be any more pathetic at small talk? How did people do this? "So…uh…what do you do for a living?"

Carla put her hand on her hip. "Oh come on, Beth. I know what you really want to ask. I've been Carla for about five years. After I trashed out my knee in college, that killed any chance of going pro. It felt like my life was over. I spent some time in therapy…lots of self-reflection." She waved her hands. "Oh, never mind. Sorry. Too much information. Anyway, I work at a management consulting firm in Austin."

Beth smiled. "That's great, Carla. You seem really happy."

"Oh, I am! It's been great to see you, Beth. I should go talk to the guys on the team. I've been mentally preparing myself for this moment for a long time, since most of them don't know what I've been up to lately. I need to go get that over with. Please give your mom my regards."

"I will." Beth waved slightly. The members of the 1985 Alpine Grove football team were about to get a big, big surprise.

～

Beth walked toward the refreshment area. She had actually managed to talk to another classmate without stuttering too much or sounding like a complete idiot. It was a miracle.

Maybe she could get through this evening without making a fool of herself, after all. She ladled some punch into a plastic cup and felt someone come up behind her.

A voice whispered in her ear, "Hey there, Bethie. It's been a while."

She put the cup down, turned and looked into Drew Emery's soft blue-gray eyes. There were little laugh lines at the corners now, but otherwise his eyes looked the same as they did in her dreams.

"Drew! I didn't expect to see you. You're…you are *here*. And you cut your hair." Was that was the best she could do? After a *decade*. Really? Beth wanted to crawl under the table and die.

He grinned and said in his laconic North Carolina drawl, "After ten years, if I hadn't ever cut my hair, I'd look like a troll doll by now."

Beth laughed and gripped her necklace, twisting it in her fingers. "I suppose." Drew still had light brown hair with sun-tinted highlights, but it was cut short, so it wasn't curling wildly around his collar anymore. And even in February, he hadn't lost his perpetual tan. Because he had filled out, he seemed more solid somehow, with less of a surfer-boy look. Although he was casually dressed, he looked like he could head up an executive board meeting. She'd always thought he was attractive, but the grown-up Drew was more than a bit disarming. Wow.

He reached around her and picked up a plastic cup. "How are you?"

"I am doing extremely well, thank you. I live in Tucson and everything is just perfect."

"Perfect?" He gave her a sidelong glance as he ladled some punch into the cup. "Really? I'm not sure I've ever heard anyone say that before." Beth knew the look in his eyes all too well. He could always tell when she was lying.

Beth shrugged and clutched her necklace more tightly. "Well, perhaps *perfect* isn't the ideal term."

"If you keep doing that, you're gonna strangle yourself, Beth." He put down the cup, reached over, and gently pulled her hand down from her necklace. "You still have that silver heart pendant, huh?"

Beth nodded and looked down at her hand in his. Her hand was trembling visibly between them. This was so embarrassing. But he wasn't letting go—he had an amazing knack for understanding when she was really scared. The simple contact was so comforting, and the racing of her heart slowed slightly.

Looking back up into his eyes, she had no idea what to say. All she could think about were her last words to him ten years ago. All those terrible things she'd said to him the day before she left for college in Arizona. Didn't he remember? Why would he even want to get near her? She tried to stand up straighter and pull herself together. She was an adult. Time to behave like one. "So…so…what…what have you been doing for the last ten years? Did you get married and have a plethora of children?"

A corner of his mouth turned up in a half-smile. "Nope. Nothing like that. But a more complete answer might take a while." He waved with his free hand toward the stage. "And I think that cheerleader is up to something."

Beth looked over at the stage, where images were flashing on a screen. The strains of "The Power of Love" by Huey

Lewis and the News increased in volume, and she wished they were farther away from the speakers. A picture of Michael J. Fox and a Delorean-based time-travel machine flashed by. The next image was a baby picture, and a woman in the crowd squealed. "That's me!"

Beth leaned toward Drew and shouted over the music. "I think someone scanned the baby pictures from that page in the yearbook."

He grinned and pointed at the screen. "Look, there you are."

"Yes." The photo was one Beth had seen many times. She was in a high chair, looking earnestly at the photographer. Her mother was wearing a rather ugly floral housecoat with ruffles and was smoking and reading a book. A mixed drink sat by her side. It looked like a parody of a Virginia Slims cigarette ad from the sixties. Mom had really come a long way, baby.

Drew leaned toward her and said, "Now I'm doubly glad I managed to 'forget' to give the yearbook people my baby picture way back when."

Beth giggled. "You never know what will come back to haunt you a decade later."

After the crowd had been warmed up with baby pictures, Danielle waved her hands and announced with a flourish that they were having a contest to see who remembered the most about 1985.

Drew moved his hand and Beth was overly conscious of the fact that her fingers were interlaced with his, and she didn't want to let go. He looked at her. "Do you want to sit down?"

She nodded and he finally released her hand. Touching the small of her back, he led her toward a table, pulled out a chair for her, and they sat down.

Danielle was galloping around the stage getting more and more animated about the contest as people started shouting out answers. "All right! Now for some Madonna questions! What was the name of her tour in 1985?"

A deep male voice shouted, "Like a Virgin!" and the other members of his table started hooting and slapping him on the back.

"Okay, what about the movie she was in—who remembers the name?"

A woman in the front yelled out, "Desperately Seeking Susan!"

Beth glanced at Drew. "I think a few of our classmates may have partaken of the open bar earlier."

Drew laughed. "I think so. Dang, it's loud. Phil Collins was overplayed so bad in 1985, I'm not sure I can take much more from the members of Genesis. I've exceeded my lifetime quota."

"He is a talented musician, but I can't say I disagree."

They sat quietly and watched as various classmates showed their knowledge—or lack of knowledge—about the mid-eighties. Beth glanced at Drew. He was tilting his head, apparently trying to decipher what Cindi Lauper was doing in a particularly unflattering photograph on the screen.

Other than her mother, Drew was the only person Beth had ever met who put her completely at ease. Something about his relaxed presence made her forget to be nervous. She hadn't appreciated it at the time, but it had been that way almost since the moment they met in their senior year. They could be in an empty room and be silent, but it was never awkward. Countless times, they'd just be sitting somewhere enjoying each other's company, without having to say a word. It was sort of surreal to have him sitting right next to her, with all the loud noise and people yelling around them.

He rubbed at the back of his neck with one hand. The scar on his pinky was still there. Beth knew that his 'adventure in road rash' had resulted in another much larger scar on his hip. The injuries were from a particularly bad bicycle wipeout when he was ten years old. When he'd told her the story, he'd pointed out that hitting the asphalt was better than getting run over by the ice-cream truck. He said that death by creamsicle was a crummy way to go, even when you're ten.

Resting his elbow on the table, he leaned forward and put his chin on his palm, staring at the screen. The resigned look in his eyes indicated to Beth that he was getting bored. He had the attention span of a housefly sometimes, although in certain situations he had amazing focus and could be incredibly patient. Beth felt the heat rise to her cheeks, recalling some of those situations.

Drew looked over at her, catching her staring at him. He raised his eyebrows. "I'm getting a headache. Do you wanna get out of here?"

~

Beth grabbed her coat and purse and Drew took her hand, leading her out of the meeting room. A woman was sitting at the check-in table, and she called after them. "Drew! Are you leaving?"

He stopped and gave the woman a dazzling smile. "We'll be right back, Lisa. I have to go check on something."

The woman blushed and simply said, "Okay."

Beth squeezed his hand. "Lisa had a huge crush on you in high school, you know."

"Oh sure, *now* you tell me."

Back then, every girl had had a crush on Drew. As a transfer student, he'd been quite the novelty. The fact that he was so handsome, funny, and kind hadn't hurt either. Beth always wondered what he saw in her, but had been too afraid to ask. As they walked down the hallway, the realization dawned on her that they were probably going to his room. She slowed her pace. "Drew, what do you have to check on?"

"You'll see."

She used to be able to read him so well, it was almost spooky. He always said it was like she knew what he was thinking before he thought it. But it *had* been ten years. What was he checking on? Did he mean he was checking on her? Maybe it was some type of code for 'let's have sex' that she didn't know about. He wouldn't do that, would he? Was 'checking on' the same as 'hooking up'? She'd been out of the dating scene for a long time. Changes had probably occurred in the vernacular. And she was with Graham now. What was Drew up to? He did have a tendency to be impulsive. Beth cleared her throat and tried to sound businesslike. "Perhaps your recollection is faulty, but when it comes to surprises I'm not an enthusiast."

He stopped in front of a door. "Bethie, relax. It's me. Don't go all robo-thesaurus on me here. I promise on my great-granddaddy's dear, departed Confederate soul that I'm not up to anything *unseemly*. Stay right here. Oh, and you'll want to put on your coat."

Beth did as instructed and waited in the hallway. She twisted the chain of her necklace in her fingers. How clueless could she be? This was totally mortifying.

A delighted yipping noise came from within the room. Drew came back out into the hall with an extremely fuzzy brown puppy cradled in his arms. "Hold her for a second. I need to get my coat."

Beth held out her arms and Drew rolled the ball of fur into them. She snuggled the puppy up to her chest. The little pup was warm and squirmy, wriggling in her arms and trying to lick her face. "Oh, what a little sweetheart you are! You are absolutely adorable."

Drew returned with his coat and a leash, which he clipped on the puppy's collar. "Keep holding her until we get outside. I learned the hard way, you don't want to let her walk the hallways when she's gotta go." He waved his hand. "This way."

"Oh Drew, she's just so cute!" Beth giggled as the puppy moved in her arms. "The Enchanted Moose personnel must really love you."

"Hey, they said they allow pets." At the end of the hallway, he pushed open the glass door for Beth and they walked outside. Taking the dog from Beth, he put the puppy on the ground, where she ran in a spastic circle before squatting. Glancing at Beth, he said. "See what I mean? When the puppy has gotta go, she's gotta go."

"What is her name?"

"Well, I've had her less than twenty-four hours, but how do you feel about Dixie?"

She crouched down to stroke the pup's head. "What do you think, Dixie?" The little dog wagged her stubby tail enthusiastically. Beth looked up at Drew. "I think she likes it."

They walked down a path toward the RV park as Dixie scampered off in random directions. Drew said, "She hasn't quite figured out the whole walking-on-a-leash thing."

"So I noticed. How did you acquire her? Most people don't bring a puppy to their high-school reunion."

"It might be more fun if they did." He took her hand and tucked it into the crook of his arm. "Better than eighties trivia, anyway."

"I certainly cannot dispute that." Beth curled her hands to her chest and huddled against the shoulder of his coat, trying to absorb any available warmth while they waited for Dixie to address the rest of her personal needs. "Ugh, it's freezing out here. And that has to be the most cherubic little canine I have ever seen."

Drew smiled down at the puppy. "Yeah, she's still in the roly-poly stage."

"You failed to answer my question. What possessed you to get a puppy within the last twenty-four hours?"

He looked at her and the reflection from the street lights glinted in his eyes. "Well, I was driving down here to the reunion and I stopped at a rest stop off I-5. It was early in the morning, and there was just one other car in the lot. I get out and the first thing I hear is this guy yelling at this little dog. I guess she'd made a mess in her crate. He was screaming at her and I thought he might do something to hurt her."

Beth looked up at his face. "But she's just a baby."

"I know. I went over to him and asked if there was a problem and if I could help. He didn't seem to appreciate that and said I needed to mind my own business. Well, he didn't quite use those exact words, but that was the gist of it."

"Apparently you didn't."

"No. I pulled out my wallet. I had eighty bucks I'd withdrawn from the ATM before I left. I showed him the money and said I'd buy the puppy." Drew shrugged. "He threw in the crate too. In case you're wondering, trying to clean out a crate in a rest-stop men's room while hanging onto a scared puppy on a leash is not easy."

Beth squeezed the thick fabric of the arm of his coat. "That's so sweet. You're Dixie's hero."

"I'm hoping one of our classmates will take her."

"You'd give her up after rescuing her?"

Drew grinned. "Hey Beth, want a puppy? She's *really* cute."

"I am, uh, not in a particularly good position to take on the responsibilities of a puppy right now."

He glanced at her quickly. "I thought you said everything was *perfect?*"

"I'm cold. Can we go back inside?"

Drew looked down at Dixie, "Are you done?" The little dog launched toward the building. "I guess so."

They walked back to the room and Drew opened the door. Beth walked inside slowly, taking in the scene. The Enchanted Moose wasn't exactly a luxury motel, but the room was a complete disaster. Clothes, books, and papers were strewn everywhere and a plastic sky kennel sat in one corner. Drew looked at Beth. "Sorry about the mess."

She smiled. "You have never been known for your tidiness."

"It's worse when your roommate needs to go outside fifty times a day. I didn't get a chance to put anything away." He moved a stack of books from the desk chair and dumped them in a corner. "Have a seat."

Dixie walked over to the corner and proudly picked up a paperback in her mouth, carrying it over to Beth. She pulled the book out from Dixie's teeth and put it on the desk. "Are you part retriever, sweetie?"

Dixie wagged and turned away to find something else to pick up and show off. Beth looked over at Drew. "Did you get her any chew toys? You might want to pick up everything up off the floor so she can't get to it."

Drew picked up the stack of books again and threw it on the bed. "Yeah, good point. I'm kinda new at this puppy-parenting thing." He moved around the room and threw the clothes and various dog paraphernalia on the bed, creating a small mountain of debris. "At least I got a room with two beds."

Beth picked up a little blue plastic bone from the floor and tossed it to the dog. "Here, Dixie." The puppy ran over, picked up the toy, and collapsed into a heap, chewing furiously.

Beth picked up the book from the desk again. "My mom just told me about these novels by A.J. Emerson. What do you think of them?"

Drew stood up and threw his suitcase on the bed next to the mountain. "Have you read them?"

"No. But my mom says I'll like them."

"I'd be curious to hear what you think."

Beth looked down at the puppy who was now snoring quietly with the chew toy clasped between her little brown paws. "Aww, this is so cute. I think Dixie has gone away down south to sleepy land."

Drew chuckled. "Yeah. She'll probably be crashed for a while. Do you want to go back to the reunion party?" The humor left his eyes. "Or do you want to tell me why everything isn't so perfect?"

Beth nodded her head. "I've missed talking to you, Drew."

"I know, Bethie. Me too."

Drew sat down on the floor, leaning back on the foot of the bed with his long legs out in front of him. Dixie got up and settled herself in his lap. He stroked the puppy's head and looked up at Beth. "So what's happened with you over the last ten years or so?"

Beth couldn't talk to him, looking down from the chair, so she got up and sat on the floor next to him. This would be easier if she couldn't see his eyes. "Well, you know I went to college in Arizona."

"I remember. The full scholarship. I believe you said you were going places."

Beth touched his arm. "I'm so sorry about the things I said, Drew. You have no idea."

He shrugged. "You weren't completely wrong, Beth. It was probably for the best."

"I thought so at the time. But I still wish I could take back everything I said. I have thought about it so many times."

"Yeah, well, I know that part. What happened after that?"

She straightened. "Okay, the synopsis is I went to college, graduated with honors, and was recruited by RTP."

He glanced at her. "So far, this is sounding like exactly what you wanted. What's the problem?"

"It was. All the things I wanted just fell into place one after another. I was always thinking about the future. When I was in high school, I was thinking 'I'll be happy when I graduate and get a scholarship so I can go to college and get out of Alpine Grove.'"

"I think the words you used were 'get out of this tedious backwater town.'"

A corner of her mouth turned up in an ironic smile. "Yes, that sounds like something I would have said then. And I did. I left town and I thought, 'if I can graduate from college with honors, then I'll get a great job.' So I studied all the time and then at the end of senior year I met Graham. I finally had a boyfriend, after an extended period of time without much, well, companionship."

Drew scratched his chin. "I see."

"And then I actually did get the dream job. I didn't even have to apply. The campus recruiters said they wanted me. I was thrilled. When I started working at RTP I figured that if I worked really hard, I could buy a house. I studied the Tucson real-estate market and found a house I liked and could afford. Then I thought everything would be perfect once Graham and I got married and had kids."

"You have kids?"

"No. I *want* to get married and have kids. After getting the job and the house, the rest hasn't quite gone according to plan. My life has been more or less the same for the last six years or so."

"Well, it doesn't sound bad. In fact, it sounds perfect for you."

"I thought it was. Well, mostly. And everything was the same until February fifth when I lost my job. I was laid off and it felt like my whole world was ripped out from under me. Most people don't understand, but working at RTP is like becoming part of a special fraternity. All of my social interactions and most of the people I know revolve around the company."

Drew stroked Dixie's fur slowly. "I read about the big layoffs at that place a few years ago."

"I know. I thought my job was secure after that. But it wasn't. My mom had asked me to come here for a visit, but I said no because of work obligations. Then after the layoff, I changed my mind. I decided to come to Alpine Grove to think. I missed Mom and I wanted to talk to someone outside of the company who would be sympathetic. Plus, I had nothing else to do at home, except feel sorry for myself. Then after I got here, my mom hurt herself and I extended my visit, so I could help out at the store."

"Working there must have been a blast from the past. As I recall, you aren't a big fan of working in retail."

Beth smiled. "That's for sure. The first day at the store, I was really nervous, but I got used to it again. But then that cheerleader Danielle tricked me into coming to the reunion."

"You know how sneaky those cheerleaders can be."

Beth turned and shoved at his shoulder playfully. "Very funny. But the thing is, even though I do hate being cold all the time, being here has actually been okay. And it helped me forget that my life is a mess. Everything I worked so hard for all those years—it all fell apart practically overnight. I'd thought I was indispensable. A vital employee. RTP is doing a big product launch at the end of the month and I told them they could call or e-mail if there was a problem."

"Did they?"

"No. At first, I didn't think about it because I was worried about my mom and the store. Then I ignored it, figuring they must be really busy. Then I got kind of angry. I kept wondering how they could possibly survive without my valuable knowledge and expertise."

"And now?"

"Since I've been away from the day-to-day grind of my job, I realized that I was busy, but maybe not as important as I thought I was. When I'm endlessly sorting books at the bookstore, I miss the intellectual aspect of what I used to do. The technology is fascinating, but now I'm in management. Or I was before they fired me anyway. You know how I am with people. I should never have taken the promotion, but in that environment, you can't just say no to an opportunity like that. Here, I've had a lot of time to think. I love my house and my job, but something has always been missing."

"What?"

"I'm not sure. I'm wondering if I've just been waiting to be happy, expecting it to show up like some magic genie because that's what happened before with the scholarship and my job. I never had to go out and get those things. They just came to me. All I had to do was just follow along."

"It sounds like you worked hard."

"I suppose I did. But I treated it like an equation. If I do X, then Y will happen. But now I have no idea what to do. I have no X." She turned her palms toward the ceiling. "Well, beyond finding a job. But doing what? My experience is so specialized, I can't just look in the newspaper. I'll probably have to move, but I don't want to leave Tucson. I like it there."

He smiled. "Well, it is warm out there in the desert."

"Yes, and sunny! And now I've met a bunch of classmates who seem really happy doing things I never would have expected. I thought I had to go to college, get a good job, and then everything would be perfect. But it's not. Other people made different choices and seem so happy. I mean, Vanessa teaches aerobics! And Carl...Carla? I never would have imagined that."

"Yeah, she's staying here at The Moose. We had a long conversation earlier. She's a heck of a lot nicer than she used to be."

"I know! She actually thanked me and apologized. I couldn't believe it."

Drew gestured toward the window. "Okay. But wait, you didn't say anything about the guy. You've been seeing the same person for six *years*? Are you living together?"

"No. His house is on the other side of Tucson. He's a professor at the university."

"Interesting."

Beth knew that when Drew said 'interesting' it never meant that he thought something was actually interesting. He just wasn't saying what he really thought. "No it's *not* interesting. What are you really thinking?"

"Nothing. I'm just happy for y'all. It's probably nice to have a long-term thing like that." He stroked the fur on Dixie's back. "I wouldn't know. I can barely handle an eight-pound puppy."

"And now here I am babbling away, dumping all my ruminations on you, just like I always did." She squeezed his arm. "I don't know why, but I can tell you things I just can't say to other people—even my mom."

"That's 'cuz you know I'll do something stupid like suggest we sneak off to Los Angeles and go see the Dead at the Coliseum or go skinny-dipping at Gray's Point."

"Maybe." Beth giggled. "But that was fun. And after the raccoon ran off with your shorts—well, I don't think I've *ever* laughed that hard."

"I don't think the lower half of me has ever been that cold."

Beth nudged him. "And then when the little raccoon stood up on his hind legs and grabbed your briefs off that shrub. I thought I was going to die of laughter. It was like he was mocking you."

"Nasty varmints."

Beth looked into his face. "I confess, I really didn't think you'd want to come back here."

"I didn't. But I had a question I needed to get answered and some stuff to do. So I decided at the last minute to come." He pointed toward the pile of papers and clothes on the bed. "I threw a bunch of stuff in the rig and hit the road. One thing Alpine Grove has going for it is quiet. Like you said, this is a good place to think. I figured I could make an appearance at the reunion and get those cheerleaders to stop harassing me. I don't know how they got my number."

"You certainly are an eclectic packer. Are you still doing those wonderful pencil sketches? I still have the one you did of me sitting on that huge rock at the lake. It's hanging on my wall at home. I got it framed."

"No." He shrugged "I don't do that much anymore."

"Didn't you study art?"

He shook his head.

"So what have you done over the last ten years?"

"Did some time at UNC. I was on the slow-boat six-year, off-and-on collegiate program." He grinned at her. "Go Tarheels! Then I traveled a lot too. You know my Dad used to buy and sell properties. After he sold the marina here, he was moving on to some other 'big thing.' I don't even remember what the deal was anymore. But he had a heart attack and he wanted me to take over the business so he could slow down. I said no. I was about to take off on a trip and there was no way I wanted to settle down and become Mr. Real Estate Mogul."

"That doesn't really sound like your style."

"No kidding. But then he had another heart attack and died."

"Oh Drew, I'm so sorry. I didn't know."

"It's okay." He shrugged. "Really, Dad always predicted it. He always said he was going to keel over from a massive coronary. Unfortunately, he was right. All that working finally caught up with him."

"So did you take over the business like he wanted?"

"Nope. I sold it. His partners were desperate for it. I said they could have it. So I took the money and ran."

"Ran where?"

"Everywhere. I wanted to travel. So I did. Criss-crossed the States. Went to India, Europe—a bunch of places."

"Wow. I can't imagine doing that much traveling. I *can* imagine you doing it, though."

"Yeah, I kinda just wanted to get away."

Dixie stood up and stretched deeply, making a little squeaky yawning noise. Drew scooped her up in his arms and stood up. "Okay, little one. We know where you need to go now."

Beth stood up next to him. "Outside?"

"You better believe it, baby. This animal has a bladder the size of a blueberry."

Glancing at the clock on the nightstand, Beth discovered it was a lot later than she thought. "I should probably be going. My mother will be concerned. I told her I'd only be here for a little while and she tends to worry."

He grinned at her. "Talk about a flashback. How many times have I heard you say, 'My mom is going to kill me'?"

Beth put on her coat. "I know. You'd think by now it wouldn't be an issue. But I know she's going to give me her patented 'I was worried' glare when I walk in the door. The statute of limitations for maternal worry doesn't ever seem to run out."

"Hold onto sleepyhead while I put on my coat. I'll walk you to your car."

Beth collected the lethargic puppy in her arms. "Drew, you don't have to do that. I know the way."

"My great-granddaddy would roll over in his grave if he knew I let a woman walk alone. The gentlemanly code of the South has a few standards left. Maybe not many, but a few."

Beth rolled her eyes. "Oh brother. You and your great-grandfather. Someday you'll have to show me a picture of this illustrious fellow."

They walked back outside, where Dixie enjoyed some more darting, cavorting, and relieving herself. Beth took Drew's arm again and let out a deep breath as an overwhelming sense of relief washed over her. He didn't seem to hate her, after all.

For ten years, she'd avoided any contact with Drew, desperately afraid to hear what he might say to her. She certainly would have deserved his wrath. But it was like no time had passed and she had never said all those horrible things to him. She didn't know how or why he had forgiven her, but it didn't matter. Maybe she hadn't lost the best friend she'd ever had, after all.

~

Beth stood next to her Explorer and bent to disentangle Dixie's leash from her ankles "She's quite a speedy little thing."

"Yeah. I keep worrying I'm gonna step on her."

Beth stood up. "I didn't ask you before. How long are you staying in Alpine Grove?"

"I'm not sure. Like I said, I've got some stuff to do."

"My mother's birthday is next weekend and Bea Sullivan is throwing a big party. I know my mom would love to see you."

Drew looked into her eyes. "Would you?"

"Yes." She leaned forward and put her arms around him. "I just can't believe you don't despise me. I've relived what I said in my mind a thousand times."

He hugged her quickly and let go. "I could never do that, Bethie."

Beth leaned back to look up into his eyes. "I'm so sorry I called you lazy. I didn't mean it."

"I believe you said I was 'a lazy, puerile underachiever' who would never amount to anything." He smiled. "After I got home, I looked up *puerile*."

"I should never have said that. I was just so upset at leaving you and my mom and everything that was familiar. I was terrified, and I lashed out at everybody. My mom has forgiven me for the things I said to her." Beth shook her head and looked down. "She said it takes two to tango."

"That sounds like something she'd say."

"I know. She also said that making amends and admitting her own wrongdoing is part of the AA steps. I don't know, but it sounds like the steps go on indefinitely."

"I think so." Drew bent to pick up Dixie. He tucked the dog next to him and wrapped his coat over her body, hugging her with one arm. "I think she's getting cold."

"Okay." Even though she was freezing, Beth didn't want to leave. "I would like to see you again. Will you come to the party?"

"We'll see." He grinned and waved expansively at the parking lot with his free hand. "In the meantime, I'll be enjoying the ambiance of The Moose."

Beth giggled. "It's so good to see you again, Drew."

"You too, Beth. Drive safely."

As Beth drove back to her mother's house, she couldn't stop smiling. Seeing Drew again had been so much fun. What a wonderful conversation! She went over everything they'd talked about in her mind. He had this way of listening with total attention, but he hadn't really said much. Although she knew he went to the University of North Carolina, he didn't say what he studied. Or what he was doing now. Or where he lived. Hmm.

She walked into the living room, where her mother was watching TV. Margaret only watched TV when she was too tired to read. She sat up and glared at Beth. "I assume they do still have telephone service at the Enchanted Moose."

"I'm sorry I didn't call, Mom."

"I thought you were only going to stay for a half an hour? 'Make an appearance and go,' I believe you said. Did you have car trouble? Did something happen that caused you to be incapable of picking up a phone?"

"No. I lost track of time." Beth smiled, unable to hide her enthusiasm. "I'm so happy you encouraged me to go!"

Margaret raised her eyebrows. "Really?"

"Yes. I saw Drew Emery."

"I thought you didn't *want* to see him."

"I didn't. But Mom, he doesn't hate me. He was so sweet and funny. And he has a little puppy named Dixie. She is so cute."

Margaret smiled. "It's wonderful to see you so happy, dear. I'm glad you had a good time after all."

"Oh, and I invited Drew to your birthday party. I hope that's okay."

"Of course, dear. It will be nice to see him again."

"I'm going to bed. At least I don't have to work at the store tomorrow. I'm going to celebrate by sleeping late."

"Okay. I won't disturb you. I know you're not in high school, Beth, but if you stay out late, please call me."

Beth walked over to her mother and bent down to give her a hug. "I will. I promise."

After a gloriously relaxing day lounging around with her mother reading novels, Beth returned to the store on Monday. The boxes were still there. She'd barely made a dent in the towering masses of them in the back room. It was discouraging.

She grabbed a box and dragged it out next to the desk to begin sorting. Beth was distracted by the pen-and-ink illustrations in an antique copy of *Alice in Wonderland* when the bells on the door jingled. She looked up and grinned when she saw Jill, her mother's best friend and AA sponsor.

"Aunt Jill! I'm so glad to see you." Jumping up from the desk, she ran toward the front of the store and hugged the older woman. "I was hoping you'd stop by!"

Jill had worked at the Alpine Grove library for as long as Beth could remember. She always wore her gray hair in a long braid that stretched down to the middle of her back. She pushed an errant gray strand back behind her ear and looked around the store. "It looks like you remembered what to do. Your mom tells me you're doing a great job."

"I don't know about that." Beth pointed at the box. "It's a good thing she can't see how little progress I've made on the book-sorting project. How many auctions has she been to?"

"I lost count. Margaret likes the buying part, but not the sorting part. She said she's a little behind."

"No kidding. So how are things at the library?"

"Same old stuff. Except I have to do more things on the computer, which I don't like. But I keep handing off all the online research to Jan. It works out, since she loves that stuff. I figure she can have it."

Beth recalled Jill's long-standing animosity toward computers. They never talked about RTP or what Beth did for a living. "It sounds like Jan is working out well then, after all?"

"Jan is the most amazing librarian I've ever met. She drives me insane sometimes, but she's great. To be fair, she's mellowed out a little since she started seeing that guy."

"What guy?" Finding a man worth dating in Alpine Grove wasn't easy.

"Michael Lawson. He owns the new ad agency."

"You mean the one in the old Frederickson's building?"

"Yup. He's gorgeous. I may be old, but I'm not dead. It's some nice viewing when he stops by the library to see her. I try not to drool on the desk."

Beth laughed. "Well good for her. I guess that means he has all his teeth, too."

"You better believe it. She met him in San Diego and he's quite beautiful." Jill flipped her braid back over her shoulder. "I need to talk to you about something."

Beth sat back down at the desk. "Is everything okay?"

"Yes, don't worry. But I want to give your mom a present for her birthday. It's a big birthday, but it's also her 20-year anniversary of being sober."

"Wow. She's getting the 20-year chip?"

"Yes. Obviously not at the party, but at the meeting next week. I want to do something really special, but I need your help. Margaret hasn't taken a vacation in a long time. Ever since Evelyn left town a few years ago, she just hasn't found anyone reliable to take care of the store. Jan found this cruise on some close-out travel web site. It's so cheap, it's almost criminal not to buy it. Mexico! Your mom would flip for it. Jan took a lot of time off a few months ago, and I've saved my pennies, so now it's my turn."

"That's incredibly generous and you both would have so much fun. Do you want me to pitch in? I'd be happy to."

"That's kind of you, but what I'd really like is for you to watch the store for a little while." Jill paused. "Your mom told me you're in-between jobs."

"Yes. That's a nice way of putting it. When is the cruise?"

"You'd need to be available March second through the sixteenth."

"Two weeks?"

"Well the cruise itself is ten days, but we have to get down and back to LA, so you'd probably have to be here for two weeks. I know it's a lot to ask."

"Well, Mom is feeling better. I was thinking I'd be able to go back home after the party this weekend and start figuring out what I'm going to do with my life. But I could come back here, I suppose."

"Would you?"

"Yes. I will." Beth nodded vigorously. "You're right. This is a really big deal, and Mom hasn't taken a vacation in a long time."

Jill leaned over and wrapped Beth in a hug. "Oh thank you, Beth! I'll tell Jan to press the button and buy the tickets. Then we can give your mom a great surprise at the party. She's going to be so excited!"

"Well, Mom made so many sacrifices for me after Dad left." Beth looked down at the desk. "It's the least I can do."

"Oh Beth, you need to let all that go. You father is a good person. Leaving was for the best."

Beth crossed her arms. "Mom always says that, but I don't see how abandoning your family is ever a good idea."

"You probably don't remember because you were just a little girl, but your parents were awful together. Your mom wouldn't admit to having a problem. Your father nagged her about rehab and it all got very nasty."

"They could have worked it out. People do all the time!"

"Not in this case, Beth. Margaret wouldn't commit to her sobriety until he left. He wanted you to have a good life. Your mom needed to be away from him to get herself together to take care of you."

Beth waved at the front windows. "Easy for him. All he had to do was cough up some money for the house and child support, and voila, he's rid of the weird shy kid."

"Beth, you've tortured yourself over this for years and it was a lot more complicated than that. He made sure that no matter what happened with your mom, you'd be cared for, but he had to earn money too." Jill shook her head. "He wasn't trying to get away from you. You refused to visit. If you say no multiple times, eventually people stop asking. Has he ever *not* called you on your birthday?"

"No. He always calls."

"Maybe you should think about talking to someone. It might help you work some of this old stuff out. You'll be happier if you do. I promise."

Beth shook her head. "I'm fine. And I was just telling one of my old high-school classmates last night that except for needing a new job, everything in my life is perfect. Well, almost anyway."

Jill gave her another hug. "I hope so, Beth. I really do. Thanks for agreeing to mind the store. I appreciate it. I have to get back to the library and harass Jan now about printing out the cruise brochure. The stupid printer jammed and I couldn't get it to go again."

"I have to pick up Arlo from the kennel tomorrow after I close up here. Could I stop by your place and take a look at the brochure? I'd love to see pretty pictures of sun, beaches and ocean."

"Sure. I'll see you then."

Chapter 4

Smells & Secrets

Several hours after Joel left for the airport, Kat decided to give Arlo provisional access to the house for a few hours during the day while the other dogs were sleeping downstairs. The dog had done okay so far and even now Arlo was contentedly sleeping on the living room rug. The little sheltie seemed placid enough at the moment. Given the horrendous mess and associated smell he had generated out in the Tessa Hut, there was no way this animal was ever staying inside overnight. A few hours of inside time was all Arlo was going to get.

Although cleaning up the Hut had been incredibly unpleasant and almost caused Kat's fingers to freeze off, she felt bad banishing Arlo all the time. There was a heater in the outbuilding, but it was still not exactly balmy out there. He was probably cold and lonely. Beth was picking up Arlo the next day, so he should have at least one opportunity to be Mr. Special Dog. And inside, they could be lonely together. Maybe if Kat started howling with him, she'd feel better.

She'd called her friend Maria, who was not sympathetic to her complaints about missing Joel. Maria had just started working at the new ad agency in town and the owner, Michael Lawson, had given her a bunch of books on psychology. Now Maria was calling Kat 'codependent' just because she wished Joel were here. Kat hadn't been in the mood to hear that and she'd told Maria to go eat her Twinkie and get back to work. But now she felt bad. Maria was her best friend and she was probably just trying to be helpful in her own unique way. Flying off the handle at her like that had been mean. Kat needed to get a grip on herself. What was her problem?

The phone rang, disturbing Kat from her depressing self-recriminations. She got up and walked to the kitchen to answer it. Joel's sister Cindy said, "Hi Kat. I'm glad you're there. Joel said I had to call you."

Kat twisted the phone cord around her finger. Given how poorly Cindy and Joel got along, that had undoubtedly been an unpleasant conversation. "Is your aunt okay?"

"Yes. Joel probably told you that the surgery went well. I'm at Eileen's house with her. But Joel is in the hospital."

"Why isn't he with you?" A heaviness settled in the pit of Kat's stomach and she sat down in a chair. "Wait. He's *in* the hospital. Are you saying he's a patient?"

"Yes. He tripped. Only Joel would end up hurting himself in a hospital."

"What do you mean he tripped? On what?"

"Johnny ran in front of him. He was being a fire engine and Joel tripped on him and hit his head. They're keeping him there overnight. So he said I should call you, since they're doing some test or something and he won't be able to call you tonight at seven thirty like he usually does."

Kat clenched the phone cord in her hand. "A test? Is he okay?"

"Yeah. It's no big deal. Just a precaution, I guess."

"You're sure? This sounds like a big deal to me."

"That's what they said."

"Could you ask him to call me as soon as he can?"

"Okay. He'll be back here at the house tomorrow morning, since he's gotta take me to the airport."

Kat wished Cindy a safe trip and hung up the phone. She felt like she was going to throw up. What if Joel wasn't okay? Didn't people sometimes die after a concussion? Brain swelling or something? Leaning her forehead down on the cool wood surface of the table, she tried not to cry. Please don't let anything be wrong with Joel.

Ugh. What was that smell? Kat peered under the table and found a gift from Arlo precisely placed right in the middle of the rug. Gross.

Grabbing the leash off the table, she hastily swiped a tear off her cheek and strode across the room. She clipped the leash on Arlo, who looked up at her in surprise. "Special Dog time is officially over, Arlo."

After putting Arlo back outside in the Tessa Hut, Kat set to work cleaning the rug. It had seen better days, since multiple generations of animals had undoubtedly committed equally if not more disgusting acts of badness upon it. But really, sneaking over and taking a dump while she was on the phone was really rude. It was going to be quite some time before she let Arlo inside the house again. Like maybe *never*.

As she scrubbed furiously at the rug, she finally let herself cry. A few tears couldn't do any more damage to this old rug. Maybe a little extra salt would help get rid of the hideous smell.

Later, after spending some time staring at her computer monitor worrying about Joel and not writing her article, Kat gave up. She walked out into the hallway. "Okay guys, work isn't happening. It's time." All the dogs got up and stretched, readying themselves for the big afternoon walk.

After donning her dog-walking outerwear, she hooked up Linus and Tessa to their harnesses, leashed up Chelsey, and opened the door. Lori and Lady shot out toward the forest trail, followed by Linus and Tessa. Kat started strolling with Chelsey, who looked up at her in concern. "I know Chels, I'm upset. Sorry. But what if something is really wrong with Joel? It's too awful to even think about."

Chelsey didn't seem to have any suggestions and they continued on. Kat tried to focus on taking deep breaths, letting the cold air fill her lungs. It was best not to think about the fact that she had to wait until tomorrow to talk to Joel. It was probably only twelve hours, but it felt like forever. Maybe she'd go to bed early. Tomorrow had to be better than today. She'd talk to Joel and then Arlo would go home. It would be a relief to have just her own dogs and cats to worry about again.

Kat and Chelsey watched as Linus and Tessa ran around with Lori ahead of them on the trail. Kat turned around. Where was Lady? The collie-mix had a habit of disappearing into the forest, but she always came back to annoy Lori some more. The two dogs had a complicated game of ambush that was fun to watch. But now it looked like Lori was playing the game with Linus and Tessa instead.

They completed the loop and Linus, Tessa, and Lori stood at the door panting happily, waiting for Kat to let them inside. She peered around the back of the house. "Okay guys, what did you do with Lady?" All four dogs wagged and gazed up at her, but didn't offer any clue about their missing canine cohort.

Shaking her head, Kat let the dogs in and removed leashes and harnesses. Chelsey went to her favorite spot under the table and the other dogs milled around settling themselves in for their afternoon naps. Kat went upstairs and out the front door. She didn't want to take Arlo out until she found Lady, since they didn't get along. And after his explosive event under the dining room table, there couldn't be anything left for him to do anyway.

Kat walked around toward the back of the house again and then back down the trail calling for Lady. Where could she have gone? It was cold out here. What if Lady had hurt herself and was trapped in a hole or something? Joel would never forgive Kat if something happened to his dog while he was gone.

"Lady, Laaaaaydeeee" Kat went around the loop trail twice, calling until she was hoarse. Frozen tears made her face feel stiff and her fingers hurt from the cold. Where could the dog have gone? They did this walk every single day. It wasn't like Lady didn't know the way home.

Kat stopped and gazed at the towering trees. This wasn't working. Maybe she should get in the truck and drive down the road. At least it would be warm. The heater in the truck mostly worked. Sometimes. Kat went in the back door and all the dogs stood up, looking concerned. "It's okay, guys. I'll find her. I promise. I'm just going to take a little drive. I'll be right back."

Kat got the truck keys out of a kitchen drawer, grabbed a leash, and went out the front door. Walking across the driveway, she was overcome with sadness. What if she lost both Joel and his dog? On the same day? Was that really what was happening now?

She went to open the door of the old green Ford and looked toward the back. Lady was curled up in a tight ball in the truck bed. Kat reached over the side. "Lady! Are you okay?" The dog raised her head and gave Kat a sleepy look. She stood up and stretched.

"Have you been here the whole time?" Kat clipped the leash on the dog. "We are going inside. Right *now*."

Kat lowered the tailgate and Lady jumped down daintily. "You are *so* not going to be off-leash again until Joel gets back here. I almost froze to death looking for you."

Lady wagged and looked pleased with herself. Kat stomped back around the house with Lady in tow and went back inside. Stupid dogs.

∼

After stewing about Lady's disappearance for a while and making herself some food, Kat picked up the phone and called Maria at the ad agency. "I'm sorry I snapped at you. What I said was kind of mean and I feel bad."

"It's okay, girlfriend. You are experiencing undue stress. Not to mention you aren't getting any at the moment and I, sadly, can relate. It's unfortunate that my financial situation has forced me to relocate to such a dating wasteland. I feel your pain."

"I know it's Monday and I know you have to work tomorrow, but can I stop by your place for a while after you get off work? No wine, just whining. I've had a very bad day and I'd like to get out of the house for a while."

"Sure. Maybe you can help me with some questions I have on decor."

"Decor?"

"Yeah. There isn't any in my sad little apartment. I need ideas. My place needs some style."

Kat grinned. "Okay. I'm not exactly Martha Stewart, but that sounds like fun."

"See you later."

After walking Arlo several more times and feeding dinner to all the animals, Kat got in the truck to head into town. She used both hands to grind the ancient transmission into reverse. "C'mon, I'm not making you plow anything, it's just reverse. Let's go."

After Kat swore at the truck a few times for emphasis, the old Ford finally obliged. Kat wished again that Joel were here. She hated driving his truck. With the plow blade on it, she felt like she was driving a tank. A curmudgeonly uncooperative tank.

Maria's apartment complex was an older boxy brick building that had been built in the early sixties. Although Maria would have preferred to rent one of the cute cottages in town, the bland one-bedroom apartment in the ugly building had the advantage of being cheap.

Kat knocked and grinned at Maria when her friend opened the door. Maria spread her arms wide, "Girlfriend!" They embraced and Kat handed her a bottle of wine. "You can partake if you like, but I can't, since I have to drive home. Mostly I just wanted to talk to you and hang out somewhere without dogs that I'm incredibly pissed-off at."

"That sounds like a good enough reason for a Wine and Whine to me." Maria took the wine and went to the small kitchen. "You never get mad at those furry things. What happened?"

Kat settled onto the sofa and sighed. "Well, this sheltie I'm taking care of is, well, for lack of any other term, gross. His owner mentioned that Arlo had 'sensitive' digestion. But what comes out of that dog smells like nothing I've ever smelled before. It's like…I don't even know what it's like."

Maria sat down next to Kat on the couch. "That's okay. You can spare me the details. I'm trying to drink. Don't spoil the bouquet of my vintage here. I'll use my imagination."

"It's bad."

"Girlfriend, you know dogs stink. They just do."

"I know. But this one is extra stinky. I don't think my nostrils are ever going to be the same. I suppose it just feels worse since Joel isn't around to sympathize." She glared at Maria. "And don't call me codependent again. I looked it up online and I was right. It's definitely *not* the same thing as missing someone."

Maria tilted her wineglass toward Kat. "Wow. You really *are* cranky, girlfriend."

"I know." Kat slumped on the sofa. "Then I thought I lost Joel's dog."

Maria stopped drinking in mid-sip. "Okay, that's definitely not good. I take it you did not, in fact, misplace Lady?"

"No. I was walking out there for ages calling her name, freezing my toes off. And Lady was in Joel's truck sleeping the whole time. I was so cold, and it was all I could do not to kill her."

"Maybe she misses him too."

"Yeah, maybe. Probably." Kat sat up straight again. "But that's not even the worst thing at all! Something happened to Joel. Cindy called. He hit his head and he's in the hospital."

Maria turned and looked into her eyes. "The engineer is okay, right?"

"That's what they say. But I couldn't talk to him." Kat leaned on Maria's shoulder. "What if something really happened to him?"

"Listen to me, girlfriend, you do not want to cross that bridge unless you have to. Assume he's fine until you find out otherwise." Maria sipped her wine thoughtfully. "But now I know why you got so mad at the wildlife. Transference. You're mad because you can't talk to the engineer so you're blaming his dog."

Kat groaned. "Oh no, not more psychobabble."

"Hey, I'm learning new stuff. The ad game is all about psychology. People buy for emotional reasons. I didn't know that. When I look at a pair of shoes, I think about how they'll look fine on me. I have lists of reasons why I need a new pair of shoes. I think my reasons sound logical, but according to Michael, I guess they aren't."

"Probably not. I've heard your reasons."

"Speaking of fine and Michael. He is fine, and I like to look at him when he talks about advertising, psychology, and stuff. So this job is working for me so far, even though it's a bit of a tragedy that he's taken. Anyway, I guess the whole transference thing doesn't explain the stinky dog."

"Maybe it does. I probably would be better able to take Arlo's digestive indiscretions in stride if I weren't so upset about this other stuff. It's not like I don't have lots of experience cleaning that house. Or bad smells."

"Well, that's a fact."

Kat waved her hands in exasperation. "It's making me insane that I can't just fly out and see Joel and make sure for myself he's okay."

"I'm sure he's fine, girlfriend. You'll talk to him tomorrow and he'll sound just the same as he always does. Which, fortunately, you actually find appealing."

Kat shoved Maria playfully. "Don't be a smart aleck. You know how I feel about him."

"I know, girlfriend. And I mean it. He'll be fine." She raised her glass. "Good thing my glass was almost empty. Spilling the wine at a Whine and Wine is a punishable offense, you know."

"I know. That would be alcohol abuse and we can't have that." Kat wrapped her arm around Maria and leaned her head against hers. "Thanks. I'm so glad you're living here now."

"You can repay me by finding me an available man in this town who actually has all his teeth."

"Yeah, that's a tough one. But I'll work on it."

~

The next evening after closing the store, Beth drove out to pick up Arlo. Her mom adored Arlo and was eager to have him back at home. Although she hadn't said anything specific, Beth got the distinct impression that Kat was quite ready for Arlo to go home as well. Beth hoped he hadn't done anything too disgusting.

The Explorer thumped through the potholes in the driveway and Beth pulled in next to the green truck. She saw Kat come down the steps and hurried to get out of the

Explorer. Arlo was barking furiously in the outbuilding. "Hi Kat. How are you?"

"I'm fine." Kat walked over to the outbuilding, opened the door, and shouted over the noise of Arlo's barking. "I've got everything all packed up for you. It looks like Arlo is happy to see you again."

Beth waved at the dog. "Arlo, for heaven's sake, be quiet."

Kat unlatched the gate, pushed in the door, and leashed up Arlo.

Arlo ran out and leaped up on Beth, who belatedly pushed him down. "Arlo, no!" She was too slow. So much for her nice clean slacks. Oh well. She looked at Kat. "I detect the scent of enzymatic cleaner. Along with the distinctive stench of Arlo."

"Probably." Kat handed her the leash. "You, uh, weren't kidding about his digestion. I've spent more time scrubbing than I have in months. I scrubbed the kennel. I scrubbed my house. I scrubbed his feet and various other body parts, which I can report, he didn't appreciate."

"I'm sorry. I have been cleaning too. My mom is going to have to give up and throw away her dining-room rug. I don't think the pumpkin works for him. I'll talk to her about taking him to the vet again."

"Just so you know, I tried keeping him in the house so he wouldn't be too lonely, but I don't think I'll be able to do that again."

"I understand. I'll be happy to pay for carpet cleaning if he did something truly atrocious."

"That's okay. My aunt had dogs for a lot of years and I think the rug has lived through worse. But thanks for offering." Kat looked down, fiddling with a pocket on her coat. "I was on the phone and not paying attention, so really it's partly my fault. Normally, Joel probably would have noticed and gotten him outside in time."

"Where's Joel?"

"He had to go out East. His aunt is sick."

"I hope everything is okay."

Kat shrugged. "I think so. I talked to him this morning. Although I'll probably faint when I get my long-distance bill. Plus I keep getting calls from companies asking me if I want to change my long-distance provider. It's like all of a sudden, they *know* they can make a fortune off me."

Beth laughed. "Maybe they do. Technology marches on."

Kat bent down to pet Arlo. "Cindy is probably home from the airport by now. She'll see you tomorrow, Arlo. Be good."

Beth loaded Arlo into the Explorer and returned to her mother's house. Kat had been too nice to say it, but she probably was hoping she never saw Arlo again. Beth looked in the rearview mirror at Arlo. "What are we going to do with you, buddy?"

The next day at the store, Beth was half-heartedly sorting through books and thinking about Drew. She wanted to tell him about the cruise for her mother. He would love that idea. She also wanted to know if he was still planning to come to the party. At some point, Beth had realized she hadn't actually given him any details about where the event was being held.

Beth called the Enchanted Moose and the surly woman at the front desk told her that Drew's phone was on Do Not Disturb, but that she could leave a message. Flustered, Beth listened to the automated voice and hung up before the beep. Could she be any more juvenile? She called back and forced herself to leave a message like a real grown-up. She gave Drew the details about the party and only stuttered a couple of times. But she did manage to get out the fact that she wanted him to come. Why did he have his phone off? She had no idea what he could possibly be doing. Maybe Dixie didn't like phones? He seemed to be alone, but maybe he wasn't. Maybe he met another woman from the reunion. Beth shook her head in an effort to stall her swirling thoughts. The idea of Drew with one of her classmates was disturbing. She didn't want to dwell on *that* hypothesis.

After sorting through a few more piles of books, Beth became increasingly annoyed at her own thoughts. If she wanted to know what Drew was doing, she should just ask him. After being a coward and avoiding him for ten years, she *still* couldn't just pick up the phone and tell him she'd like to talk to him? What was wrong with her? She should just ask him to call her back. Why didn't she do that before? Beth sighed and threw a book into the recycle pile. Could she be any more socially inept?

She picked up the receiver and dialed the number for the Enchanted Moose again. "Yes, I'd like to speak to Drew Emery, please."

"You again?"

"Yes. I apologize. I inadvertently failed to include a salient detail in my message."

The phone rang again and as she listened to the automated message she tried to formulate what she was going to say. After the beep, she stammered, "Drew, hi, um, I know, it... it's me again. Beth? I just was wondering, well, wondering if you might, I don't know…maybe…maybe. Well, if maybe I could see you before the party? Or talk to you? There is something I wanted. Um…yes…something I wanted to tell you about. I'll be at the store. Here. It is in the same place. Well, you know that. Maybe you could stop by? Or maybe call? I will be here the same hours. You know. Ten to five. Okay, anyway…that was it. I am sorry to bother you. 'Bye."

Beth hung up and put her forehead on her palms. That had to be the most convoluted inarticulate message in the history of the universe. If he actually did show up here, she'd be embarrassed to even look at him. Returning to Alpine Grove seemed to be causing some regression in her already meager interpersonal skills.

Later that afternoon, the phone rang and Beth smiled at the sound of Drew's voice. He said, "You called?"

"Yes, I mostly just wanted to say hi." She looked up as the bells on the doors jingled and said, "Oops."

"Is something wrong?"

She whispered, "A customer just walked in. I shouldn't be on the phone."

"Let me guess, your mom will kill you."

Beth giggled. "Sorry, but you know my mom is really strict about calls. No talking on the phone when customers are in the store. Can I call you right back?" She watched as the woman perused the shelves. Putting her hand over the mouthpiece, she said, "Please let me know if you need anything." The woman nodded and pulled a book down from a shelf.

"Beth, are you there?"

She could hear the annoyance in his voice. "I'm sorry, Drew. Did you know your phone is on Do Not Disturb?"

"I know."

"Well, ah, could you take it off, so I can call you back? I'm sure it will only be fifteen minutes or so. I'll call you just as soon as this customer leaves."

"All right."

Beth said goodbye and hung up. She returned to sorting books and watched as the customer slowly worked her way around the store, methodically pulling out titles and reading the back covers. The woman appeared to be in her late forties or early fifties. Didn't she have anything else to do? She had to have looked at a hundred-twenty-five books, yet she still wasn't carrying anything. Beth said, "Can I help you find something?"

The woman shook her head, causing her brown hair to brush against her chin. "Just browsing."

An hour-and-a-half later, the woman smiled, looked down, and said "thank you" before strolling out of the store, having purchased absolutely nothing. Beth sighed and picked up the phone to call Drew. As usual, she got the surly woman and then the answering machine.

Oh well. She'd tried. If he was that intent on not being disturbed, she'd just have to talk to him at the party. If he showed up, he'd find out with everyone else about her mom's cruise to Mexico. Beth smiled as she started gathering up her things in preparation for closing. Mom was going to be so thrilled.

∼

Saturday at the store, Beth waved through the window at people who were walking to the Italian restaurant for the party. She had no idea how Bea Sullivan had managed to talk

Jerry, the owner of the restaurant, into closing it for a private event, but she had. Bea had remarkable powers of persuasion.

Beth was sitting near the window sorting books and Margaret was at the desk reading a novel. Her mother was feeling better and had been working afternoons at the store for the past couple of days. She assured Beth that she could return home to Tucson whenever she liked.

The idea of being warm again was enticing and Beth got her return ticket set up for Monday, which would give her tomorrow to pack and make sure everything was arranged for her return to Alpine Grove in March for the cruise. Since it was a surprise, she couldn't talk to her mother about it yet.

After this peculiar, yet somewhat nostalgic, blast back to her past, Beth wasn't sure how she felt about returning to her real life. This trip had been a good distraction, but when she returned home, she'd have to face the harsh truth that her life was a mess. What happened next? Looking for a job was obvious. But what would she do with herself? No work. No school. What did unemployed people do all day? The only bright spot was that it would probably be amusing to relate her Alpine Grove experiences to Graham and give him more insight into her formative years.

Beth had convinced her mother to ask Cindy to drive her to the bookstore after walking Arlo, so Margaret wouldn't have to walk there alone. Beth had driven to the store the last two days so she could drive her mother home at the end of the day. However, Margaret insisted that she could walk the few blocks up the street to the restaurant.

Beth gathered up her things and got ready to close up. "It's no big deal to drive, Mom."

"I'm not an invalid. I feel much better. And I want the fresh air. I'm certainly not going to drive to the store after you leave, so I'd better get used to it."

"You could drive here for a little while. Why not?"

"Parking is bad enough. I don't want to take up a space that could be used by a paying customer."

Beth sighed. This was another of Mom's retail rules. "All right. But if you start feeling sore again, you should drive."

Margaret glared at her. "You're hovering again, dear. Please stop it."

"Sorry. I just want to make sure you're okay."

They strolled slowly up the street and then crossed over to the other side. Margaret stopped in front of Bea Haven Gifts. "Look at her window display. Isn't it lovely? I need to do more with mine."

"You always say that. The bookstore window looks great. Bea has lots of glittery gift items she can use. Books don't sparkle."

"I suppose."

They walked into the Italian restaurant and Margaret was immediately surrounded by well-wishers. Beth took her mom's purse and coat and retreated to a table. She sat down and put her finger to her eye, trying to get her contact lens back into the right place again. The stupid things had a knack for leaping out of her eyes at the worst possible moments. Blinking a few times, her vision cleared and she saw Drew walking over to her.

She waved and smiled eagerly. "You made it!"

"Hey, Beth. This is quite a crowd." He sat down. "I can't stay long. Miss Dixie is napping, but I need to get back to deal with her."

"Oh, but you'll miss the big surprise."

"What's that?"

Beth reached over and put her hand on his arm. "Jill is giving my mom a cruise to Mexico. Isn't that wonderful?"

"Yeah, your mom will love that."

She smiled. "I'm going to brave the cold and the inevitable unpleasant spring snowstorm and watch the store while she's gone."

"You're coming back here? That's surprising."

"Just for a couple of weeks. Jill asked me about it the other day. I tried to call you, remember?"

Drew looked away toward the crowded room. "Yeah, sorry about that. I had deadlines."

Beth squeezed his arm. "Deadlines for what? You never told me what you do."

"I write. And as you may recall, I have a lot of experience with procrastination, so unlike raindrops on roses, deadlines are not a few of my favorite things."

Beth smiled. "You used to refer to yourself as a world-class expert in that area."

He looked back at her. "Yeah, some things never change."

"What do you write?"

"Novels."

Beth's jaw dropped. "You're a novelist? Really? Would I have read anything you've written?"

"You said you hadn't."

"When?"

"When you took my book out of Dixie's sharp little teeth." He grinned. "That pup has good taste in mysteries."

"*You're* A.J. Emerson?"

He wiggled his eyebrows. "Don't tell. It's a secret."

"I'll say. That is definitely *not* you on the back cover."

"Yeah, I know. It's some model they got."

"So you didn't call me because you were writing?"

Drew stretched his legs out under the table and leaned back in the chair. "Sort of. I was staring at the screen anyway. I'm having a little problem with writer's block, you might say. My publisher is not amused. I'm on the last book of a six-book contract and I can't figure out how to end it."

"Can I help? You helped me back in high school. Maybe I can return the favor?"

"No. I just gotta pound through it and get it done." He shrugged. "Mostly, I'm worried about disappointing my readers."

"You must have a lot of fans. Danielle told me she read about you in *People* magazine."

He cocked his head and scratched his ear. "Yeah, that interviewer was one fry short of a Happy Meal, so I kinda came off sounding like a moron. But my publisher loved the publicity. They were talking about another contract, but now they might be rethinking that idea."

"I'm sure that's not true. My mom said she loves your books. She's got the next one on pre-order, so she gets it as soon as it's released."

"That's good to hear." Drew moved to get up. "On that note, I should go give her my regards and get going."

"Already? But you just got here." She grabbed his hand. "Wait, Drew! I'm leaving on Monday. Can I see you again? I don't even know where you live. I don't want to lose touch for another ten years."

He sat back down, squeezed her hand, and looked into her eyes. "I don't think that's a good idea."

"Why not? Can't we be friends? It's been great catching up with you again. Like no time has passed at all."

He let go of her hand. "But it has."

"So what? I'd love to hear more about your books. You always did tell the best stories. I remember sitting up there at Make Out Point looking out at the lake and you were telling me this whole complicated tale about your cousin Bart." She grinned. "It was hilarious. You have the weirdest family."

He scratched his chin. "I may have embellished a little."

"So Bart didn't hang upside down in trees pretending to be a bat?"

"I may have made that up."

"What about Frances and her promiscuous friend Barb at the hair salon?"

"Yeah, she was slutty. But largely fictional." Drew shrugged. "I really have to go, Beth."

"Could we exchange phone numbers?" She started rummaging around in her purse, looking for a pen.

"Let's just say goodbye, okay?" He placed both hands on the table and pushed himself up.

She looked up into his eyes. "I don't understand. Are you still angry? I wouldn't blame you if you were. But I told you, I am truly sorry. Can't we be friends now?" She needed all the friends she could get.

He sat back down heavily. "No, I'm not angry at you anymore. I got over that a long time ago. You were right that I had a lot of growing up to do. I had a bunch of stupid, unrealistic ideas back then. But our lives are different now. I move around a lot. You have a house and a guy waiting for you back in Arizona."

"So what? That doesn't mean we can't keep in touch." Beth had so few people she could really talk to that the idea of losing Drew's friendship *again* made her feel slightly sick. It was just like when her friend Michelle moved away after tenth grade. After that, Beth didn't have anyone to sit with at lunch. That was when she had starting hiding out in the library, so people wouldn't see that she had no friends.

Drew placed his forearms on the table and leaned forward. "What's your boyfriend's name again?"

"Graham."

"Would you want to have Graham's old lovers contacting him? How would you feel about that?"

Beth shrugged. "Well, if they were in the past, it would be fine, I suppose. I mean I know he was married before."

"How much contact does he have with his ex-wife?"

"He never talks about her."

"I'm sure that's on purpose."

"So you really never want to see me again?"

"I don't think we work as 'just friends,' Beth." He shook his head. "Everything that happened back then—it was just all too intense. There's way too much history with us."

Beth felt a tear slip down her cheek. She blinked rapidly and her contact lens flipped out of her eye. "Stop! Don't move!"

"Jeez Beth, *really*? This used to happen all the time. Why don't you get those soft contact lenses that don't fly out of your eye every ten minutes?"

Beth stretched out her hands, feeling around the tablecloth to find the contact. "They don't work for me. I couldn't see as well. It was like I was looking at things underwater, which gave me a headache."

Drew bent down and peered under the table. "In this dim light, we're never gonna find the fool thing."

"I'm sure we will. Just don't step on it!"

Drew lifted his feet up under the chair and leaned down, running his hand along the floor. "Okay. I got it." He handed the tiny green lens to her. "Dang, those things really get airborne."

Beth dunked the contact into her water glass on the table and put it back in her eye. She blinked a few times and smiled with relief. "Thank goodness. I hate not being able to see."

Drew put his hand on hers briefly, then stood up again. "Okay. I'm really leaving now. You take care."

She stood and faced him. "This is ridiculous. I don't want to say goodbye to you *forever*."

"Well, you sure had no problem doing it before."

Beth looked down at the floor. "I know. It was a terrible mistake. One that I wish I could take back."

"You can't just press a rewind button, Beth. Life's not like that." He put his fingertip under her chin and tilted her head up so he could look into her eyes. "But if you have an emergency or something and really need to reach me for some reason, you can always find me through my publisher. I know your mom has the books at the store."

Beth reached out, wrapped her arms around his neck, and looked into his face. "I don't want to do this again, Drew. I'm going to miss you too much."

The distressed look in his eyes softened. "I know, Bethie. Me too." He bent his head and kissed her lips quickly before he pulled her arms away from him and stepped back from her. "Have a safe trip back to Tucson."

As he crossed the room to the crowd around her mother, Beth touched her fingertip to her lips, which still tingled from the contact. He was right. Some things never changed.

She watched as Margaret hugged Drew and gestured animatedly. They chatted briefly, and a few minutes later he was gone.

~

Beth and her mother returned from the party late. Margaret was exhilarated and said it was the best birthday party she'd ever had. Beth was exhausted from the stress of socializing, but pleased at how well the party had gone. No one seemed to want to leave and only when Jerry started closing up the restaurant did everyone start reluctantly exchanging hugs and filtering out onto the street. This was probably the most late-night action the main street of Alpine Grove had seen in half a decade.

On the short drive to the house, Margaret went on and on about all the people who had been there. Beth had spent much of the evening near the door smiling and attempting to chat with most of the people she'd ever met in Alpine Grove, along with quite a few she hadn't. It was probably going to take a week for her introverted soul to recover from all that human contact. She was looking forward to a relaxing Sunday of sleeping in, reading, and packing for her trip home.

After the conflicting emotions related to seeing Drew again, it would be a relief to be in her own space to decompress. Not to mention warm. She smiled at the idea of sitting outside and letting the relaxing warmth of the desert sun wash over her face.

The next morning, Beth made waffles for breakfast because they were one of her mother's favorite foods. Margaret loved any excuse to flood a plate with maple syrup, and she felt that waffles were superior to pancakes because the little indentations were ideally designed to hold onto the sugary maple goodness.

After stuffing themselves, Beth and her mother prepared to settle in for a reading session. Beth was dying to find out what Drew's novels were like. She asked her mother to see if she could find any of the A.J. Emerson books she had at the house.

After a protracted search, Margaret finally unearthed the first book in the series from the gigantic pile of paperbacks she had stacked on the settee in her bedroom. She handed it to Beth. "Well, at least I found the first one. I'm not sure where the second one went. Maybe I lent it to someone. You really want to read the second one too, because of how this one ends."

"Don't tell me what happens. I have a bunch of stuff to do today, anyway. Mostly I want something to read on the plane. I'll bring it back when I return in March. Anyway, I'll start with this one and see if I like it. "

Margaret grinned. "Oh you will, dear. I can't wait until he releases the sixth one. I'm so glad you called the distributor. I want to be sure I have copies for the store as soon as it comes out."

Beth laughed. "I always knew it. You really only order those new books for yourself. Can you imagine if you didn't own a used bookstore? You'd spend everything you had on books."

"That's sadly true. As it is, I can support my reading habit and still earn a living." She sighed. "Although less so in February and March. When you return, I don't think you'll have much to worry about as far as sales and dealing with customers, since it's the slow season."

"Oh Mom, you worry about this every year and then it picks up again. By summer, you'll be complaining about how you can barely move around in there because it's so full of people."

"I know. You'd think I'd be used to the cyclical nature of Alpine Grove business by now. But when I look at the paltry receipts every day, it's difficult not to panic."

Beth put her arms around her mother's shoulders. "I probably shouldn't say this, but the lack of customers did make it less traumatic for me to ease back into retail. Maybe next year you can think about doing something creative to coincide with that Chamber of Commerce Mardi Gras celebration you told me about. I'm sure your store isn't the only one hurting at the moment."

"We'll see." Margaret waved her hands, shooing Beth away. "I'm not going to think about that right now. I'm keeping you from your novel. Go relax and enjoy! You have a long trip tomorrow."

Beth went downstairs and settled into her favorite cushy chair to read. The next thing she knew, Margaret was bending down next to her. "Beth? Didn't you hear me?"

She reluctantly pulled her gaze from the page. "What?"

"Would you be willing to walk Arlo? It's getting late and he's starting to look anxious."

"What time is it?"

"Two."

Beth cast her gaze around the room. "Oh no! Has he done something revolting? I don't smell anything."

"Not yet, dear. But you might want to hurry."

Beth jumped up from the chair, marked her place in the book, and set it aside. She speed-walked across the room to get a coat and the dog's leash. "I'm sorry. I completely lost track of time."

Margaret gave her an I-told-you-so smile. "I knew you'd like those books."

Beth leashed up Arlo, who was obviously quite relieved to be going for his walk. They went outside and slowly began the trek down the street. "Sorry, buddy. I got wrapped up in Drew's book."

Arlo was not interested in excuses and continued sniffing at a particularly fascinating patch of snow. Beth stared off down the street, waiting for him to finish. She was thinking about the intricate mystery story and wondering what would happen next. How on earth was Drew going to get the main character, Preston Truitt, out of the mess he was in? And the woman too. What about Liz Logan?

The trip home was uneventful, and as the plane circled Tucson International Airport, Beth looked down at the familiar mountain ranges, trying to see if she could determine where her house was located from the air. The flight from LA was short, and she was so close to being done with Drew's novel, she just wanted to get back home so she could finish it. What a page-turner.

When Beth walked into her house, it was as if she hadn't left. It felt like so many things had happened in Alpine Grove, yet time appeared to have stopped here at home in Tucson. She put down her suitcase and tried to remember what she had as far as food.

Opening the refrigerator, she discovered that some things *had* changed. That was disgusting. When she left, she had assumed she'd only be gone for a few days. Extending her trip to Alpine Grove had not only been expensive, it had not done much for the items in the produce drawer. Gross.

She set to work throwing away slimy lettuce and a package of strawberries that had developed a pelt of white fuzz along the top. The sad little berries looked like they were wearing tiny fur coats. Reading was going to have to wait until after she went to the store. She also should pick up a copy of the Tucson newspaper and look at the employment classifieds. That exercise would undoubtedly be futile and depressing, but she had to start somewhere. With a sigh, she grabbed a pad and pencil and started making up a grocery list.

Chapter 5

The Silver Bird

The next morning, Beth rolled over in bed and looked at the clock. She never slept in like this. Maybe all the travel had worn her out more than she thought. It had felt funny not setting her alarm the night before, but it wasn't like she had to get up and go to work.

After she returned from the grocery store, she checked her e-mail. That certainly didn't go well. The only e-mail she'd received from RTP during the time she was in Alpine Grove said that she needed to return her laptop. She had replied with the date she would be returning to Tucson and explained that she'd give back the laptop then. Now her work e-mail account was disabled. The messages on her answering machine related to the issue were equally unpleasant. A stern-sounding fellow in the IT department called to let her know she needed to return her "RTP company property" as soon as possible.

It sounded like a threat, but what were they going to do, fire her?

Beth needed to copy some files off the laptop before she returned it, so they were going to just have to get over themselves. She'd get the stupid thing back to them today, but first she was going to finish Drew's book. She pulled the novel off her nightstand and returned to the story.

She turned the last page and sat up in bed. "Are you kidding me?" Slapping the covers closed, she mumbled, "I don't believe it, Drew. Really? *That's* how you end it?"

Today's errands obviously were going to need to include a trip to her favorite Bookman's bookstore for the next installment in the series. Her mother hadn't been kidding about needing to read the second one. No wonder the publisher loved Drew. There was no way a reader wouldn't want to know what happened next. He'd probably made that publishing company a mint.

Making a conscious effort to disengage her mind from Drew's intricate North Carolina-based story world, Beth settled into the tedious task of copying her personal files from the RTP laptop. She had a lot of information related to her dissertation that she might need if she wanted to get her PhD someday. Then she was going to wipe the hard-disk drive. Thanks to the data-mirroring tools she had helped develop, RTP had duplicates of all of her work-related files stored on the company intranet anyway.

Beth smiled as she tapped the keys. One advantage of having done so much work on storage encryption algorithms for RTP meant that it was highly unlikely anyone would ever be able to get access to any intellectual property she didn't want them to have. There was no way they were getting access to her research. When she erased files, they weren't just gone, they were *really* gone, so they couldn't be restored by even a geeky expert. Sure, she had moved into management, but she hadn't forgotten all her sneaky tech tricks.

After transferring the files onto her own personal computer and storing her backup copies in a drawer, Beth was ready to head out to return her "RTP company property" to its rightful owner. She was nervous about going back to the science and technology park after her ignoble exit on the day she was laid off. Seeing everyone was going to be awkward and she wasn't looking forward to talking to her boss Joan again. They had been friends as well as coworkers, but now that she didn't work at RTP, that was likely to change. After she'd been laid off, she'd thought about calling some of her colleagues, but most of them were really just acquaintances. They talked about work, but she never saw them socially. And now she was an outsider, so they'd have nothing in common at all.

Giving back the laptop had to be done. She packed up the small computer in its bag for the last time and tried to pretend she was just driving off to work like any other day. She sat in her car and looked around the interior, remembering the day she had acquired it. Graham had gone with her and applauded her choice of a sensible sedan for her first brand-new car. The 1992 Ford Taurus had been a problem from the day she drove it off the lot.

Beth hated the "ugly purple thing" as she thought of it. But because it was a lease, she had been able to afford the payments. They hadn't had the color she actually wanted, so she'd ended up with a Taurus that was a sort of sickly reddish purple, which had faded to an even less attractive color in the desert sun.

As Beth drove to the science and technology park, she considered the fact that the lease on the Taurus was coming up at the end of the month. The leasing company was encouraging her to buy the car, but she needed to look up the Blue Book value at the library, because it seemed like what they wanted to pay off the ugly purple thing was utterly absurd. Soon, in addition to having no job, she'd have no car either. Being able to get a new car with no job wasn't promising. Perhaps she'd spend some more time scouring the classifieds. The employment ads had been predictably useless, but maybe she'd do better in the used-car section. And this time, she was not going to get talked into buying something ugly.

Beth returned from her errands minus one laptop and plus four A.J. Emerson books. After the tense discussion with Joan, her now-former boss at RTP, Beth had needed some retail therapy, and books had always been her solace.

Beth had spent way too much time perusing the shelves at Bookman's. The place was huge and teeming with book-loving people, which was comforting in an odd way. After the bookstore, she'd gone to the library to research the value of the Taurus and peruse a few *Consumer Reports* and car magazines. She needed to learn more about the used-car market and get some ideas for alternate transportation.

As Beth drove across town toward home, she went over her conversation with Joan in her mind. Clearly, Beth's termination from RTP was going to have an effect on her friendship with Joan, just like she'd anticipated. Yet another friendship gone.

Making friends was always so difficult and Beth's universe suddenly felt a lot smaller without the camaraderie of her co-workers at RTP. Even if those people weren't friends exactly, they were human beings. If she remained unemployed without contact with anyone, she'd probably turn into some kind of bizarre shut-in. She'd never expected to be in the position of completely starting over at this point in her life.

After she got home, Beth spent some more time with the classifieds. The job listings were demoralizing, unless she wanted to start a new career in fast-food service. Ugh. At least the car ads were more interesting. She circled a few possibilities and took a deep breath. Time to start calling. Picking up the phone and talking to people she didn't know always made her uneasy. The first person she talked to claimed the paper had misprinted the price. Making a special effort to enunciate slowly and clearly, Beth said politely that no, she was not in the position to pay twenty-five-thousand dollars, even if the vehicle was a "classic." Moving on.

She made a few more calls and found a car that looked promising. The woman who owned it had purchased the car new and had kept all the service records over the years. Her name was also Elizabeth, so maybe it was a sign. They had laughed about the fact that Elizabeth actually preferred to be called Elizabeth, not Betsey, Liz, Lizzie, Liza, Eliza, or Beth.

The car was a 1988 Acura Integra with fairly low miles. Although the Acura was older than the Taurus, it was in the right price range, so Beth would be able to pay cash from her savings. It might just work. Beth got into the ugly purple thing and drove out toward the university. She passed by some of her old stomping grounds at the U of A and navigated to an older neighborhood. The car was sitting out front, and Beth tapped her hands on the steering wheel in excitement. It was adorable!

Beth knocked on the door and introduced herself to the owner, who smiled and put out her hand. "Hi Beth, I'm Elizabeth. Do you want to look it over?"

The two women walked around the car. Beth had no idea what she should be looking for or at, but the car seemed to be in okay shape. Although there were some dings in the silver paint, at least the car didn't appear to have been in a wreck.

It felt right. Elizabeth said, "Would you like to take it for a drive?"

"Yes, please. That would be great. But, um, I haven't driven a car with a manual transmission in a while." That was an understatement. Drew had taught her on his horrible old Datsun, but that seemed like a lifetime ago.

Elizabeth handed her the keys and walked around to the passenger side. "It will probably come back to you. And every car is different anyway. I stalled out this one when I was pulling out of the dealership. It was kind of embarrassing."

Beth giggled. "Thanks. That makes me feel a little better."

After adjusting the seat and mirrors, Beth put the car in neutral and pushed in the clutch. "Okay, here we go."

As Beth slowly drove through the residential neighborhood, she started to relax. Elizabeth was right, the nuances of driving a manual transmission were starting to return, particularly since she didn't have to take the car out of second gear at the moment. Beth pulled over and parked so Elizabeth could explain all the various heating and audio controls on the dashboard. After trying everything out, Beth turned to Elizabeth. "I like the car. Why are you selling it?"

Elizabeth patted the dashboard. "The Silver Bird and I have had some good times together, but I just got a new job that pays better, so I'm celebrating by buying a brand-new Acura. The dealer gave me such an insultingly low offer on the trade-in for the Silver Bird, I told them I'd sell it myself and get back to them. I'm sure all those pretty new Acuras will still be there on the new-car lot when I return."

Beth smiled. "I didn't enjoy my experience with car dealers much either. I leased my car and I'm looking forward to giving it back. They're not going to be happy."

"So are you interested? I've had a lot of calls on her."

"Yes. I'm sure my boyfriend would tell me I should drive it more, but I can tell it's in good shape. I'll take it. But first I'd like to get it checked out by a mechanic, if that's okay. There's a foreign-car place on Speedway I drive by all the time."

"That's fine. They should certainly know Acuras."

Beth started the car and drove it back to Elizabeth's house. They exchanged numbers so they could work out the appointment with the mechanic, and assuming all went well, transfer ownership. Since Beth was paying cash, the car would be all hers. No leasing company and no payments. She couldn't wait.

~

When she got home, Beth was eager to share her automotive news with Graham. The last few times she'd talked to him, he had sounded distracted and couldn't talk long. He was being vague, but she had the impression that something was happening at the university again. And whatever it was definitely displeased him. She really wanted to see Graham in person and find out what was going on.

She called his office and talked to his assistant, who said he had left early. Hopefully he wasn't sick. Dialing the number to his house, she tapped her foot. The new car was so cute. She couldn't wait to drive it somewhere fun by herself so no one—except the Silver Bird—would discover that Beth might not have quite perfected her shifting technique yet. And at last she would have a car with a sunroof! If she was going to live in a place with 350 days of sunshine, she really should have a car with a sunroof.

Graham answered the phone and Beth greeted him eagerly. "I have great news."

"Hello Beth. Did something exciting happen in the realm of the unemployed? I thought for sure you'd be working your way through your fifth or sixth novel by now."

"No. Just one. I've been busy." He didn't need to know about all the new A.J. Emerson novels sitting on her dining room table right now.

He chuckled. "Oh yes, with all that work you have to do, right?"

Beth sighed. It was obvious from his tone that Graham was in one of his difficult moods. "No, obviously I'm not currently toiling away at RTP. However, I have other items that must be addressed in order to find gainful employment again. Most notably an automobile."

"You have a car. The Taurus. I was with you when you got it."

"I know. The lease is up. I plan to give it back."

"But why? It's an excellent car and it's perfect for you."

"No. I bought a new car today. Well, almost. I haven't signed anything yet."

"Beth, are you insane? You just lost your job. Why would you spend money on an extravagance like a new car *now*?"

"Technically, it is not new. It's a 1988 Integra two-door. It's so cute, Graham, you should see it. I love it!"

"You're buying an eight-year-old junker? Really, Beth, what were you thinking? What if it dies on you?"

"It has low miles and I did research on used cars. *Car and Driver* magazine named the Integra to its annual "Ten Best" list in 1988. And *Consumer Reports* gave it good marks for reliability too."

"Why didn't you talk to me about this decision? Didn't you want my input?"

"I figured you were busy." Beth twisted her necklace and gripped the heart pendant with her fingertips. "It will be my car, not yours."

"I know that. But I have vastly more experience in these type of transactions. Didn't you think about that?"

"Not really."

"Oh Beth, I'm surprised at your impetuousness. This isn't like you."

"The car is going to be checked out by a mechanic. I'm certainly not going to purchase it if there are fundamental problems."

"Fine, Beth. I need to get back to what I was doing. Did you want something else or just to tell me about your *cute* car."

"I was hoping we could see each other."

"Not all of us have the free time you do, Beth. I have commitments."

Beth sat down heavily in the chair. What was wrong with him? "Graham, what is going on? You haven't been acting like yourself."

"Things are complicated at work. I'd rather not go into it."

"Wouldn't you feel better if we talked about it? We used to talk about university politics all the time. You said I had good insights. It feels like you're shutting me out."

"Beth, that's not true at all."

"I haven't even had the chance to tell you about my trip to Alpine Grove with the reunion and everything that happened with my mother."

There was a long pause and finally Graham said, "All right. I suppose I have some time later this evening if that works with your busy schedule."

"Do you want to come by here?"

"Certainly. I'll be there around seven thirty, darling."

Beth hung up the phone and looked around the room. She'd been home for less than twenty-four hours and already newspapers and books were strewn everywhere. The place was a mess. At least she'd hosed out the refrigerator yesterday. Graham was unlikely to be amused by fruit wearing furry outerwear.

By seven thirty the house was sparkling and Beth was exhausted. She'd barely had time to grab a quick shower, so she wouldn't be all sweaty and disgusting when he arrived. Now, garbed in a light cotton sundress, she felt good about the appearance of both her home and herself.

Beth settled into her favorite chair and picked up the second A.J. Emerson novel. Maybe she could get in a few pages before Graham arrived. She was dying to know what happened to Preston Truitt. The poor guy was having serious problems at the end of the first book. And the relationship between him and the woman, Liz Logan, was getting extremely interesting.

The doorbell rang, startling her out of the story. Glancing at the clock, she noted it was 8:30. Graham was an hour late. Had she misunderstood the time?

Beth opened the door and wrapped her arms around him, hugging him hard. He kissed the top of her head and handed her a bottle of wine. "My apologies for being late, Beth."

"It's okay. I'm so glad to see you and glad you could make it this evening. I have so many things to tell you. Have a seat." Beth went to open the wine and poured Graham a glass. "Here you go."

"Aren't you going to have any?"

"You know that doesn't tend to be a good idea."

"Oh, come on. Just one glass. We should toast to your new hunk of junk."

Beth turned and poured herself a half a glass. She held it up. "Here's to the Silver Bird!"

"That's lyrical."

Beth sat down next to Graham on the sofa and leaned toward him, smiling. "Isn't it great? The owner named the car. I think she took good care of it too. It sounds like she's going to miss it."

Graham rolled his eyes melodramatically and sipped his wine. "Really, all this about a car?"

"Maybe it is a little silly." Beth turned away from him and gazed down at the burgundy liquid in her glass. Graham knew his wines. It was good. "So tell me what is going on at work."

"The usual." Graham waved his hand west in the general direction of the university. "Just a bunch of unfounded accusations!"

"About what?" But Beth had a bad feeling she knew.

"You know this happens almost every year. Some little student gets a crush on me and then claims I made advances."

"Did you?"

"Of course not!" Graham leaned forward, resting his elbows on his knees and holding the stem of his glass with both hands. "I can't believe you're even asking. That was more than six years ago and you know there were extenuating circumstances. I did not make any overtures toward you until you were no longer a student, and I was cleared of any wrongdoing. And then I got divorced on top of it."

Beth swirled the wine in her glass. "Yes. I remember. How is your ex-wife doing?"

Graham waved his glass at her. "You can't be serious. You said never to mention the name of that 'vile malingering woman' in your presence ever again. I believe it was during the now-legendary Fourth of July dispute of 1989, in which I discovered the scope and truly wicked nature of your temper."

"I said that?" Beth looked away from him. "I suppose I might have."

He got up and poured some more wine. "And yet here we are, still together. Still perfect for one another. Nothing has changed."

"Yes. Here we are."

Graham sat back down and sipped his wine. "With budget cuts, I think the jackals are just looking for ways to get rid of professors. There's always a bunch of up-and-comers willing to work as adjuncts."

"You're just upset that you were passed over for tenure again."

"I am working on my paper. It will be done soon."

"Perhaps they are tired of waiting for you to publish something. I told you I could help you with it, if you like." She lifted her wine glass with a flourish. "And right now, I have quite a bit more free time."

"Thank you for the offer Beth, but this is out of your area of expertise." He waved a hand dismissively. "The technology is *so* advanced and your arguments are unformed and sophomoric."

Beth hated that word. Sometimes he treated her like some ill-behaved student. "Maybe I'm not as well-versed on the subject as you are, but *sophomoric* is a bit extreme, don't you think?"

"It's not a problem. My assistant is helping me."

"And I suppose her arguments are *not* sophomoric?" Beth swirled her wine, observing the droplets as they slid down the side of the glass. "I was not suggesting that I write the paper, Graham. I could help you with research and editing. But it sounds like you have everything well in hand."

Graham drained his wine and got up to get more. "My, aren't you feeling snippy this evening? Apparently, your trip back to Podunkville did not improve your disposition."

"Actually the trip was more enjoyable than I expected."

"Yes, didn't you have lots of small-town anecdotes you wanted to share about bygone days and your glory years as the Cedar Tree valedictorian?"

"Cedar *County*." Beth looked up into Graham's face as he sat back down. What was wrong with him? Maybe she shouldn't have mentioned his ex-wife. "The trip was... eventful, I guess you might say. I told you about my mother's accident."

He closed his eyes and leaned his head back on the sofa. "Yes. I'm glad she is on the mend. It was kind of you to stay and help."

"Her birthday party was a great success. I think everyone in town had a wonderful time."

Graham opened his eyes and sipped his wine. "I'm sure it was the social event of the season."

"The other thing I wanted to let you know is that I am returning to Alpine Grove in March because my mother's sponsor—her friend Jill—gave her a cruise. They're so excited about the trip." Beth smiled. "Mom is over-the-moon happy. It was so sweet!"

"You're going back there? Again? That's going to cut into your job search, isn't it?"

"Well, yes. But I told you, RTP gave me a generous severance package, so I have some time. And soon I won't have a car payment!"

"Of course your savings are also depleted, thanks to your impulsive purchase today."

Generally Beth tried to be patient with his moods because she didn't want to rock the boat. They'd been together for a long time, so naturally they had their ups and downs. She tried not to voice her discontent, since he often found her complaints childish. Sure, sometimes they didn't communicate well or engaged in playful banter as a form of teasing, but this was different. Graham was being downright nasty, and Beth had reached her limit. "What is bothering you? All you have done is snipe at me since you got here."

Graham's eyes widened and he sat up straighter on the sofa. "I told you, work has been stressful, darling."

She put her hand on his. "I'm sorry. Is there anything I can do?" He took work so seriously. Maybe she wasn't being fair.

He put down his wine and turned to look at her. "Perhaps we could have another glass of wine."

Beth nodded. "All right." Maybe everything was fine, after all.

~

The next morning, Beth awoke to sunshine streaming through the window. She stretched her arms above her head, grabbed the headboard, and grinned. Sleeping in late felt so decadent after years of getting up promptly at five in the morning. Unemployment wasn't all bad. She could get used to getting a solid eight hours of sleep every night. When Graham left, he'd kissed her goodbye and promised to call. Because of work schedules and her trip, they hadn't seen each other in a while and after she'd called him on his behavior, he seemed to make an effort to be charming and agreeable.

Beth reached down under the bed and pulled out the A.J. Emerson novel she'd hidden under there. The fact that the chemistry between Preston Truitt and Liz Logan practically sizzled off the page probably had enhanced Beth's romantic feelings toward Graham. He didn't need to know that she was thinking about Preston. All women had little fantasies like that, didn't they? She opened the book and threw the bookmark on her nightstand. Preston and Liz just had to work this out. They just *had* to.

After Graham arrived and made comments about her indulgent reading behaviors, Beth had discreetly moved the book from the chair where she'd been reading and thrown it under the bed before he noticed. It was odd that he was so fixated on the idea of her returning to the ranks of the employed. For the first time she could remember, Beth had absolutely no responsibilities. Why shouldn't she enjoy it? It wasn't like she hadn't done anything. She'd tackled the dreaded resume project and a draft was safely stored on her computer, although she wasn't completely happy with it yet.

Later, the phone rang and Beth reached over to answer it. Elizabeth had made an appointment with the mechanic to get the Acura looked at and they agreed to meet at the foreign-car place later in the day. Beth reluctantly put the book aside. She really needed to get going. With a sigh, she pushed back the bed covers and went to take a shower.

That afternoon the mechanic decreed the Acura basically sound. It would need new brake pads soon, but was otherwise fine. Beth called Elizabeth and told her she was going to the bank to get a cashier's check. Everything was falling into place. After she picked up Elizabeth and she signed the title over to Beth, they would drop the Taurus at the Ford dealer, drop Elizabeth back at her house, and then Beth could take the car and its title home with her. The Silver Bird would be hers!

By the time she got home, Beth was exhausted. What an action-packed day. Buying a car was complicated, but exhilarating. It had been a long time since she'd done something completely on her own with no input from anyone else. No consensus, no compromise, and no meetings. There were a number of things she did not miss about corporate life.

However, she may have annoyed a few Tucson drivers on her way home. People didn't appreciate it when she stalled out at traffic lights. The guy behind her had really lost his sense of humor when she stalled in the middle an intersection and the left-turn arrow started flashing. He had gesticulated wildly and looked like he might have some type of neurological episode.

The congestion in Tucson certainly had not improved since she'd lived there, but by the time she was shooting down the suicide lane on Broadway toward her home on the east side, she was starting to really enjoy driving the Acura. It was so much more fun than the Taurus, and once she figured out shifting, she could really zip around. What a difference. She had arranged with the dealer to sign papers and return the Taurus keys the next day, but at least the ugly purple thing was in their lot and out of her driveway.

After a satisfying evening of devouring the second A.J. Emerson novel, Beth set the book aside. Now that she'd read the second installment in the series, she couldn't deny the fact that Drew had obviously drawn rather heavily on his own experience in writing the character of Liz Logan. Liz was essentially a much sexier, prettier version of Beth. Preston seemed to be drawn to her in spite of himself. The woman did have an unfortunate habit of getting in the middle of his investigations. But the connection the two characters had with one another was undeniably drawn from real life. She and Drew had never solved mysteries together, but he always used to say that Beth understood him like no one else.

In the novels, the character of Liz Logan was described as five-foot-seven with dark-brown hair, deep-set green eyes, and a curvaceous, buxom figure. She even had a freckle on her upper lip. Beth looked down at herself. There was a fine line between curvaceous and out of shape. Plus, her eyes weren't truly green. They were really a sort of weird greenish-brown shade. The tinting of her contacts helped push her eye color more toward the green end of the spectrum, which was much prettier, she thought. In the books, Liz was extremely intelligent, but not a shy, bookish social misfit. It was kind of Drew to omit some of Beth's less-redeeming qualities.

The last page of the novel said that A.J. Emerson enjoyed hearing from readers. Like the other authors in the publisher's "family," he could be contacted through the new web site or a P.O. Box in New York City. Well, Drew *had* said she could reach him through his publisher. She didn't exactly have an emergency, but she really wanted him to know how much she loved the books.

Beth got up and turned on her computer. She no longer had an RTP e-mail address, but she did have a personal e-mail account. Mostly she used it for buying novels on the new book web site Amazon.com. RTP didn't need to know about her book-buying habit, so she had set up another e-mail account. There was no way she could ignore a site with one million titles and discounts on best-sellers, after all.

She typed in the address for the web site listed at the end of the book. The design was hideous. Given all the money Drew must be making for his publisher, they really should think about getting it redone. She held out a Preston Truitt book in front of her. Like the other novels, the cover design was arresting. Putting the covers onto a dreary gray background on the web site sucked all the life out of them. Yuck. Mom would be appalled at displaying books so poorly, even online. Beth clicked the contact form and found A.J. Emerson's name in the list of authors.

Drew had said his pen name was a secret. Maybe she shouldn't put her real name or e-mail address into the contact form. After digging up some documentation to remind herself how to do it, Beth quickly created an e-mail alias that would redirect to her e-mail account, but disguise her real name. She chuckled at the name she selected: *TheRealLizLogan*. If Drew ever actually saw the e-mail, which was debatable, at least he'd know exactly who it was from. Sometimes technology was just too much fun.

Beth paused, trying to think of something to say. So many things were swirling in her mind after reading the second novel. She began typing.

```
Dear Mr. Emerson,

    I wanted you to know that I am now a
dedicated devotee of your Preston Truitt
series. I have read True Alibis and True Blues
so far. They are fast-moving and engrossing
with clever, crisp dialogue. I am particularly
fond of the interplay between Preston and Liz.
They are amusing and yet dedicated to pursuing
every piece of evidence. I love Preston's
irreverence, creativity, and tendency to bend
the rules when it suits him. I am so gratified
that my mother suggested I read your books
and lent me the first one. I have purchased
the other four that are available and look
forward to accompanying Preston on the rest
of his journey into the sixth book when it is
released.

    Your fan,

    Liz
```

Beth pressed the submit button on the contact form and sent her e-mail out into the ether. Given that about fifty other authors were on the contact form, she doubted Drew would ever actually see her e-mail. But at least she got what she wanted to say out of her system. Since he seemed to be having so much trouble with the final book in the series, she wanted to give him a bit of encouragement and let him know how much she was enjoying what he'd written so far. As he had pointed out, Drew excelled at procrastination. Being his editor must be an exercise in frustration. Drew also had a tendency to get depressed and withdraw when things weren't going well. Maybe her e-mail could do a little to buoy his spirits.

The next day, Beth stopped by the dealership to say her final goodbye to the ugly purple thing and her lease payments. Afterward, she sat in the parking lot enjoying the beautiful weather. Here in the desert, it was a glorious sunny day with temperatures in the high sixties. Meanwhile, according to the weather reports, it was snowing in Alpine Grove. Beth was delighted to be missing that.

She grinned happily at the Rincon Mountains and turned to look north at the Santa Catalinas. For the first time in an extremely long time, where she went and what she did was completely up to her. Patting the Acura's steering wheel, she said, "How would you feel about a trip up to Windy Point, little car?"

She headed east out Tanque Verde Road to the Catalina Highway, which went up to the top of Mount Lemmon. The drive up the winding road reminded her a little of the road up to Alpine Grove. Because the top of Mount Lemmon rose more than 9,000 feet above the desert floor, driving up to the tiny town of Summerhaven was like visiting another realm, far removed from the heat and congestion of the city below. She'd never told Graham, but when she felt homesick for Alpine Grove, she sometimes took the drive up Mount Lemmon just so she could see a few pine trees. When she was an angry, unhappy teenager, she hadn't appreciated the forests and the beauty of the area where her hometown was located. But after being away, she found she sometimes craved the sight of the lush green trees again.

The road up to Summerhaven passed many campgrounds, hiking trails, and recreation areas with panoramic views overlooking the city. One of her favorite spots was Windy Point, which was about fourteen miles up the road. The parking area was surrounded by stacks of huge boulders, rock spires, and cliffs that offered views down to the desert below. She parked the Acura and walked to the Windy Point overlook. The spot was aptly named, and her hair swirled around her face. She rummaged in her purse for an elastic, yanked her hair back into a messy ponytail, and gazed out across the wide vista.

Somehow, having the vast expanse of blue sky and the landscape spread before her seemed symbolic of the rest of her life. Up until now, Beth's choices had been obvious and easy. She thought about Vanessa, who had started teaching aerobics in college. Never in her wildest imagination would Beth have considered that as a career choice, but Vanessa seemed happy. Not to mention in good shape.

Beth pulled at the waistband of her slacks. Since she had a little extra time now, maybe she could sign up for an exercise class. Graham said that PhD candidates didn't go to classes with a bunch of fat sweaty old women. Beth didn't understand his rationale or what one had to do with the other. But it was time she started taking better care of herself. An exercise class was a good first step. That summer after senior year, she and Drew had gone hiking everywhere. Now she wasn't sure she'd even be able to make it up the waterfall trail back in Alpine Grove. How pathetic.

The reality was that, right now, Beth could do almost anything. Suddenly, not knowing what was next seemed liberating instead of terrifying. She hadn't lied when she'd told Drew she wasn't completely happy. Something was missing from her life. Pretending that everything was perfect was not the same as being truly contented and fulfilled. Carl had obviously made some drastic changes since high school. And Drew had traveled all over the world. Beth hadn't gone anywhere, even around the Tucson area. All she'd done was work. Now she could go somewhere. Anywhere. She had enough money to do whatever she wanted, at least for a while.

But what *did* she want?

Maybe she could start small. That adult-education flyer she'd gotten in the mail described a stained-glass class that looked interesting. She loved stained glass and had a number of pretty pieces hanging in her windows. It might be fun to make one of her own.

Beth walked down the steps from the overlook and back to the car. It was sort of sad that she had no hobbies beyond reading. Her mother was a furious gardener and, by her own admission, a terrible guitar player. But she loved both activities.

Cleaning the house and checking e-mail didn't count as hobbies. Now that Beth had some time for herself, maybe it was finally time for her to expand her horizons beyond basic maintenance tasks, working, and reading.

～

The next morning, Beth mustered the energy to go to an exercise class at a gym that wasn't too far from her house. She got a day pass to try it out and see if she could actually stand it. Forcing herself to exercise always sounded like a good idea until she actually did it. The only good thing was that people who were busy exercising were too out of breath to want to make small talk with her.

The class said it included cardio and low-impact, whatever that meant. Mostly it seemed to involve a lot of loud music and running around. At first Beth felt like a moron, but then she sort of got into it. After she got home and collapsed on the sofa, she could tell from the dull ache in her muscles that she was going to be incredibly sore. How did Vanessa do this every day? Where were all those endorphins that you were supposed to get from exercise that made you feel good? Beth closed her eyes. Oh well. Maybe next time.

Later when she opened her eyes, she realized she'd fallen asleep. She really was in terrible shape. And also in desperate need of a shower.

After cleaning up, she decided to face the resume problem again. She knew the basic facts about what she had done at RTP, but making it sound enticing to anyone outside of that insular environment was proving to be a bit of a challenge. Besides, she wasn't sure if she wanted to do the same type of work for another company.

Moving into management at RTP probably hadn't been a good idea, and most of the huge companies with the budget for high-end technology like she'd worked on at RTP were defense contractors. Building missiles that could blow up small countries did not hold much appeal.

With a sigh, she turned on the computer and pulled up her resume. Having read many resumes from eager RTP applicants over the years, she knew that this sad little piece of paper had about three seconds to get someone's attention before it was dumped into a pile with 200 other rejects. The prospect was daunting.

She clicked the icon to check her e-mail and laughed when she saw a missive to *TheRealLizLogan* from

TheRealAJEmerson. She eagerly clicked to open it and smiled as she imagined Drew saying the words in his teasing over-the-top Southern-storyteller voice.

```
    Dear Liz,

    I was just happier than a tornado in a
    trailer park to read your e-mail. Here in my
    disheveled hovel, I had just run out of ways
    to put off writing what I should be writing.
    Desperate for diversion, I logged in and waded
    through the author e-mail folder, because
    as a responsible up-and-coming novelist I'm
    supposed to do that. Except I usually don't
    because there are way too many e-mails for one
    sleep-deprived guy to read, much less answer.
    Except when I am desperate for diversion,
    which brings me around full circle.

    Because my publisher knows authors are
    a fickle lot, every week they forward all
    our e-mails to a fan-mail service, so if you
    happen to get another e-mail from my publisher
    that says something like "Thank you for being
    a fan, XXOO, A.J." that was probably pasted in
    by a baby-faced intern named Aurora, who gets
    her knickers in a knot whenever they tell her
    that it's her turn to answer author e-mail
    again. I've seen this first-hand. I swear on
    my great-granddaddy's dear, departed soul that
    I am not making this up.

    ~ The Real A.J. (not Aurora)
```

Beth wiped a tear of amusement from the corner of her eye. Clearly, Drew had *not* finished his book yet. Maybe he was still holed up in Alpine Grove at The Moose. At least she had an e-mail address for him now. Maybe they could be online friends. She smiled at the idea. Having Drew as a digital pen pal could be extremely entertaining.

The next morning, Beth rolled over in bed and groaned. Clearly, her body was not going to put up with a daily exercise class. Maybe she'd try for every-other day to start. Today, perhaps she could limp over to the adult education center and sign up for the stained glass class, since it didn't start until after her trip to Alpine Grove. Then after that, maybe she'd go for a short, easy hike somewhere. Everyone raved about the trails out at Saguaro National Park, particularly when the wildflowers started blooming. After living in Tucson for all these years, she'd never been to the park, even after they enlarged the area and changed Saguaro National Monument to a national park. She really needed to get out more. It was another glorious warm blue-sky day, and she couldn't wait to hop in the Acura and open the sunroof.

Beth returned from her excursion with many little spiky things attached to her socks. Her feet were sore, but she knew a lot more about saguaros and desert ecosystems. Before she went on another hike, she'd have to invest in some desert-proof hiking shoes.

After turning on her computer, Beth attempted to really buckle down on the resume project. A few large city newspapers had been putting their employment classifieds online and she dug deep to find some listings from the *Los Angeles Times*. But once again, most of the tech jobs were at aerospace companies. More defense contractors. Beth sighed. Maybe she should try reaching out to some RTP colleagues. Job-search books always said getting a job was all in who you know.

She opened her e-mail program and smiled at Drew's e-mail. She leaned back in her chair and flipped her pencil around in her fingertips absently. How should she respond?

Dear A.J.,

Your reply was a refreshing surprise and a fascinating glimpse into how busy one can be doing things that do not need to be done in order to avoid doing something one actually is supposed to be doing.

With that said, although I'm sure she is a lovely woman, I was delighted to hear from you and not Aurora.

Given your current state of overwork, it might be unsettling for you to hear that at this very moment, I find myself in the curious situation of having nothing to do for the first time in my life, thus giving me more time to simply ruminate on the vagaries of human nature. As I sit here idly twirling my pencil, it occurs to me that procrastination often stems from laziness, perfectionism, or fear of failure.

You obviously do not exhibit laziness or perfectionism, or your prior five novels would not exist. That leaves the third option, which I think is unjustified if my own reading experience is any indication. Just something to ponder as you toil onward toward completion.

Your fan,

~ Liz

P.S. Write something. Write anything. You can fix it later.

Beth spent a little more time going through her e-mail contacts seeing if there were any likely candidates for "do you know if anyone is hiring?" e-mails. Groveling for employment was so dreary. Maybe tomorrow she'd pick up the university catalog for next semester. It was too bad she'd had to drop out this term. She missed going to classes and wandering around the U of A mall. Sometimes after class, she used to sit on the steps of Old Main eating her lunch, watching students wander by before she rushed back across town to work at RTP. It could have been a peaceful interlude, but at the time she'd been too busy worrying about the latest crisis at work to enjoy it.

The next morning, Beth diligently went off to exercise class again and then rewarded herself for her virtuous pursuit of good health by indulging in a lethargic afternoon of reading. The third A.J. Emerson novel was just as good as the first two. She looked over at her computer. Maybe Drew had replied to her e-mail by now.

She turned on the machine, quickly clicked the e-mail icon, and tapped her foot, waiting for everything to connect. Grinning when she saw the return address, she accessed the e-mail.

```
Dear Liz,

    Your ruminations were a bright light in an
otherwise dark day. It's snowing here and the
lights have been flickering. I was getting as
nervous as a long-tailed cat in a room full of
rocking chairs because as you have surmised,
I have a deadline. And it's tough to use a
computer without electricity.
```

> Here's something they don't tell you about
> the romantic world of publishing: editors
> have no sense of humor. None. I'm not making
> this up. In fact, I'm pretty sure my editor
> is actually made out of cast iron. She gave
> me a lecture today and I have to say that
> lady was just about as mad as a mule chewing
> on bumblebees. So you'll forgive me if I keep
> this short. Right now, I have words to write.
> And with that, I'm off like a herd of turtles.
>
> ~ A.J.
>
> P.S. Dixie says "hi." Or it might be, "I
> need to go out." Gotta run.

Beth shook her head. Drew was so predictable. He was going to wait until everyone was utterly desperate for him to produce something. And then when he did, it would be totally brilliant. He'd admitted that was how he managed to pull off straight A's that last semester he'd attended Cedar County High School. Meanwhile, she'd studied like crazy to keep her 4.0 GPA, and she'd had to do hours upon hours of extra credit work to avoid doing an oral presentation for her AP English class. Thank goodness Mr. Albertson had finally agreed to the extra credit, or she would never have been valedictorian.

The contents of her postscript to him was actually something Drew had said to her back then. After they had gone to the senior prom together, Beth found out to her horror that as the valedictorian she had to give a speech at graduation, in front of all her classmates and their parents. That stupid oral report in English she'd worked so hard to avoid paled in comparison. Giving a speech in front of *everyone* was a shy girl's worst nightmare come true and she was terrified. Writing the speech had been agonizing, as well. Drew had helped, and pointed out that you can't edit a blank page.

They probably both still had the opus memorized after Beth had practiced it four-hundred-thousand times with him. On the big day, she pretended she was looking into his sympathetic blue eyes as she spoke. After she'd uttered the last word of the speech, she just stood there, staring incredulously out at the audience, stunned that she'd actually pulled it off without throwing up or fainting. At some point, the principal had finally come over and shoved her off the stage. Beth cringed at the memory.

In many ways, giving that speech was the most difficult thing Beth had ever done. Since then, every time she had to do something that scared her, she thought about it. Speaking in front of people was her worst, most paralyzing fear, and yet she had overcome it enough to give the speech.

Some things like that were seared into your consciousness and never left you. It was one of many unusual experiences she'd shared with Drew. Now that she knew he didn't hate her, Beth wanted to talk to him again. That summer they were together, they'd had so many long conversations while they were sitting looking out at the lake. They spent hours laughing and philosophizing on life, family, education, dreams for the future, and memories of the past.

They had pondered things they thought were unjust or unfair and marveled at things they thought were incredible. Talking to Drew had always been so easy and fun. He listened with complete absorption in that extraordinary way he had. And somehow he understood how her admittedly odd mind worked. It wasn't like that with anyone else she'd ever met, before or since. Now that she'd seen Drew again, she finally let herself admit exactly how much she'd missed him.

According to the weatherman on TV, it was snowing again in Alpine Grove. Based on the e-mail, Beth had a pretty good idea that Drew was still there. Although she was dreading seeing the snow on her return trip, she definitely wanted to see him again.

Chapter 6

Back Again

After the short flight to LA, Beth got into another grossly expensive rental SUV and set out for Alpine Grove. Her mother and Jill were probably on their way down the hill, cruising toward their hotel somewhere in LA. Mom had actually closed the store early for the first time in years. She and Jill were going to stay overnight in the city before getting on the ship the following day. It would have been nice to see her mother before the trip, but the flights didn't work out. Maybe Beth and her mother would pass each other on the road somewhere.

As Beth got closer to Alpine Grove, the effects of the recent snowstorms became apparent. The plows had been busy, which was a relief, but the sky was gray and ominous. After all the time she'd spent running around the desert with the sunroof of the Acura open, the heavy gunmetal-hued clouds seemed even more dour than usual.

She cranked up the heater and tried to will herself to view the snow in a more positive light. Snow was pretty. Clean and white. Pure and pristine. Not to be confused with cold and dirty. Or slippery and treacherous. Beth sighed. Even though the first day of spring was technically in March, it didn't feel like it. Snow could put you in a festive holiday mood in December, but it was just exhausting and irritating by the time March rolled around.

Beth pulled the car into her mother's driveway, which she was happy to note had been plowed. The path to the house had been shoveled as well. The last thing her mother needed was another fall. At least there wouldn't be any ice in Mexico.

Grabbing her luggage from the passenger seat, Beth got out and went up the steps to the house. She unlocked the door and was greeted by the sound of Arlo barking. "It's me, Arlo. Calm down." The dog was looking anxious. Uh-oh. Beth knew that look.

Dropping her suitcase on the floor, she grabbed a coat and the dog's leash, wasting no time in getting the sheltie outside. She opened the baby gate at the kitchen doorway and Arlo rushed by her toward the door. "Okay, buddy, I know. We're going."

They went for a walk and Beth was reminded again how poorly she dealt with wintry weather. It was cold. Her mood darkened to match the gray skies as she strolled slowly through the neighborhood with Arlo. It was going to be a very long two weeks here, particularly if the sun didn't come out. Sometimes the sun went into hiding for extended periods in late winter and early spring. She looked up at the sky. Maybe the mega clouds would just leave for a change.

After returning to the house, Beth found a long note from her mother listing things that needed to be done related to the house and the store. Ugh. Mrs. Oliphant's gout had gotten bad enough that she was in the assisted-living place south of town for a little while, but she still wanted her books. Mom was like the bookmobile, carting books all over the Alpine Grove area.

Maybe all the unemployed leisure time she'd been enjoying was making Beth lazy. At the moment, the list of tasks seemed hard and complicated. None of the items were a big deal, but she didn't want to handle any of it right now. At least tomorrow was Sunday and the store was closed. Beth was going to embrace her day of rest. Looking down at Arlo, she said, "What do you think, buddy? I think it's time to make a fire, curl up, and hunker down with another one of Drew's books." The sheltie wagged his tail, apparently agreeing with Beth that staying warm was a mighty fine plan.

By Sunday afternoon, Beth had devoured the last of Drew's Preston Truitt novels. And she was dying to know what happened next. Maybe Drew was still at The Moose. Without her computer, she couldn't e-mail him. And since she didn't have her RTP laptop anymore either, she was completely disconnected from the online world for the first time in an extremely long time. But there was still the telephone. If Drew still had his phone on Do Not Disturb, she was just going to march over there and knock on the door. After reading the books, she *had* to see him.

Beth picked up the phone book and looked up the number for the Enchanted Moose. The surly woman at the front desk explained that Mr. Emery had checked out a week ago. And no, he did not say where he was going. She also told Beth that it was a violation of his privacy to even ask and there was no way she'd tell her where he went, even if he had said. After apologizing meekly, Beth hung up the phone and stared at it for a moment. She'd been so sure Drew was still here in town. It was stupid to be so disappointed when he'd made it extremely clear that he didn't want to see her again. And now she was going to have to wait with the rest of the world to find out what happened to Preston and Liz. Argh!

The next day, Beth went through the familiar routine of feeding Arlo and heading off to the bookstore. The weather was still dreary and threatening to precipitate in some way. The meteorologists remained undecided as to whether it was going to be rain, sleet, snow, or some form of generalized partially frozen slop. Whatever it did weather-wise, no sun was going to be involved.

Beth walked into the back room and noticed that the boxes of books were unchanged, sitting exactly where she had left them. Obviously, Mom had made zero progress on that front. So Beth still had the interminable sorting project to look forward to, along with another dump run. Yippee. The only thing worse than going to the dump was going to the dump when the pavement was icy.

She unlocked the front door and settled into the chair behind the writing desk. If Mom was reading instead of sorting books while she was here, Beth could too. Something had happened in Drew's first novel that she wanted to look up again.

Several hours later, she had helped a few intrepid customers who had braved the cold in search of reading material. Because she was reading one of his novels, she also had sold a few of Drew's books. Depending on his royalties, he'd might have earned fifty cents today here at the store. Beth smirked at the thought of telling him that in an e-mail. He'd be amused.

She looked up and did a double-take. She'd just been thinking about Drew and there he was on the sidewalk, accompanied by an extremely tall woman with sandy blonde hair. Given her body language, she was flirting madly with him. Maybe Drew *had* found a girlfriend here. He waved toward the store and picked up Dixie in his arms. With one hand, he held the door open for the woman and they walked

in. The woman looked disturbingly like Joel Ross and was
followed by Arlo, who was moving slowly, even for him. Beth
stood up as Arlo toddled around the humans toward her. So
that was Cindy, huh?

Crouching down to greet the dog, Beth said, "Hey buddy.
Did you want to come by for a visit?" She straightened and
looked at Cindy. "Hi, I don't think we've actually ever met,
but I've heard a lot about you. I'm Beth, Margaret's daughter."

"Yeah, I've heard about you too." Cindy pulled Arlo away
from the bookshelves, "Drew wanted to stop by here." She
waved toward Drew, who grinned. "This is Drew Emery."

Beth could feel the heat rising to her cheeks at the amused
twinkle in his eyes. She knew that look. With a polite smile,
she said, "Yes. We've met before. In high school, actually."

Cindy turned to Drew. "You never told me you knew
Margaret's daughter. She went out with my brother."

Drew readjusted Dixie in his arms and raised his eyebrows
at Beth. "Oh really? Did she now?"

"That was a long time ago." Beth turned to Cindy. "At
the time, I believe you were visiting Alpine Grove rather
regularly and surreptitiously."

Cindy put her hand on her hip. "Yeah, I'd met someone
who lived here. I suppose Joel told you about that."

Beth nodded. "How is Joel, by the way? Kat said he was
in the hospital, but he was going to be okay. Is he still staying
with your aunt?"

"Yeah, he's fine. Same as ever. My aunt is doing better
too, so he should be able to come home soon. Which would
be good. He's grumpy on a good day, but just insufferable
now."

"When I saw him, he didn't seem particularly grumpy. He looked quite happy actually."

Cindy rolled her eyes. "Ugh. He and Kat are so nauseating. You'd think the world was going come to an end if he didn't call her precisely at seven thirty. Then she almost had a nervous breakdown when he was in the hospital."

Beth glanced quickly at Drew, who still looked amused. From his expression, it was clear he was not interested in Cindy. She pointed down at the dog. "So, ah, Arlo is getting that anxious look."

Cindy bent to look at Arlo. "Uh-oh. I have a lot of other dogs to get to. I should go." She looked at Drew. "Maybe I'll see you and Dixie again tomorrow."

He inclined his head slightly. "Maybe you will."

Cindy hustled Arlo out of the store and Beth grinned at Drew, unable to hide how thrilled she was that he was still in Alpine Grove. "So A.J., is this some type of salacious dog-walking date?"

"Not exactly, Liz." He looked down at Dixie, who was falling asleep in the crook of his arm. "More like our dog-walking paths crossed."

"The bookstore is a long walk from The Moose. Where are you staying?"

"I was feeling like a hack, so I came by here looking for something to read by a skilled writer for inspiration. I ended up talking to your mom for a while. She told me that Mrs. Oliphant was worrying about her house while she's in that assisted living place, so I offered to house-sit. I checked out of The Moose. The kitchenette there was starting to get to me anyway. There's only so much you can do with a hot plate."

Beth tilted her head. "You were avoiding writing, weren't you?"

"Yeah. Pretty much. You know how I am." He waved one arm toward the windows. "But I finished the stupid thing. My deadline was Saturday and I did it! The book is with the editor. Gone. Not my problem. Well, at least until she sends it back for revisions."

Beth clapped her palms together. "Oh Drew, that's fantastic. I knew you'd do it. You always do."

"Well, there's nothing like having your own words thrown back in your face for motivation."

"I wondered if you might remember that." After putting up with her endless angst, how could he *not* remember?

"I haven't forgotten much, Beth." He looked down at Dixie and stroked the pup's head as she snoozed in the crook of his arm. "But thanks for the e-mails. It helped me finally just suck it up and get it done, instead of agonizing over every little nitpicky thing."

"Okay, I just *have* to know how the series ends. You have to tell me…do Preston and Liz end up together? I finished the fifth book and I'm just dying to know what happened."

"Not really."

Beth leaned back on the desk and crossed her arms. "What do you mean not really?"

"Liz dies in the last book."

Beth dropped her arms, stood up straight, and glared at him. "*What*? You can't be serious. You killed her off? You actually *killed* Liz?"

He shrugged. "In the context of the novel, it seemed like the right way to end the story."

"I just can't believe this. Your readers are going to want to kill you. *I* want to kill you. How could you *do* that?"

"Jeez Beth, it's just a book."

Beth crossed her arms again and shook her head. "Unbelievable."

"Well, since you're good and pissed-off now, I guess I'll amble on back to the Oliphant residence. It was good to see you again. Take care."

Startled from her dark thoughts related to the demise of Liz Logan, Beth stood up again. "Wait! Don't go."

"Beth, I can't stand here holding this pup forever. Dixie is gonna wake up or my arm is gonna fall off. It's hard to say which will happen first."

"Oh. Okay. Well, would you like to come by for dinner? We could celebrate the completion of your novel. And meeting your deadline against all odds."

"That's probably not a good idea."

"Oh come on, Drew. I think finishing the book deserves some type of recognition. It's a big deal!"

His doubtful look faded and he smiled. "Well, I am feeling kinda celebratory and there wasn't anyone around I could really tell about it other than my editor, who mostly just said it was about time. Except maybe with a few extra adjectives thrown in for emphasis."

"I can imagine."

~

That evening the doorbell rang and Beth ran to answer it, followed by Arlo, who was barking hysterically. She opened the door and Dixie ran by her into the house, trailing her leash behind her.

Drew shrugged and walked through the door. "Oops."

Arlo ran after the puppy, excited to see his walking companion again. Dixie turned and play-bowed, yipping at the larger dog, encouraging him to chase her.

Beth giggled as she bent to remove the puppy's leash. "Well, Dixie is definitely awake now."

"That animal has two speeds. Full blast and full stop. Twenty minutes from now she'll collapse in a corner somewhere and pass out."

"Hopefully she won't give Arlo a heart attack first. The poor guy is already panting hard."

"Now you know how I feel. Between finishing my book and keeping up with this tiny dynamo, I feel like I've been rode hard and hung up to dry."

"But she's so cute!" Beth waved toward the living room. "Come on in."

As he walked through the house, Drew turned his head, looking around. "It's weird to be here again. A lot of things look exactly the same, but little things are different." He pointed at a chair. "Like that wasn't here before."

"Yes. The old one got so stained, Mom couldn't stand it anymore. She didn't want to recover it again, so she finally bought something new. It's actually a great place to sit and read now."

"That would explain the stack of books on that end table."

"Yes. One of many stacks of books. Mom needs more shelving. Or fewer books." Beth glanced around the floor. "Where did Dixie go?"

"I dunno. She's a wily one and this house is pretty big. Is there a way we can seal ourselves in one room, so I can keep an eye on her?" He waved in the general direction of the street. "I got one of those plastic expandable baby gates for Mrs. Oliphant's house and I move it from one doorway to another. It's a little complicated, but hey, I warned Mrs. O that I had a puppy. I guess she's more worried about her pipes freezing than whatever damage Dixie could do. She might be underestimating Dixie though."

"Come into the kitchen with me. The soup's almost done. Mom has a hinged gate here on the door to keep Arlo confined to the linoleum when she's at the store. There have been a few, uh, deleterious acts committed against the dining room rug."

They rounded up the canines and closed the gate behind them. Drew gave Dixie a chew toy and she settled into a spot and began gnawing. Arlo stood next to Beth, hoping for some form of food to magically fall on the floor in front of his nose. She looked down at the dog. "You had your dinner. Go lie down."

Drew sat down at the little bistro table. "That smells great. You must have gone to a lot of trouble."

"Not really. When I was here before, Mom made about fifty gallons of cream of potato soup and froze it. Fortunately, I know when she did it and what the containers look like. She never labels anything. It drives me insane."

Drew laughed. "It's well documented that you're a little more Type A than your mom."

"I know. But really, how hard would it be to write "Tomato soup, July" on a little piece of masking tape and put it on the container? When I was here last time, I was trying to figure out what to make for dinner and in the freezer there are five plastic storage items with something reddish inside.

Five! Mom said they were either tomato sauce from last summer, gazpacho she made around Christmas, or maybe some leftover V-8." Beth threw up her hands. "Really, Mom? Come on! If I'm making pasta, I don't want the V-8."

"Well you coulda had it, you know."

Beth rolled her eyes. "Oh please."

He grinned. "Your mom is organized about some things. She couldn't run a bookstore if she weren't."

"True. And remember when she made you dig up the perennial bed out front? She knew precisely where each and every plant was supposed to go." Beth smirked. "You were *not* happy about that."

"That was a lot of digging. I think I planted a hundred and fifty plants that day, and it was hot. I swear I thought I was gonna die of heat stroke."

Beth stirred the soup. "You kept saying you had to help your father at the marina. Even Mom knew you were just trying to get out of it."

"I'm sure I don't remember that."

"Yes you do. I know you. You never forget anything, which was even more apparent when I read your books. I really want to talk to you about them." Beth leaned back on the counter. "But that reminds me. We have to raise a glass and toast to the success of book six!"

Beth went to the pantry and got a bottle of wine. "You have to take this with you when you go. It can't be here in the house when my mom gets back."

"Or we could just drink it."

"I don't drink much." Beth rummaged around in the cabinets. "I don't think Mom actually has wine glasses. Hmm. Okay. How about a tumbler of wine?"

"It's a glass. I think it should work."

Beth poured the wine and handed him a glass. "Real wine aficionados would be appalled. They say the shape of the glass affects nuances of the flavor."

He looked down at the liquid. "Looks drinkable to me."

Beth raised her tumbler. "Congratulations, A.J."

"Thanks, Liz."

They drank and Beth put her glass aside and turned back to the stove to stir the soup. She said over her shoulder, "Did your editor say anything about the book?"

"Nothing beyond 'Thank God you finally finished it.' I think it's going to be a while before she gets over her mad."

"I'm sure once she reads it, she will love you again. The way you end these things, you just have to read the next book."

"Well, it's the last one." He looked down at Dixie, who had fallen asleep on her chew toy. "I don't want to talk about that anyway. You'll just get pissed-off again. I can do without another woman mad at me at the moment. And my editor is nothing, compared to you."

Beth turned and pointed the spoon at him. "What's that supposed to mean?"

"Oh come on, Beth. You've got a really long fuse, but when you go off, you can dish out a whole lotta whup-ass."

"I guess that's fair, after the things I said to you. And you aren't the only person who has mentioned that."

"Ya think?" Drew leaned back in the chair and crossed his long legs at the ankles, holding the tumbler of wine in both hands on his stomach. "Presumably, after all those years, your boyfriend might have noticed that you have a bit of a temper. Unless he's only got one oar in the water, that is."

"He's quite intelligent actually. We have long conversations about technology. And the various machinations of university life."

He sipped his wine. "Sounds interesting."

Beth glanced at him sharply. Interesting? Okay, maybe there was one thing she couldn't talk to Drew about. Fortunately, he'd probably never meet Graham. They'd be like oil and water. "I think the soup is done." She ladled the soup into bowls and carried them to the little table. "Here you go."

Drew sat up and put his wine aside. "Thanks, Beth. This looks great. After eating my own cooking—and I use that term loosely—at the Enchanted Moose, this is a welcome change."

They ate quietly for a few moments. Beth stole a glance at Drew across the table. He had a melancholy expression on his face. Something was bothering him. Suddenly, he looked up, catching her staring at him. "Beth, what is that godawful smell?"

Beth looked over at Arlo, who wagged his tail. "Uh-oh. We might want to expedite our consumption. I think Arlo needs to go out."

Drew stood up and took his bowl to the sink. "Dang, that'll kill your appetite real fast. And melt down your nasal passages. Yeesh, dog, what is *wrong* with you?"

Dixie woke up, stretched, and ran around the room a few times, attempting to find the exit. Drew grabbed her and picked her up. "Not so fast, Little One. You're coming too."

~

They bundled up, leashed up the dogs, and went outside. The clouds had cleared off and the air was frigid. Beth looped Arlo's leash over her arm and pushed it up to her elbow, so she could ram her gloved hands into her pockets. Even buried in multiple layers, her fingers were still cold. Misty breath swirled in front of her face. "It's freezing out here."

Drew hunched his shoulders against the stiff breeze that whipped down the street. "No kidding. It's colder than a witch's, uh well, yeah, it's mighty cold."

"Two days ago, I was wearing shorts and driving around with my sunroof open."

He grinned. "That sounds dirty."

"What? No, I got a new car." Beth smiled. "I love it! It's a little Acura and it's so much fun to drive. I even remembered how to drive a stick." She nudged him with her shoulder. "Good thing you taught me how on the Blue Bomb."

"Don't speak ill of the dead. My Datsun may have been a piece of crap, but it was *my* piece of crap."

Beth giggled. "It took us to a lot of fun places."

"Most of the time." He tugged the lapels of his coat up around his chin and glanced at her. "So if you got a car, does that mean you found a new job?"

"No. My old car was a lease and the lease was up. This one was used, so I could pay cash. That means no payments! And it appears to be in great shape."

"Sounds like a good way to go." He looked down at Arlo. "Is he empty? Because some body parts I'm rather fond of are gonna start freezing off if we don't get back inside soon."

"I agree. Let's go."

They returned to the house and Beth busied herself lighting a fire in the fireplace. Drew sprawled out on the sofa. "How's the job search going?"

Beth crouched in front of the hearth and rubbed her hands in front of the warmth. The fire looked like it was going to stay lit. "Not very well. I have not seen much that I want to do."

"Which is what?"

She stood up. "I don't know. That's part of the problem."

"Oh, come on. You always know."

She shoved at Drew's leg. "Move over. I know I don't want to work for a defense contractor. And RTP doesn't want me. I have no idea. I signed up for a stained-glass class."

He straightened a little and the weary look left his eyes for a moment. "Really? That sounds like fun."

Beth looked at his face again. Something was definitely wrong. "You seem a bit subdued. Did the soup make you feel bad? Sometimes Mom can be a little heavy-handed with the spices."

"It was great, Beth. I'm just tired. Usually I take a trip to somewhere far away after I finish a book, to clear my mind. But I have Little Miss Dixie here. And then I agreed to house-sit."

She grinned. "So you're trapped in Alpine Grove. Gosh, that sounds awfully familiar."

"Very funny. I always get like this when I finish a book. When I write these things, I get all involved in the story and then when it's done, everything feels a little empty for a while. It probably sounds stupid, but I miss all the characters." He rearranged himself and put a throw pillow behind his head. "We sure spent a lot of time on this couch."

Beth smiled. "I know. That summer, being a latchkey kid was not so bad."

"Neither was naked Monopoly."

"I spent a lot of time looking at that clock on the mantle, worrying my mom was going to walk in on us."

"I spent a lot of time thinking about you naked." He raised his eyebrows in response to Beth's expression. "What can I say? I was eighteen."

"So was I. It feels like a million years ago." She touched the back of his hand. "Until I'm sitting here with you and it doesn't feel like that at all."

Drew pulled his hand away and glanced at the floor, where Dixie was quietly gnawing on the sofa leg. "Dixie, *no!*" He reached down, picked up the puppy, and put her in his lap. He looked back at Beth. "I think your mom is going to kill me."

"Uh-oh." Beth examined the shredded upholstery. "Maybe I can find some way to fix it before she gets back."

Drew pulled out a piece of stuffing. "I don't know about that, unless you have some serious sewing skills I don't know about." He held the dog out in front of him with both hands. "After that unfortunate pillow episode, we talked about this, Dixie. Fiberfill is not good for you." The little dog wagged and wiggled in his grasp and Drew snuggled her up to his chest.

"She ate a pillow at The Moose?" Beth giggled. "I knew they were going to love you there."

"A pillow, among other things." Drew stroked the puppy's head. "When I checked out, the woman at the front desk may have said some unflattering things about Dixie's heritage."

"With all the traveling you said you do, I am surprised you opted to keep Dixie. I thought for sure you would have talked one of our esteemed classmates into taking her by now."

"I couldn't do it. Plus I've been thinking about getting a house. Actually having a home-base somewhere." He looked down at Dixie, who had fallen asleep. "Preferably with a really big fenced yard."

"That's so sweet. I know I love my house. I've been enjoying it even more lately, since I'm not running off to work every day."

"Being a lazy underachiever does have a few advantages."

"Ha-ha. You're just so humorous. I have already apologized for that more than once."

"I know. I'm just saying that spending a little time just thinking and doing nothing isn't always such a bad thing. You didn't mind all those times we spent just sitting around, looking out at the lake, after all." He grinned. "Well, when we weren't making out anyway."

"I thought about that when I was driving around Tucson the last few days."

"What? Making out?"

She leveled an oh-spare-me glare at him. "No. Our conversations and all the things we did that summer. For years, I've been so busy with work, I haven't seen many of the Tucson-area attractions, even after living there for so long. There are some great hiking trails, for example. I enjoyed the hikes we used to take."

"Desert hiking is great. Have you ever hiked during a full moon? It's amazing, although you do have to watch out for snakes."

"Thank you for sharing that herpetological tidbit. How disturbing. Perhaps I'll confine my explorations to daylight hours." She pushed off her shoes and put her feet up on the coffee table, wiggling her toes in the thick socks. "I guess it just feels like I've missed out on some activities I used to like."

"I hate to break it to you, but that's part of your Type-A thing."

"I know. I think after that summer with you and my freshman year of college, I may have overcompensated."

"Overcompensated for what?"

"Being irresponsible."

"Right. *You* were irresponsible. And you say *I* make up stories."

"I didn't adjust to life away from home as well as one might hope. In my desperate and largely futile efforts to make friends, I made some poor choices."

"My leg is falling asleep. This little animal sleeps like the dead." Drew readjusted Dixie on his lap and looked at Beth. "What choices? You mean like going out with Cindy's brother?"

Beth shook her head. "No, that was mostly just a demoralizing blow to my ego because Joel dumped me so quickly and efficiently. I mean in Tucson. The University of Arizona's reputation as a party school isn't unwarranted."

He smiled. "Oh really? Are you saying you may have partaken of a few open bars?"

"Yes. There was a bar near campus that ran a promotion on Wednesdays. Anything with white alcohol was discounted, and for a period of time, I became quite a White Wednesday enthusiast."

Drew stroked the fur on Dixie's back. "That would cover a pretty wide range of liquor."

"Yes, it does, and I think I tried most of the possible beverages containing them. There was one night that I had a little bit of difficulty finding my way back to my dorm. I ended up, well, resting on the lawn in front of a fraternity building. I was lying there, the world was spinning, and I was trying not to vomit. At some point, I realized that my contact lens had popped out."

"Wow, Beth, you even lose your contacts when you're wasted?" He chuckled. "Why does this not surprise me?"

"I found it. Although technically, it was actually the next day. I remembered where I was and returned."

He looked at her. "Beth, why are you telling me this?"

"I don't know. Maybe to let you know that you haven't cornered the market on irresponsibility." Beth waved her arms in exasperation. "I feel like I haven't talked to you in so long, I have to catch up."

Drew moved Dixie's small furry body off his lap and into his arms. "Well, on that note, now that Dixie has eaten your mom's sofa, it's been a full day. I should probably go. After all that writing, my inner slacker is calling. I have large plans to do a whole lot of nothing tomorrow, except keep my dog from eating her way through Mrs. Oliphant's house too. Thanks for dinner."

Beth reached out and touched his arm. "Do you have to go already?"

"You have a store to run tomorrow. And you've gotta be sick of talking to me by now."

"No I'm not. That never happens. I want to find out more about you. Here I am running on and on again. But I don't know how you are doing."

Drew stood up, cradling Dixie in his arms. "Now that I met my odious deadline, I'm fine. It's been fun talking to you again, but like I said before, us spending time together isn't a good idea. There's a whole lot of precedent that indicates that although we are incredibly compatible in certain, well, let's just say, 'lustful' ways, we're really different people. You made that abundantly clear to me a decade ago. And because of that whole historical lust factor, I doubt your boyfriend would be too excited to find out that you spent the evening with me."

Beth stood up to face him. "I don't plan to mention it. He certainly does not divulge his extra-curricular activities with me."

"What?"

As soon as the words came out of her mouth, Beth knew they were true. She'd been kidding herself for years. "Graham has been cheating on me for a long time. I haven't wanted to believe it and ignored every indicator. But I know he is."

"Did the guy *tell* you that?" Drew looked down and stroked Dixie's head with his fingertips.

"Not in so many words. But I'm quite sure of it." She had been pretending everything was fine for far too long. But it wasn't.

Drew shook his head. "I know it doesn't reflect too well on me, but I gotta say, you've got some seriously bad taste in men, Beth."

Beth gently took the sleepy puppy from his arms and locked her gaze with his. "Not entirely. I think my choices simply deteriorated over time. I was looking for something that didn't exist. Expecting people to be something they are not."

"What's that?"

"You."

Drew's eyes widened and he caressed her cheek with his fingertip. "Are you serious? After all the things you said to me before? Do you really feel that way?"

Beth nodded and smiled. "I am not making this up."

His gaze slid downward and he stepped forward, bending to kiss her while arching around her body to avoid crushing Dixie, who was starting to squirm in Beth's arms.

The kiss was even more exhilarating and arousing than the ones in Beth's dreams. Scorching and intense, the kiss deepened, and it was all Beth could do to continue to hold Dixie. Breathing heavily, she pushed against Drew's chest with one hand. "I'm going to drop your dog on your foot if you keep doing that."

He grinned and took the puppy from her. "It was so cold, I didn't want to walk over here. I drove and Dixie's crate is in the car. She likes to sleep in there, which is good, because all of a sudden, I have a serious hankering to play naked Monopoly again."

∼

Later, after bringing in the crate and settling Dixie in for a nap, Drew ran up the stairs, followed by Beth. He stopped at the doorway of her bedroom and walked in. "It looks exactly the same."

Beth shrugged. "Mom keeps saying she's going to turn it into a sewing room, but she doesn't really sew. I told her if it ended up as yet another storage haven for books, I would never stay here again."

He turned and ran his hands under her shirt as he bent his head to kiss her. With a lascivious smile, he whispered, "I think I'd like to pass 'Go' and collect my two hundred dollars now."

Beth mumbled, "The Reading Railroad seems quite appealing as well."

Drew released her from his embrace and stripped, throwing his clothes in a heap on the floor. "If I land in jail, you know what happens then."

Beth looked at him appraisingly. "Well, it seems jailbirds work out. I'm afraid I have not been quite as diligent about an exercise program until fairly recently." Approximately one week ago.

He pulled her to him, "You look fine to me, Bethie. Way better than fine." He turned and yanked the covers down on the twin bed, "Dang, it's freezing in here. Does that radiator work?"

"I doubt it. Sometimes Mom talks about getting it repaired when she mentions the sewing-room idea."

Drew leaped into the bed and jerked the covers up to his chin. "You better get in here fast before icicles start forming on my toes."

Beth began removing her clothing, slowly and carefully folding them and putting them on her dresser, enjoying Drew's look of appreciation. Shivering, she crouched down next to the bookshelf and pulled out a copy of *Gone with the Wind*.

"Please tell me that's not the same ones."

She looked over her shoulder at him. "No, I had some condoms in my purse and I was afraid my mother might look around in there for some reason. So I hid them in the hole in the book. I still feel bad for cutting it up."

Drew grinned. "I don't. The South could rise again, you know."

As she crawled into the small space left in the bed, she could feel the heat of Drew's body course down the length of hers like a current of electricity. He wrapped his arms around her and said in a low voice, "It's about time. You were making me crazy. I was thinking of breaking out a Community Chest card and assessing a school tax on you."

"You would never do that. But it does appear that your building and loan has matured. You know that Chance cards never lie."

"So I get a hundred-and-fifty bucks?"

Beth grinned as another shivery thrill went down her spine at the touch of his fingertips on the curve of her back. "Oh yes, if you keep doing that, you definitely do."

Much later, Beth was awakened by Drew crawling over her to get out of the narrow bed. She put her arms around his neck and pulled him down to kiss him, "Where are you going?"

"I heard Dixie rustling around in her crate downstairs. Did you know that puppies have to go out every four hours or so?"

"No."

"Well, I gotta tell you, it's a depressing thing to find out when it's four degrees outside."

"When you return, maybe I could buy a hotel."

He stroked her cheek, "I'd like that."

The next morning, Beth woke up to the sound of Arlo barking downstairs. She and Drew were intertwined, and although she hated to extract herself from the cocoon of warmth, if she didn't, Arlo would undoubtedly commit a heinous act in the kitchen. Moving her leg against Drew's, she attempted to wiggle her toes against his ankle. "Drew. Wake up. You need to move. I'm trapped and I think Arlo is awake."

He disentangled his legs from hers, rolled over on his back, and put his arm behind his head. "Fly, be free."

Beth crawled out into the cold and stood next to the bed, popping her contacts out of her eyes into her palm and closing her fist around them. "Ugh, I forgot to take them out last night. My eyes feel like sandpaper." She groped around the nightstand for the case and put them away. Putting on her glasses, she glanced at Drew, who had an amused half-smile on his face. "What?"

"It's just kinda cute when you're all cold, naked, and blind, that's all. Like a baby bird."

She gathered up her clothes and bent to kiss him, running her fingertips through the hair behind his ear. "Don't look so smug. We all know little miss 'bladder the size of a blueberry' has to go out again by now too."

Drew groaned and sat up. "I hate morning. Why do they make it so early? Could you throw me my shirt?"

After a frigid outing, Beth left Drew in charge of the dogs so she could go take a shower. She was barely going to make it to the bookstore on time, since she had definite issues keeping her hands off Drew's enticing body. That certainly hadn't changed, either. It was like she'd degenerated from a normal rational adult into a lust-obsessed teenager again.

As the warm water washed over her, Beth wondered what her problem was. Maybe she was just an extraordinary slut. For years, she'd managed to rationalize sleeping with Graham, even with all the student rumors and after they'd had some rather horrible arguments. Last night with Drew, it had been way too easy to forget Graham entirely.

The sheer magnitude of her denial was unbelievable. Why had she pretended he was perfect for so long? She was a smart person. You'd think she might have noticed she was fooling herself. And now she was equally willing to jump into bed with Drew, even though she knew next-to nothing about him. Did she have no self-control whatsoever? What was wrong with her?

In the clear light of day, it seemed she was a complete idiot when it came to matters of the opposite sex. Although Beth had a habit of blabbing endlessly whenever she was near him, Drew was remarkably circumspect about what he had revealed to her. Questions swirled in her mind. How long was he going to be in Alpine Grove? Where had he lived before the reunion? Where was he going to live after he was done house-sitting? Did he plan to write more novels? Maybe not, given that he just killed off one of the main characters in his series.

What did it mean that he had just killed the fictional version of her? And what *was* he going to do with himself? Did Drew have any plans at all? Or was he just as aimless as ever, floating through life on the largesse of his family's wealth? Not everyone had that luxury. She certainly didn't.

At some point, she'd need a job. She wasn't a kid anymore. What if she couldn't pay her mortgage?

Beth scrubbed the shampoo into her hair vigorously, as she became increasingly annoyed with herself. Drew was right—her taste in men was abominable. A few conversations with him and she was right back where she'd been when she was a stupid, irresponsible teenager. Had she learned nothing? She was supposed to be a mature adult with a house and a grown-up life. What was wrong with her? Perhaps she'd inherited her ineptitude in relationship choices from her mother, along with her inability to drink socially like a normal person. Thanks, Mom.

After getting dressed, Beth padded down the stairs in her stocking feet. Where were her shoes?

Drew was sitting on the sofa reading a book, with Dixie in his lap. Arlo was nowhere to be seen. Usually when the dog disappeared it was because he knew he'd done something bad. Uh-oh.

Drew looked up, "Hey, look at you, all squeaky clean."

"Yes. Quite a contrast to you. I'm really late. Have you seen Arlo?"

"He was right here a second ago." Drew waved toward the kitchen. "Dixie was playing with him until she ran out of steam."

Beth stomped around the living room. Where were her shoes? "My shoes are gone too. Did your dog eat them?"

"I don't think so. Is something wrong?" Drew set the book aside. "You seem quite a bit less...uh... happy than you were earlier."

Beth looked over her shoulder and snapped, "Afterglow only gets you so far, then real life intervenes."

"What?" Drew stood up and carried Dixie over to her crate. The puppy strolled inside and collapsed into a somnolent pile of brown fur. He closed the door and followed Beth into the dining room. "Dang, that's a serious stink. I think we know where Arlo went. So to speak."

Beth was standing in front of the table with her fists clenched and her eyes squeezed shut. "I am so angry right now, Drew. Please do not say anything for a second. I need to collect myself or I'll say something terrible again."

Drew put his arms around her rigid body. "It's okay, Bethie. I'm guessing your mom has probably stocked up on rug cleaner."

Beth burst into tears, sobbing into his shirt. She blubbered, "I ffff...ound my shoes."

"That's good, right?" He rubbed her back, kneading her tense muscles gently. "Dixie didn't eat them, did she?"

"No!" Beth wailed. "Arlo! That...horrid...dog. What's wrong with him? He brought them in here so he could take an elephantine dump *in my shoes*."

Drew released his hold on her and bent to look under the table. "Nice placement."

Beth snuffled and her angry tears turned to a giggle and then into peals of laughter. "Oh Drew..." She hugged him as she tried to catch her breath. "I don't know how you do that."

He tucked a strand of hair behind her ear. "Hey, I'm just standing here."

"I had worked myself up into a serious mad, as you would say." She looked into his eyes. "This was just the last straw. I was so mad at myself and all ready to say a lot of things to you that I'd hate myself for later. And I *never* want to do that again."

"Like what?" Drew waved his hand. "Never mind. Forget I asked. I don't want to know."

"The primary issue is that I know almost nothing about you."

He smiled. "Well, I think you found out quite a few things last night. What else do you want to know?"

"Not *that* way…"

The phone rang loudly, and Beth looked through the doorway at the big kitchen clock. "I'm late! I need to clean this up *right now*."

"It's no big deal. I'll help you. Thanks to Dixie, I have quite a bit of experience."

The answering machine clicked on and Beth heard Bea Sullivan's voice asking if everything was all right at the bookstore. Beth wanted to scream in frustration. Her forays into irresponsibility always led to disaster. Mom was going to be furious when she found out Beth hadn't even managed to open the store on time. That was probably the most serious retail rule violation she could make.

∼

After locating Arlo, speed-cleaning the carpet, and securing the dog in the kitchen, Beth left for the store. Drew loaded up Dixie for the return to Mrs. Oliphant's house. He said he'd stop by the store later during Dixie's walk if the weather warmed up. Beth drove to the store, even though her mother would consider it a waste of gas and a store-proprietor parking faux pas.

She unlocked the front door a half-hour late and sheepishly called Bea Sullivan at the gift store to let her know everything was okay. Almost immediately after Beth hung up, a woman walked in. It was the slothful browser, who seemed to view this bookstore as her personal library, rather than a retail establishment where people actually paid for merchandise.

Beth was not in the mood to watch the woman move slowly through the store for an hour and a half again. Glaring at the woman from behind the desk, Beth tried to telepathically tell her to get out. There were phone calls to be made. The woman's straight brown hair brushed her chin as she bowed her head to read the front flap of a hardback. She had to have looked at the cover of almost every single book in here by now. Twice. The store just wasn't that large.

Because of the various distractions related to Drew, Beth hadn't dropped off the books her mother had asked her to take to Mrs. Oliphant. Beth had been so excited about dinner with Drew that the task hadn't even crossed her mind. It was also clear that Beth needed to take Arlo to the veterinarian. The dog had just been outside a few minutes before the latest dining-room disaster. Did Arlo simply view the rug as his personal toilet, or was something actually really wrong with him? It was hard to tell, and she was starting to worry about the little guy.

Beth dragged a box of books from the back room and began sorting. If Sloth Woman ever left, Beth could try to call the vet and make an appointment. Maybe if she dropped Arlo off in the morning, Cindy would be willing to pick him up from the vet's office. Unfortunately Cindy did not seem to be Beth's biggest fan, but maybe a significant cash incentive would improve her disposition and willingness to help.

Beth heaved another book into the recycle stack. Maybe Mom wouldn't notice if she just took all of the boxes to the dump. It would certainly save a lot of time. This was ridiculous. Ninety-eight percent of them were too damaged to be salable. But then, there had been that antique copy of *Alice in Wonderland* with the beautiful illustrations. That single volume had been a little sparkling gem in an immense field of ugly rocks. Beth sighed. What if she threw away something wonderful? Much as she would prefer to be rid of this onerous activity, there was no way she could avoid looking through every single book in every single box.

An hour later, the woman was still in the store, aimlessly wandering through the aisles. Beth couldn't stand it anymore. She cleared her throat. "Excuse me. Are you looking for something in particular?"

The woman looked surprised and said in a soft voice. "No. Just looking."

Beth picked up a tattered paperback from the box. "We have more books in the back." A whole lot more books. Thousands. Millions! "Would you like to see them?"

The woman's expression lit up, transforming her appearance. "Oh yes. I just love looking through used books."

Beth smiled. "Well, today is your lucky day. Let me get you a chair from the back."

After settling the woman in with a folding chair and a box of books, Beth said, "This is embarrassing. I didn't even ask your name."

"I'm Linda…Linda Howland."

"Are you related to Walter?"

"Yes, he's my husband. Or he was."

Beth cringed inwardly. She was so bad at small talk. "I'm sorry. I think I knew your daughter. Karen. She was a few years behind me in school."

"Yes. She moved away after she graduated."

Beth held up a book. Or what was left of one. "This volume is exemplar of the type of book we can't sell. No cover, missing pages, and shredded binding. Books like these can be added to the recycle pile in that box over there."

Linda nodded.

Sure, Beth was shy, but in comparison to Linda, Beth was practically a raging extrovert. Maybe this is what she'd be like if she'd never been forced to confront her fear of speaking in front of people. That was a somewhat aberrant thought. Like the path not taken if Drew and her mother hadn't pushed her to do the speech in high school. Beth had tried to quit or make excuses so many times and they both had kept telling her she could do it. At the time, she hadn't appreciated their support, but now she did.

At least Linda was helping with the endless book-sorting project. The quiet woman seemed to enjoy the process of sorting through the books. A little smile touched her lips as she flipped through the pages.

Beth helped a few customers as Linda continued to softly riffle through books. The only sounds were the thump of volumes periodically hitting the recycle box. After a customer left, Beth turned to Linda. "I know it's a bit rude, but would it be a problem for you if I make a couple personal phone calls? I need to make an appointment with the veterinarian for my mother's dog."

Linda nodded her head in mute assent.

Beth arranged to drop off Arlo with the local vet, Dr. Cassidy, the next morning. If Cindy stopped by with Drew, Beth would have her chance to beg Cindy to pick up Arlo before the vet closed for the day. If Cindy wouldn't do it,

Beth had no choice but to close the store for a little while. Her mother had a deep loathing of signs on shop doors that said "Back in fifteen minutes." She always shook her head and said, "Fifteen minutes from *when*?" Oh well. Beth's failures as a shopkeeper just kept growing. *Sorry Mom.*

At a movement outside, Beth looked up from her sorting. Drew was outside the glass door, picking up Dixie. The bells jingled when he walked into the store. As he strode across the room to the writing desk, Beth's pulse quickened as memories of the night before flashed through her mind.

He smiled. "Hey there. That's quite a pile of books you have here."

Beth wanted to run around the desk and engage in an overt and passionate display of affection right there in the middle of the store, but refrained. Linda probably wouldn't appreciate that at all. "Hi Drew. This is Linda. She's helping me sort. We've gone through quite a few boxes and that heap over there is the recycle pile. The serpentine path through the storeroom is almost getting to the point that one might regard it as a navigable walkway again."

Linda smiled politely. "Hello."

"Pleased to meet you." Drew waved at the pile. "Given how much work it is to write something, it's kinda depressing to see that."

"They'll be recycled, though."

"Great. Each one is eighty- or a hundred-thousand words of someone's creative effort getting turned into corrugated cardboard. Kinda makes you wonder why anyone bothers to write anything."

Beth looked quickly at Linda and walked around the desk. She took Drew's arm and led him toward the front of the store. "Are you distressed about something?"

He readjusted Dixie in his arms. "Probably just tired. I didn't get much sleep last night."

Beth hoped Linda wouldn't notice the flush rising on her cheeks. She whispered, "I enjoyed some of the modernized naked Monopoly rules."

"Me too, Bethie. Although if you want to play again, maybe next time we could go for a larger game board. In a room with functioning heat."

Beth giggled. "That would be a welcome change. By the way, did you see Cindy out there in dog-walking land? I have an appointment to take Arlo to the vet tomorrow. I need to drop him off before I open the store."

"Nope. I didn't see her today."

"I have to make other arrangements, then. This afternoon I need to take books to Mrs. Oliphant."

"Want company? That woman loves Dixie and she's a hoot. I hope I'm that sharp at ninety-two."

Beth smiled. "Everybody loves Dixie. And yes, it would be wonderful if you came with me. I don't know Mrs. Oliphant very well. As you know, I'm not the most talented conversationalist in situations like that."

"You've always been kinda hard on yourself about that stuff. Don't worry. Mrs. O is great."

"I tend to think it's an accurate assessment of my social skills." Beth glanced back at Linda and took his hand. "I want to thank you for being so kind to me this morning when I was upset."

"He's just a dog, Beth. You don't need to get so worked up. Some days dogs are cute as pie. And some days they take a crap in your shoes." He grinned. "Life's kinda like that when you get right down to it."

Chapter 7

Choices

As Kat drove down the 405 toward LAX to pick up Joel, she remembered exactly how much she hated Los Angeles drivers and the associated gridlock they created. No matter how much time you allowed, other drivers seemed to do their utmost to delay any trip into the city. It would be equally exciting trying to find the correct airport terminal and then a parking lot that wasn't twenty-five leagues away from the gate.

Air travel was horrible and it just seemed to get more unpleasant all the time. Kat wound her way through the maze of airport traffic and noted the controversial new LAX control tower with its unusual curved roof and the Theme building with its spidery arches and flying saucer motif. George Jetson would feel right at home in this airport.

As Kat walked through the long hallways toward terminal 5, she witnessed the wide range of human emotions that can be found only at a busy airport. There were happy reunions, furious delayed travelers, anxious people standing in line, patient airport personnel trying to soothe upset passengers, and the occasional breathless runner trying to catch a tight connection. Finally, Kat arrived at gate 53B and sat down heavily. Many hours after leaving home, she had actually managed to get here before Joel's flight landed. It was a miracle. By now Cindy should be at the house walking the dogs. She said she would be anyway.

Kat pulled a book out of her bag and tried to settle into the uncomfortable plastic chair. With all the announcements over the loudspeaker and parts of the gigantic human being next to her oozing into her space, it was hard to concentrate on the novel. After a few minutes, she gave up, put the book away, and walked over to stare at the arrivals monitor for a while. Only a few more minutes. Joel had been gone for more than a month, and she felt as if it had been forever since she'd seen him. Although they'd talked every night, she was both thrilled and anxious about seeing him again. Her stomach was all tied up in knots worrying that something might be different after so much time apart. What if he was used to being alone again? What if he wasn't attracted to her anymore? Or he couldn't stand the idea of being around so much fur? Life with Kat was sort of strange in a lot of ways, after all. What if he'd changed his mind? This whole line of thinking was totally ridiculous, since it wasn't like she hadn't talked to him. And yet talking with someone on the phone wasn't the same as being together in person.

On the monitor, the status of Joel's flight switched to 'landed' and the announcement came over the loudspeaker. Kat turned to look at the gate. As a flight attendant opened the door, Kat's heart-rate increased. She stood on tip-toe, trying to see the passengers as they walked through the doorway. At last she saw Joel, who was turning his head, looking for her. Spotting Kat in the crowd, he locked his gaze with hers and grinned. Kat yelped in excitement as all her fears and anxieties evaporated. She started pushing her way forward through the crowd around the gate. After shoving the last person aside, Kat leaped into Joel's arms, causing him to drop his suitcase on the floor.

After a truly memorable kiss, Joel released Kat and whispered in her ear. "We're really in the way here."

Kat reluctantly let go and took his hand. "Oops. Okay, I'm moving."

He picked up the suitcase and threw the strap over his shoulder. "Let's get out of here."

They walked through the terminal and out into the bright sunlight. Kat looked up at Joel. "The truck is not exactly nearby. Sorry."

Joel readjusted the suitcase strap on his shoulder. "I don't care. It's such a relief to be off the plane and out of airports. I almost missed the connection in Detroit. It's a good thing I didn't check any luggage. Who knows where it would be by now?"

"No place good."

Joel stopped walking and Kat turned to look at him. "Everything okay?"

He wrapped her in a hug and rested his chin on her head. "It's just so good to be back here with you. I missed you so much."

Kat stepped back and looked up into his face. "I know. Let's try to avoid separation again for a while, okay?"

"I'm not going anywhere again for a long time, if I can help it."

Kat was relieved to have Joel drive back to Alpine Grove. She turned to him. "I'm delighted to be relinquishing driving duties back to you."

"It sounds like you adjusted to the truck okay."

"If by 'adjusted' you mean the range of ways I have found to swear at it, then yes, I've adjusted."

Joel laughed. "At least it's still running."

"True. There was some doubt the day I had to call Jack and ask him to come by and drag it out of the giant pile of slop in the driveway."

"Yeah, that didn't sound like much fun for anyone."

"Have I mentioned that it has been raining?"

He glanced at her. "More than once."

"The rain-on-snow motif hasn't done much for my perfectly plowed driveway. You missed the three days when it was looking really good. I was proud. Now it's a mish-mash of sloppy slush ruts."

Joel reached across the seat to hold her hand. "Did you find Dolly Mae yet?"

Kat nodded her head. "I did. That dopey cat went up into the attic. Remember the weird scrabbly noise I heard coming from up there? After I talked to you, I sucked it up and got out the horrible old ladder so I could go up and investigate. I braved the creepy spider haven and didn't see anything, so I went downstairs again. Then Maria called and we chatted about her lack of social life for a while. After I talked to her, I put the ladder away in the Tessa Hut."

"I guess Dolly Mae followed you up there?"

"Apparently. I didn't think she would do that. I mean, I didn't know a cat could climb such a large ladder. Who knew? I wish I had seen her do it. She's not that big and she must have had to really stretch out some paws to reach."

"Did she start meowing or something?"

"No. I heard all these massive thumping noises from upstairs, which scared the crap out of me. I was afraid the scrabbly thing might have found some hefty friends and decided to have a party. I do not need gigantic varmints having some bizarre critter orgy in the attic."

"I'm guessing that was Dolly?"

"Yes. Hunting makes a lot of noise. On a positive note, I think she caught whatever was up there. She looked really proud of herself."

Joel grinned. "Good kitty."

~

As Joel drove up the hill toward Alpine Grove, the weather began to deteriorate. Kat turned to look at him, "Welcome back to the land of extreme precipitation."

"All the rain and snow is what makes it green."

"I keep telling myself that. Be glad you missed the freezing-cold weather before this. Even the dogs were annoyed. They don't believe me when I tell them it's not my fault when their dainty little paw pads are cold. I think Tessa takes temperatures in the single digits as a personal affront."

"So has Lady been behaving better?"

"I haven't given her the chance to be bad." Kat squeezed his hand. "Sorry, but your dog hates me now. She really does not appreciate being walked along with Chelsey on a leash. We are way too slow and boring for her."

Joel shrugged. "I'll work with her again. She never has run off like that before, even when she was young."

"I think she was looking for you. Maybe it's a collie thing. She thinks you're Timmy trapped in a well somewhere and it's her responsibility to find you. But the whole *Lassie Come*

Home thing doesn't work out too well when you're three thousand miles away."

He glanced at her. "I'm not sure I buy the Lassie theory."

"Sorry. It's all I've got."

They drove through downtown Alpine Grove and headed north toward the house, listening to the windshield wipers flapping back and forth in the driving rain. It was foggy and the two-lane road was lined with tall ridges of sodden dirty snow that had built up from months of winter plowing.

Kat pointed at the road ahead. "Look out! There's a coyote."

Joel braked hard and the truck fishtailed as he maneuvered it to the side alongside a driveway. "That's not a coyote, Kat." He opened the door and leaped out of the truck, running along the shoulder. Grabbing the animal, he collapsed into a snow bank, hugging it to his chest. Kat turned off the truck and got out.

As she walked up to them, she realized that Joel was not hugging a strange dog. It was his collie-mix Lady. She crouched down next to them. Lady's fur was sodden and she was squirming in Joel's arms, obviously delighted to see him, but a bit annoyed at being manhandled in the snow. Joel was soaked and his hair was hanging in dripping strands in front of his face. Kat stroked the wet fur on the dog's head. "Is she okay?"

He nodded. "I think so. Let's get her home."

Joel carried the dog back to the truck and loaded her into the cab. Kat got in, collected her long hair back behind her shoulders, and wrung it out while Joel started the truck. She looked over at him and realized he was shaking and his cheeks weren't wet from just the rain. Lady had curled up in a ball on the bench seat and Kat reached over the dog to touch Joel's arm. "I think she's fine—just really, really soggy. I bet she'll sleep for hours."

He swiped at his eyes quickly with the base of his palm. "Why is she way out here?"

"I left everybody locked in the house, happily snoring away. Cindy was supposed to come by and give them a walk around lunchtime. I told her that she had to walk Lady on a leash now, after your dog ran off on me." She'd made a big point of it, so it wasn't like Cindy didn't know.

Joel shook his head and mumbled, "Unbelievable."

They drove the rest of the way back to the house in silence. Kat had found that when Joel was really upset, it tended to be a good idea to leave him be for a while. As they bumped through the ice ruts and slush in the driveway, Kat said, "Sorry about this. It's kind of a mess."

"Well, Cindy got in and out of here okay in that piece of garbage she calls a car."

Kat mentally cringed. Okay, Joel was definitely still angry. "I'll towel off Lady and get the woodstove going again to help dry her off."

He looked at her and the hard expression on his face softened. "Thanks, Kat."

They went inside and the other dogs greeted them with a cacophony of barking. Joel dropped his suitcase and laptop case in the entryway and walked off toward the bedroom, pausing for a moment to look at a piece of paper that was lying on the dining room table.

Lady ran down the steps and stood in front of the gate, waiting to be let into the downstairs hallway. The other dogs stood on the other side of the gate wagging, obviously thrilled that their missing cohort had returned. Kat opened the gate and got an old towel while the dogs engaged in a flurry of canine greeting.

After giving the dogs who had *not* just run away an outing and dealing with the wood stove, Kat went back upstairs. Getting out of her wet clothes was her next trick. She looked at the note on the table, which was from Cindy. She said Lori had been anxious to go outside so Cindy had unlocked the doggie door. Lady had run out after the border collie before Cindy could grab her. It sounded like the whole thing was an accident and Cindy had to leave to pick up Johnny from school.

Kat looked over her shoulder toward the bathroom. The shower was running. She wiggled her cold toes in her soggy sneakers, which made a squishing noise on the wet foam insoles. Ugh. Joel had the right idea. A hot shower sounded fantastic right now.

She skimmed the note again and jumped at the sound of the phone ringing. Cindy's voice greeted her. "Kat, did you see my note? I'm so sorry! I wanted to see if you're home yet. I can come back out and help look for her, but I had to pick up Johnny first."

Kat sat down in a chair. "You don't have to do that. Lady is here. We found her out on the road on the way home. She's fine. Just extremely wet."

"Should I come out? Joel is probably really mad at me."

Kat gazed at the ceiling. "You could say that. It might be a good idea if you leave him alone for a little while. I'll talk to him."

"It was an accident. I didn't think Lady would run out like that."

"I understand. Lady has not exactly been on the 'A-Plus Good Dog' list lately."

"I'm so sorry, Kat. I feel terrible. Thanks for talking to Joel."

Kat hung up the phone, took off her sneakers and socks, and gazed at her pruney, waterlogged feet. She looked up at the sound of a door opening. Joel walked from the bathroom to the bedroom, and with a sigh, Kat got up and walked to the bedroom doorway. "So are you ready to speak?"

He yanked the sleeve of his flannel shirt on and held out his arms. "Yes. I'm sorry."

Kat walked into his embrace and wrapped her arms around his waist. "You're warm."

"You'll feel better if you take a shower. I'll make us something to eat. All I've had is airplane food and I'm starving."

Kat stood on tiptoes to kiss him. "Thanks. I'm so glad you're home."

Later, after a shower and dinner, Kat curled up with Joel on the sofa. She snuggled into his flannel shirt and leaned her cheek on his chest. He wrapped his arm around her and she looked up into his face. "So I know you saw the note from Cindy. She called while you were in the shower."

"Great. Did you tell her to go away?"

"Yes. I said you might still be a teensy bit mad."

"Just a teensy bit." Joel stroked Kat's cheek. "Lady could have been hit by a car out there. It was pouring and we could barely see her. *I* could have hit her. I could have killed my own dog."

"I know. I get that. And I'd feel horrible if I had been driving. But Cindy didn't do it on purpose. It was an accident.

I told you about the day I thought I lost Lady. It almost gave me a heart attack. I thought you might die from a brain injury and I'd lose your dog all in the same day. It was pretty much the worst day ever."

"I know. But I'm fine."

"So is Lady." Kat pointed at the furry ball of collie on the floor. "She's napping hard, even now."

"I know. I realize that dogs don't live forever, but when I saw her out there, it just tore me apart. It was too much like when I found her."

"You found Lady? I don't think you ever told me that. Where?"

"Out near The Shack. You know where it's located—it's the middle of nowhere. That's where people go to dump critters they don't want. They drive out to the end of some country road and 'set them free.' It's horrible. Lady was about seven or eight months old, so she was beyond the cute puppy stage. After she wasn't adorable and fuzzy anymore, someone decided to ditch her. It makes me sick, but people do it."

Kat sighed. "I know the obnoxious canine adolescent phase can be unpleasant, but humans are worse."

"True. I asked all over town if anyone had lost a dog. No one has come forward yet in five years or so. I think she's mine."

"Definitely yours. She has no interest in me."

"That's not true. You feed her."

"I suppose Lady is pleased that you found a dog-feeding helper who happened to have some canine friends for her to play with."

Joel ran his fingers through her hair, pushing a long dark strand behind her ear. "You're a lot more than that to me."

Kat smiled. "Your dog isn't the only one who loves you, you know."

"I know. I love you too."

⌇

After closing the store and sending Linda home, Beth walked Arlo and went to pick up Drew and Dixie at Mrs. Oliphant's house for the trip out to the assisted living place. Beth pulled up along the curb. Like her mother's house, Mrs. Oliphant's home was in the older part of town. The Craftsman-style house had cream clapboard siding with dark wood trim that showcased a large covered wraparound porch. Huge old maple trees rose above the fenced backyard and probably provided lots of shade in the summer. Behind the wooden fence, the tattered ropes of an old swing hung from one of the massive tree branches.

Drew opened the door and picked up Dixie's sky kennel by the handle, carrying it down the sidewalk to the car. He put the kennel in the backseat and got into the Explorer. "Hey Beth. That's a whole lotta books back there. Good thing Dixie is confined, or she'd be thinking it's a mighty fine buffet."

"Yes, I'm so glad you're helping me take all these books to Mrs. Oliphant. I note that she is requesting *True Enemies*. According to my mother, she's a dedicated A.J. Emerson fan."

"Well, you gotta figure after reading four of them already, Mrs. O isn't gonna punish herself with another one of the stupid things if she doesn't like them."

Beth glanced at him. "Your books are not stupid things. Is something bothering you?"

"Nope. Just a big day of underachievement for me. I walked my dog. Read some stuff. Answered some e-mail. Laid around. Just your typical slacker activities."

"I told you I really don't think you're lazy. Honestly. I truly don't. And you've written five novels. Lazy people don't do that. Back then, I was upset and scared. I had to say goodbye to you and I made a horrible mess of it."

Drew looked out the window. "I think it might be cold enough to snow again. At least Dixie will be pleased about that."

Beth acknowledged the unsubtle change of subject with a nod. "Has she eaten the house yet?"

Drew turned to look back at Beth. "Nope. She's been pretty good. I think she's finally catching on to the going outside thing too. She lets me know instead of just letting loose, so at least I have a chance to get her outside before it's too late."

"I'm sure that is good news for Mrs. Oliphant's flooring."

"Yeah. She told me the place was built in 1925. If you can imagine it without all the overstuffed antique old-lady furniture in it, the house itself is kinda cute. It's got really high ceilings and hardwood floors. There's mahogany trim around all the windows and doors and this huge deck off the back. I bet it's nice in the summertime. At least the deck is covered, so it's not a gigantic pile of snow right now. That makes those late-night puppy outings easier."

Beth laughed. "I'll bet."

"I think Mrs. O. hasn't used the upstairs much in a long time. It's kind of amazing that she's been living in the place for as long as she has. We should all be so lucky to stay healthy for so long."

"Yes, I think about my mom's health a lot."

"Your mom is thirty-two years younger than Mrs. O. You think too much, Beth."

"What's that supposed to mean?"

Drew raised his hands in front of him. "Nothing. Never mind. I'm just in a bad mood. You know how I get sometimes."

"Why?" Beth pulled the SUV into the parking lot. "I thought you had a nice relaxing day."

"I don't want to get into that now. Let's just give Mrs. O her books, okay?"

Beth watched as Drew unlatched his seatbelt and got out of the car. He seemed particularly annoyed whenever the subject of his books came up. Something was definitely going on with him. Maybe she could get him to talk later and answer all of her other questions as well. It wasn't like she had been a bright ray of sunshine today either. The dreary gray weather certainly didn't help.

Drew leashed up Dixie and let her peruse the parking lot for a few minutes before helping Beth with the books. They went into the assisted living center and the woman at the front desk directed them to Mrs. Oliphant's room. The young nurse smiled. "Dot is going to be so thrilled to see you with all those books and the puppy. You'll make her day!"

Beth and Drew walked by an elderly woman in a wheelchair who smiled and reached out her hand toward Drew. "Oh, look at the puppy!" Drew put down the bag of books and crouched next to the chair, holding Dixie up next to the woman's arm so she could stroke the dog's head. "Her name is Dixie."

Dixie wagged and wiggled, enjoying all the attention. The woman looked at Drew. "Oh, I had a dog just like this named Coco when I was growing up. Look at how sweet she is. So soft. Thank you for letting me pet her."

Drew stood up. "Any time, ma'am. Dixie loves any excuse for attention."

Beth took his arm. "You seem to meet women of all ages, thanks to Dixie."

"She's a puppy. What can I say? Puppies are total chick magnets."

Beth giggled. "I always learn new things when I'm around you."

They walked into Mrs. Oliphant's room. The elderly woman was sitting up in bed surrounded by books. She looked up as they entered. "Drew! What are you doing here? And you brought Dixie too!" She reached out her arms. "Let me see that adorable ball of fuzz!"

Drew grinned. "Okay, but you asked for it." He placed the puppy on the bed. "You be good, Dix."

Beth said, "Hello, Mrs. Oliphant. It has been many years, but I'm Elizabeth Connolly. My mother asked me to bring you the books you ordered the other day." She held up her bag. "Where would you like me to put them?"

Mrs. Oliphant moved one of her hands from Dixie's head and patted the bed next to her. "Right here. Show me what you brought."

"Okay." Beth moved around to the other side of the bed and set down the bag. "Do you want me to move some of these other ones?"

"No. I want to be able to reach them all. Take those out and line them up. I want to look at the covers."

Beth began pulling the books out of the bag and laying them on the bed. "Drew, I think we forgot one of the bags."

"Gimme the keys, Beth, and I'll go get it. Keep an eye on small-fry there and make sure she doesn't make a break for it."

Mrs. Oliphant was snuggling Dixie to her. "Dixie would never do that, would you, sweetheart?" Dixie's stubby tail went back and forth wildly as she tried to stand on her hind legs to lick the woman's face.

Beth said, "Is she being too much trouble? I can take her for a minute if you want to look over the books."

"Did you bring the A.J. Emerson one? I want to read that book next."

Beth sat on the edge of the bed and held Dixie, who was starting to look sleepy. "I think it's in the other bag. I just read it though, and It's extremely good. I think it's my favorite of all of them."

"Yes, I told Drew he needs to stop fretting about these things. He's got a gift with words, for heaven's sake. I always wished I could write like that. I dreamed of writing novels, but it didn't happen for me. I'm fated to be a reader."

Beth looked up. "You know he wrote the books?"

"Of course I do. He's living in my house. Did he finally finish the sixth one? The poor thing was just beside himself."

"He said he sent it to his editor last weekend."

"Well good. I told him he needed to work out the issues and not let things get left unsaid." Mrs. Oliphant stroked Dixie's brown fur slowly. "That's what keeps you up at night as you get older and you outlive everyone you know. Not the things you did, but the things you *didn't* do and the things you didn't say and you wish you could have."

"Well, it certainly sounds like it will be an interesting story." Beth didn't want to tell her that Drew killed off the character of Liz Logan. It would undoubtedly infuriate Mrs. O. just as much as it did her.

"I'm sure it will be. I think he just needed to talk to someone about it. He's a wonderful person."

Beth was a bit taken aback. Drew really had some hard-core fans, even among senior citizens. "Well, it does sound like he receives quite a bit of fan mail from readers."

"I don't mean as a writer. Don't take him for granted, Liz."

"It's Beth, actually."

Drew smiled as he walked into the room with the bag. "It looks like Dixie fell asleep on you. That little pup is really a short hitter." He handed the bag across the bed to Beth. "More for your collection."

Beth laid out the rest of the books. "Okay, here they are. Thank you for purchasing them. My mother always says you are her best customer."

"Thank you for bringing them all the way out here. When you get to my age, you never know if you're going to get through the end of a novel, much less a series." She shook her finger at Drew. "That book better be out soon. I'm not getting any younger."

Drew smiled. "It's out of my hands at the moment. I'll let you know when I get it back for revision."

"You'd better. Now come here and give me a hug before you leave. I've got reading to do."

Drew bent over the bed to hug the older woman and then gathered Dixie in his arms. "See you soon."

The woman shook her head. "We'll see. Choose to be happy, Drew."

They said their goodbyes and Beth and Drew left with Dixie. As they walked down the hallway, Beth said, I've never heard 'Choose to be happy' as part of a leave-taking."

"Mrs. O always does that. She says that happiness is a choice and that she wished she had realized that much earlier in her life. So that's what she tells everyone when they leave her room. The nurses think it's cute. I figure it's probably good advice. She says that when you get as old as she is, you better say what you really think. Whether you tell people you love them or hate them, you don't have time to beat around the bush anymore."

"That sounds like something she would say. She's certainly very forthright." Beth took his hand and swung it back and forth between them. "So now that your little dog has charmed most of the residents of this building, can I make you dinner again tonight?"

"I should take this charming little dog home, Beth. Maybe another time."

Beth lowered her gaze, feigning interest in the industrial carpeting. What had happened? Had she done something wrong? Something had distressed Drew and he clearly was not planning to divulge whatever it was this evening. So much for getting all her questions answered. Apparently, it was going to be a lonely night in her arctic childhood bedroom.

∿

The next day Beth resolved to get through more of the items on her mother's to-do list. Linda reappeared and spent the day sorting books. The woman was so quiet, half the time Beth forgot she was there. It was sort of odd, but peaceful, since Linda seemed to dislike small talk as much as Beth did. Two extremely shy people didn't make a lot of noise.

Beth took Arlo to the vet and closed the store early to pick him up, mentally apologizing to her mother for her many failures as a retailer. It had gotten so cold outside that it wasn't as if customers were lining up to buy books anyway. The main street of town was largely devoid of pedestrians. People were obviously hunkering down, waiting for the weather to warm up. Late winter weather was nothing if not capricious.

At the vet clinic, Dr. Cassidy had asked a lot of questions about Arlo's environment to determine if he was experiencing undue stress. Beth told the woman about her mother's accident, but opted not to mention that there also had been a strange man in the house. It seemed wise to omit that detail, lest the entire town find out about Beth's evening with Drew. It was Alpine Grove after all, and discretion was always an advisable course of action.

The veterinarian had not found anything conclusive, but gave Beth a new medication to try. Maybe it would help. After Beth got back to the house with Arlo, all she could think about was talking to Drew and finding out what was going on. She'd been fretting about it all day.

Exhausted from his veterinary ordeal, Arlo stalked off to his bed and curled up into a ball to pout. Beth sat on the sofa and stared at the telephone. This was absurd. She was a grown woman who had managed an entire department at RTP. Why was she behaving like an adolescent again? Maybe being in this house caused her to lapse into her teenage patterns of social angst. She pushed her hair behind her ear and dialed the number to Mrs. Oliphant's house. At least she wouldn't have to talk to a churlish receptionist. The phone rang fourteen times before Drew finally picked up.

"Hi Drew. I'm glad you're home."

"Yeah, I'm here. I have got to buy an answering machine for this place."

"Are you in 'do not disturb' mode again? Are you writing?"

"No."

Beth twisted the phone cord in her fingers. His voice sounded odd. "I was, well, hoping I could see you. It seemed like something was bothering you yesterday."

"It's not worth worrying about, Beth."

Beth paused. She knew what was going on. "Drew, it's me you're talking to. I know what you're doing. You've retreated into the dark recesses of Gollum's lair again, haven't you?"

"You know, sometimes it's just plain annoying that you knew me in high school. Yeah, I suppose. So what? Don't you have something else you need to do?"

Beth leaned forward and put her elbows on her knees. "You haven't left the house all day, have you?"

"Dixie and I visited the backyard quite a few times. Does that count?"

"No. It doesn't. Did you get out of bed and get dressed this morning?"

There was a pause and he mumbled, "Well, sort of, I guess."

"'Sort of' means no, you did not. You need to take a shower and greet the new day, which is now almost over. I'll make you dinner. Can you be here in an hour?"

After another long pause, he finally said, "All right. But if Dixie chews up more of your mom's furniture, it's your own dang fault."

"I'll see you soon."

Beth set to work in the kitchen while Arlo supervised closely, his indignation about the vet visit seemingly forgotten. She chopped vegetables and considered the conversation with Drew. He had a tendency to retreat from things he didn't want to deal with, preferring to avoid confrontation by sleeping or reading. The summer they were together, Drew had disappeared from her life after a particularly awful fight with his father. Beth had been beside herself with worry because in the days leading up to the parental strife, he and Beth had spent almost every possible moment together.

As it turned out, Drew had been in his bedroom the entire time, which she had discovered when she finally gave up on calling and got up the nerve to go over to his house. There she had found him unshaven, unwashed, and extremely unhappy. After talking with her about the argument, he returned to his typical easygoing behavior. He referred to it as emerging from Gollum's lair, and Beth hoped the same thing would happen again today.

At the knock on the door, Arlo jumped up and ran to the door, barking like a wild thing. Beth followed and let in Drew, who was carrying Dixie. His hair was wet and he had obviously just shaved. Closing the door behind him, he put Dixie down and shook his head. "I hope you're happy. My hair is now a bunch of icicles that are dripping down my neck."

Beth put her arms around him and kissed away some of the droplets. "I'm not going to apologize. It's good to see you." She nibbled his earlobe for emphasis.

"That's good to hear. Maybe coming over wasn't such a bad idea after all."

She took his hand and led him into the kitchen. "Please bring the canines in here. I was hoping I could talk to you while I finish making dinner."

With a dubious look, he complied. "Come on Dix, let's go. No sofa-leg snacking for you today."

"Do you want the rest of the wine? You forgot to take it with you. It needs to be finished and the bottle removed before my mother returns."

"All right."

Beth poured a tumbler of wine, set the sauce on the stove to simmer, and sat down at the bistro table across from Drew. Handing him the glass, she looked into his eyes. "Tell me what happened."

He took a sip of wine. "When?"

"I don't know. You tell me. What caused you to retreat to Gollum's lair? Something happened. What was it?"

"Do we really have to talk about this?"

Beth nodded emphatically. "Yes, we really do."

"Fine." He paused for a moment then waved his hand. "Sometimes the whole being connected thing is depressing, you know? I thought I'd have a few weeks before I'd hear anything about the novel. But no. My cast-iron editor is e-mailing me her thoughts as she goes through the manuscript."

Beth raised her eyebrows. "You mean she doesn't like it? I find that hard to believe."

"Believe it. She hates it. Just hates it." He leaned forward and put his elbows on the table. "Wait 'til she gets to the part where I killed off Liz. Jeez, that woman is gonna blow a gasket."

"Well, you can revise it. That's part of the process, right?"

"Yeah. But it's going to be agonizing. The whole thing kinda makes me feel sick, just thinking about it. Writing it was bad enough. I've never had this much trouble writing anything before. It was horrible."

Beth put her hand on his across the table and locked her gaze with his. "Is there any way I can help?"

Both of them jumped at the jarring sound of the telephone ringing. Beth leaped out of her chair. "Just a minute."

Beth tried not to gasp when she realized that it was Graham's voice at the other end of the line. She glanced at Drew, who was staring disconsolately down at his wine glass. "Oh, ah, what a surprise to hear from you. I thought perhaps you had lost my mother's number."

Graham chuckled. "I'm not quite the absent-minded professor you say I am, you know. I have it right here in my day planner. You should know that."

"Ah yes. And yet you didn't call once the last time I was here. Unfortunately, this is not an…an ideal time for me to talk. I'm in the middle of making dinner right now."

"You sound unaccountably disturbed, Beth. I thought your mother was on a trip and you were there by yourself. Just you and the dog."

"Yes, Arlo is right here." She waved her hand at the sheltie for emphasis, "Right Arlo?" Arlo and Dixie jumped up and began barking in unison, the older dog's deeper barks mingling with Dixie's high-pitched yips.

Graham said in a stern voice. "Who else is there? I'm not stupid Beth. That's two dogs. Not one. Are you keeping things from me?"

Beth scowled as white-hot anger flashed. She said sharply, "Keeping things from *you*? How dare you even ask me that?"

Drew looked up at Beth with concern and mimed, "Who is that?"

Beth shook her head at him and turned around. "It's honestly quite astonishing that you finally opted to call. But your timing is atrocious. I really must go." She hung up the phone and walked back to the table. "I'm sorry about that."

"So I'm guessing you haven't told the guy in Tucson about our little game of Monopoly, have you?"

"No. I haven't talked to him until now."

Drew crossed his arms in front of his chest. "Yeah, I kinda wondered if you would forget to mention it. Might as well get back at him for a little while first, right?"

"No. Frankly, I haven't thought about him at all. I've been worried about you."

"Don't bother, Beth. We both know it's only a matter of time before you'll get angry about something and lay into me again." He bent to pick up Dixie and looked at Beth. "And to be honest, I can't stand to go through that again at this point in my life. Seeing you has made that really clear to me. I can't. And I won't."

Beth stood up. "What are you talking about? Being together has been extraordinary. I've missed you so much."

Cuddling Dixie to his chest he said, "I missed you too. But I was right before. This isn't going to work. When you almost tore into me again the other day in the dining room, I knew it for sure. You told me you were close to telling me off again. And I don't need that. You kicked me to the curb once Beth, and I have no reason to believe you won't do it again. I'm just a fun diversion until you get your real life straightened out and start going places again."

Beth grabbed his arm. "No Drew, that's not true at all. Don't go. Can't we talk about this?"

"I don't feel like talking anymore. That poor old dead horse has been beaten enough. Dixie and I need to get back home so I can figure out how in the name of all that is holy I can turn the gigantic cow pie that is my novel into something that won't send my editor to the nuthouse."

"Drew, stop! Just stop. Please talk to me." Beth wiped a tear from her cheek. "You always do this. You run away. Just this once, could we please try something different? I promise I will try harder not to get angry."

He stood motionless, except for a small muscle that twitched in his jaw.

Beth reached out and stroked Dixie's head. "Look, even your dog is upset."

Drew looked down at the puppy, whose brown eyes were wide, peering up at him. "Aww jeez, I'm sorry Dix. I'm being a rotten human."

~

After Drew sat down again, Beth quietly finished making dinner. She placed a plate in front of him. "Are you over your mad enough to talk yet?"

A corner of his mouth turned up. "Getting there. Food will help. Thanks."

They ate in silence and took the dogs outside for a short walk. Beth held Drew's arm and leaned her head on his shoulder, huddling against the cold as they waited for Arlo to finish. "The vet gave me some new medication for Arlo. She also said he might have been stressed about things going on in his life."

"Aren't we all?"

Beth smiled. "Well, at least you are gainfully employed."

"For the moment. If my editor has any say, I'm thinking the odds of another six-book contract might be dwindling."

She rubbed his arm. "It will be okay, Drew."

"Unless we freeze to death. Is he done yet? Glaciers move faster than this animal."

They went back inside and Beth made a fire in the fireplace while Drew ensconced Dixie in her crate. The little dog curled up into a small brown fuzzy ball in a back corner, obviously ready to settle in for the evening.

Drew sat down on the sofa and Beth pulled his arm around her, so she could lean back on his chest. She squeezed his hand. "Are you ready to talk?"

"Yeah, I suppose. If we have to."

She turned in his arms and reached out to stroke his cheek. "First off, I'm sorry about the call tonight. I promise I will call him back at a more appropriate time and tell him it is over."

Drew readjusted himself on the couch, so he could see her face. "Beth, what are you saying? I mean, you're not dumping the guy because of me, are you?"

"Not specifically. It's more like I'm doing something I should have done a long time ago. Despite all the evidence staring me in the face, I resisted the idea that Graham was wrong for me. I was convinced that he was mature and responsible and that's what I needed. So I continued in a strange limbo state, assuming things with him would get better."

Drew shook his head. "Isn't this all sorta sudden?"

"I suppose to you it is. But I've been pretending everything was okay for a long time. I'm not sure why. It seems my powers of denial are truly quite exceptional. Maybe seeing you woke me up to that. I don't know. But I was serious when I said that being with you again has been an amazing experience."

"Yeah, but I was serious too. Do you honestly think we have any kind of future together?" He took her hand. "I mean, I thought so when I was eighteen, but I was unbelievably naive. Not to mention seriously wrong, which you explained in excruciating detail at the time. I don't really see how anything with us would ever work. That's part of what has been bugging me."

Beth squeezed his hand. "Why not?"

"Well, you'd get angry and then I'd leave and go somewhere. Then you'd hunt me down and try to kill me. It would be a big story in the Alpine Grove newspaper. "Valedictorian dismembers failed novelist." I'd end up just another Cedar County murder statistic."

Beth turned to look at him. "Oh Drew, you're exaggerating. It's not that bad."

"The word *volatile* leaps to mind. I mean, you're a passionate person, which in certain contexts is pretty fantastic. But I'm not sure we could even live in the same house for more than a day." He grinned. "Unless we spent most of the day in bed, in which case, no problem."

She smiled in response. "Spending the day in bed does sound delicious, so I certainly can't argue that point. But what if we try an experiment? You could stay here for a few nights. Then I won't have to wonder if you've disappeared again. And you can tell me about your mysterious past that you continue to avoid discussing, so I can stop inventing things and getting angry based on your prior adolescent behavior. I'd really like to find out more about who you are now."

"All right. But you, in turn, will have to work on not getting angry about every single little thing that goes wrong. Because if you live with me, things will go wrong and you will remember some unpleasant realities like I am a slob and really not a morning person. I'm sure you'll discover a whole host of other habits you won't like either. I am a lot of things, but perfect sure isn't one of them."

"I think I need to stop striving for perfection. Mrs. O is right. Happiness is a more realistic goal." Beth kissed him. "And right now, I am happy being here with you."

"Me too, Bethie. I suppose it can't hurt to try."

The next morning, Beth got up early so she could make her phone call to Graham. Although he had gotten up to take Dixie out multiple times throughout the night, true to his word, Drew rolled over and mumbled, "Go away" when she asked if he was ready to greet the day at seven thirty in the morning.

Beth knew Graham would already be in his office trying to get a head-start on projects, so it was a good time to call, before anyone else was there. She dialed the number, which went directly to Graham, since his assistant didn't arrive until eight. After she greeted him, he said curtly, "My, aren't you up early? I see you managed to fit me into your busy schedule after hanging up on me last night."

"Yes. This is a courtesy call to let you know that I don't want to see you again after I return to Tucson. You also are relieved of any further calling obligations."

There was a long pause, and finally Graham said, "Is this your way of breaking up? You have got to be kidding, Beth."

"Not at all. I truly do not ever want to see you again."

"I knew it. You weren't alone last night, were you? Did you find some yokel up there in the trees? So I was right—you *are* cheating on me. Nice, Beth. Really classy."

"No Graham. No yokels." Beth gazed out the kitchen window, where a small mountain chickadee was flitting around in a bush. "And your comment is quite ironic, because I was talking to someone about you and realized a truth. All those rumors that have been circulating around campus are valid. I've had every indication that you were cheating but refused to open my eyes. The most painful thing, I think, is that you undermined my trust, underestimated me, and clearly think I'm stupid. You never thought I'd find out because you are utterly convinced that you are so much smarter than I am."

"Spare me, Beth. What indications? You have no proof of anything."

Even though Graham couldn't see them, Beth held up her fingers, so she could count off a list. "Your distance, lack of interest in me, changing plans at the last minute, the inability to reach you at odd hours, flirting with students, the odd behavior of your co-workers toward me, the fact that you stopped attending social events with me, your endless criticism of me and my choices, and last, but not least, my intuition."

"Give me a break. That's not proof. It's all a bunch of speculation."

"It is enough proof for me. And the biggest thing of all is that even after all this time and many speculative discussions, you have never been willing to verbally express any type of commitment to me at all. You have never even met my mother or anyone close to me who would ask questions about your intentions."

"Is this you harping on marriage again? I told you I already tried marriage and it didn't work."

Beth sighed. "I don't think wanting a commitment should be such an outrageous thing if you truly love me. I wanted so badly for us to be in love and I kept thinking things would get better if I gave us more time. But I've finally realized that will never happen. To get married would require standing up in front of witnesses and legally and morally expressing that you want to enjoy a lifetime of physical and intellectual commitment to me, excluding all others. I think that last point is the troublesome one."

"Fine, Beth. You've succeeded in terminating our relationship. But nothing about us had better come back around to the university, or you'll be sorry."

"You can save your threats, Graham. My lips are sealed. However, you might want to share that sentiment with your other girlfriends, particularly if they are not as gullible and don't trust you as much as I did. For me, that trust no longer exists. Goodbye."

As she hung up the phone, Beth sat down at the table and put her head on her arms. For the first time, she cried quietly, letting herself mourn the loss of the man she had idolized and adored years ago. But she knew she had done the right thing. She'd been fooling herself about being happy with Graham. He wasn't the person she'd originally thought he was, at all.

Even if Drew was right and they couldn't stand to be together long-term, she'd never go back to Graham. Being alone was far better than being with him. That chapter of her life was definitely closed.

Chapter 8

Revisions

A t about nine, Drew stumbled down the stairs, looking disheveled. Beth looked up from her perch on the sofa. "Good morning."

"Coffee."

"There is a fresh pot in the kitchen."

He waved a thank you and mumbled, "Mmmfph."

Returning to the living room with a mug, he sat down next to Beth. "Are your contacts bugging you? Your eyes are all red."

"I'll be fine."

"Well, you look ready to roll outta here."

"Yes, I need to leave in about twenty minutes to open the store. I'll leave you a key to the house. You can come and go as you please. Just be sure to put Arlo in the kitchen behind the gate." She grinned. "And, by the way, Cindy arrives to walk Arlo at noon. You know how Alpine Grove women tend to swoon over men who have all their teeth, but you might spoil her impression of you if she sees you like this."

"Yeah. Gotcha. Good to know. We'll be outta here before then. I need to get over to the house and see what horrible things my editor is gonna tell me today. I get a new installment every day to sort of draw out the agony."

Beth reached out to caress his cheek. "Don't take it so hard, Drew. Maybe we can talk about it tonight."

He took her hand and kissed her palm. "Thanks Bethie. Yeah, I'd like that. Would you be willing to read the draft?"

She clasped her hands together. "Oh Drew, would you let me? I'd love to."

"I'm warning you though. It's a first draft."

She grinned. "I understand. Everything has to start somewhere. A wise person once told me that you can't edit a blank page."

Drew set his mug on the coffee table so he could give her a slow, mind-numbing kiss. "I'm not that wise. But I am getting better at Monopoly. Thanks for making up the guest bedroom last night."

"I prefer staying in there. I think I'll tell my mother she can turn my old room into a sewing room after all."

Drew laughed. "Sewing machines don't care about heat."

"Very true." She kissed him again. "I'll see you later."

"I'll be here."

It was another quiet day at the store with Linda, who arrived again to sort books. After a few hours, Beth was too curious to remain silent any longer. "Linda, I've offered to pay you for your time and I know you won't take money. But if you don't mind me asking, why are you here doing this?"

Linda looked up from her book. "I want to get out of the house. It's too empty."

"Have you thought about getting a job?"

Linda shook her head vigorously, her straight brown hair whipping back and forth. "No. I hate dealing with the public."

Beth smiled. "I've noticed. And I definitely understand. I feel the same way. I spent most of my high-school years hiding back there in the storeroom, doing my homework. My mom loves her customers, but I was terrified to even look at anyone. Even now, I still feel like an idiot half the time when I'm collecting someone's money during a purchase."

"No! You're great." Linda waved the book in her hand toward the street. "I just never know what to say to people. For everyone else, it looks so easy. It didn't matter most of the time when my primary job was to be a mother. Then the kids left and Walter left. Now it's just me."

"Are you sure you don't want payment? Like I said, I really am happy to compensate you for your time. It wouldn't even come from the store receipts, so don't worry about that. I'd pay you from my own pocket just because now I have this unreasonable need to finish this book-sorting project before I leave in a week. I think that thanks to you, it might actually be possible."

"Thank you for offering, but I got a very generous settlement from Walter. It's just nice to be here away from everything. I feel useful. I was starting to worry that I'd become one of those weird old ladies who are afraid to leave the house."

"Well, I don't think that would be the case, but I do appreciate it. My mother will *never* go through these books."

Linda giggled. "She'll be surprised when all the boxes are gone."

"I think *stunned* may be a more accurate description."

That evening, Beth went back to the house and found Drew in the kitchen making dinner while Arlo and Dixie looked on. She walked up behind him, put her arms around his waist, and kissed his neck. "You appear to be working with food. Did you learn to cook at some point in the last decade?"

He turned and kissed her. "I have been known to embark on fine culinary creations. This isn't one of them though, so don't get your hopes up. We're having spaghetti."

"That sounds wonderful, largely because I didn't have to make it."

After dinner, Drew pulled his laptop down from a bookshelf. "I put this out of puppy range, but if you want to read the dreadful novel, you can. I don't have a printer, so you'll have to read it on the screen."

Beth jumped off the sofa and took the laptop from him. "Oh yes, definitely. Let's plug it in over here."

After Drew had turned on the computer and opened the file, Beth sat down on the couch with the laptop in front of her on the coffee table. "I'm going to save a new version so I don't accidentally overwrite anything."

He shrugged. "Okay. Do whatever you want. After I finished it, I made a zillion backups because I'm paranoid like that. If you want to put in notes or something on your copy, go for it."

Beth pulled the laptop off the table and leaned against Drew with the laptop resting on her thighs. "I can't believe I'm the first person to read this."

"Well, other than my editor. In today's installment, she called one section in the third chapter *improbable*, and that was the nice part of the e-mail." He put one arm around her and held a novel in his other hand. "I'm gonna drown my sorrows in quality literature."

"That's a completely subjective value judgment. What are you reading?"

He held the book cover in front of her. "This."

"Ugh, Drew, even my mom hates E.L. Jakes. She said the books are awful. And she never says that about *anything*."

"Supposedly, this one is selling like crazy. It's on all the best-seller lists, but so far I'm pretty sure your mom isn't wrong. We'll see how it goes. Maybe it gets better."

Later, Beth was hunched over the coffee table reading and typing notes into the manuscript file. She glanced over at Drew, who had fallen asleep with one arm flung out to the side. He looked so peaceful lying there all sprawled out and relaxed.

Beth's gaze moved to the floor, where Dixie was contentedly sleeping in a pile of shredded paper that had been the E.L. Jakes novel. It looked like confetti.

Beth jumped up and yelled, "Dixie! How *could* you?"

Drew started awake with a groan as the puppy leaped off her paper nest and ran off toward the kitchen, followed by Arlo. Drew sat up. "What happened?"

Beth pointed at the pile of paper on the floor. "Look! Your dog completely consumed that book."

"Yeah, she kinda has a thing for paper." He leaned to peer over the side of the couch. "I must have dropped it on the floor when I was resting my eyes."

"Obviously!"

He shook his head slowly. "You know, I hate to be critical of another author, knowing how hard it is to write a book and all. But Dixie is right. That thing was trash. Now we don't have to feel bad about throwing it away."

Beth took a deep breath and sat down again. "I guess I wasn't paying attention. I'm sorry I yelled at Dixie."

"If you take her outside, I bet she'll forgive you."

Beth shut down the laptop. "Nice try. It's late. I'll take Arlo. You take Dixie."

Drew moved his legs off the couch, putting his feet on the floor with a thud. "Fine. At least they're saying it's gonna get warmer tomorrow. The word *thaw* was even used. I hope they're right, for a change. The weather reports here are about as useful as a trap door on a canoe."

"At least I'm not the only person who complains about the cold."

"I'm from the south, Beth. When the temperature drops below sixty degrees, there's panic in the streets and we start bundling up in parkas."

Beth giggled. "And my mom says *I'm* wimpy."

∽

Over the next couple of days, Beth fell into a routine of working at the store during the day and reading Drew's novel at night. Despite his dire predictions, Drew was easygoing and fun to be around. Yes, he was a slob, but he also knew he was a slob, so he'd crack stupid jokes about it, probably in an effort to get her to lighten up, as he would say.

Saturday night, Beth was hunched over the laptop again, completely engrossed in the story. Arlo was curled up on the floor, next to her feet. Although she had made a number of suggestions for improvement throughout the manuscript, Drew's writing was no less engaging than in his prior books. She ran across the improbable section in Chapter Three and talked to Drew about it. There was no way Liz Logan would do something like that. Absolutely no way. Drew had said he'd take her comments 'under advisement,' causing Beth to do a mental eye roll. It was such a Drew thing to say.

Dixie was snoozing on the couch curled up next to Drew, who was supposedly reading, but actually was 'resting his eyes' again. Beth smiled at them. It was adorable seeing the fuzzy brown puppy curled up in the crook of his arm.

Beth stretched her arms above her head and turned back to the novel. The tension in the story was building and although it was late, she had to find out what happened in the next chapter. How were they going to get out of this one?

A few minutes later, Beth gasped and yelped, "No! That's not possible!" She put her hand over her mouth as tears slid down her cheeks.

Drew moved and Dixie squeaked in protest. He sat up and rubbed his eyes. "Sorry, Dix. Sleeping there comes with some risks." He looked at Beth. "What happened? Dixie is right here."

Beth waved at the laptop. "Oh Drew, the way Liz dies. It's just…just…*terrible*. I mean, I know you told me you killed her off, but that is just too heartbreaking."

"Well, given the look on your face, I guess it had some emotional impact anyway."

"Emotional impact? How could you *do* that to Liz?" Beth rubbed her eyes and a contact lens flew out and landed on the floor. "Stop! Don't move!"

Drew scrubbed his hand across his face. "Dang, Beth. Not again."

Arlo sniffed at the tiny green circle next to him, then slurped it up with his long pink tongue. Beth shrieked, "Arlo, *no*!" The dog got up and ran to the kitchen.

Beth stood up with her arms at her side, fists clenched, as currents of rage flowed through her body. She willed herself not to scream and took a deep breath instead. "Do you have any idea how *expensive* those things are?"

Drew looked up at her. "No. But you have glasses."

"I *hate* my glasses! They look terrible on me and they hurt if I have to wear them all day."

Moving Dixie aside, Drew stood up and put his arms around Beth. "You know how Arlo gets about stressful situations. If you don't go apologize to that animal, he's gonna go crap in your shoes again."

Beth relaxed against him and put her head on his shoulder, giggling helplessly. "Oh nooo…not crap in my shoes. Maybe I'll find my contact lens in there."

"Well, just so you know, I am *not* helping you look for it this time. I mean it. I'm not kidding. No way."

Beth took another deep breath, rested her hands on Drew's shoulders, and kissed him. "Perhaps I'll just wear my glasses for a while."

The next morning, Beth stretched over Drew to reach her glasses on the nightstand. He grabbed her around the waist. "Careful with that knee, missy, or there aren't going to be any more trips down Boardwalk or Park Place for you in the future."

She put on her glasses and rested her forearms on his chest, looking down into his face. "I'm so happy I don't have to go to the store today. One entire, glorious day off."

He ran his fingertips through the hair at her temple. "It's supposed to be a day of rest. Why are you waking me up at the butt-crack of dawn?"

"The sun woke me up. Look out the window. There is sunlight! We should go somewhere. I haven't gone anywhere except the store since I've been here."

"We could go down to the lakeshore trail. It's probably cleared off by now. We could look at the water. Dixie would probably love it."

Beth patted his chest excitedly. "Yes, let's do that! I haven't been there in years."

"I think we should wait until it warms up some." He carefully pulled her glasses off and laid them back on the nightstand. "And right now, I can think of other things I'd like to do that don't involve going outside into the cold."

Beth moved to meet his kiss. "Yes, I do see the merits of body heat."

Later that afternoon, they were slowly strolling along a trail that wound alongside the lake. Arlo was plodding along, methodically checking each tree and shrub, while Dixie was excitedly darting ahead and running back when she reached the end of her leash. Beth looked at Drew. "Your dog is behaving like a yo-yo."

"Yeah, she's gonna gas out here if she keeps doing that. I think Arlo's dawdling is boring her."

"Let's go sit on that bench for a minute. Arlo is getting so slow, I think he might need to rest. I want to absorb some Vitamin D and talk to you about the scene I read last night."

He sighed. "I'm not gonna like this, am I?"

"Probably not. But you just can't leave it like it is. What did your editor say?"

"I think you're ahead of her on reading this thing now. She's got a whole lot of books she's working on, not just mine. Given your response, I'm not looking forward to the next e-mail from her."

Beth looped Arlo's leash over her arm and leaned back on the bench in an effort to soak up the maximum amount of sunlight from the weak rays filtering through the trees. "After five books, I've grown attached to the character of Liz. Plus, she reminds me of me."

Drew lifted Dixie onto his lap. "Ya think?"

"Well, except that she's much prettier than I am and she doesn't exhibit a number of my less-endearing qualities, such as awkwardness in social situations."

"She doesn't sound like a dictionary when she's pissed-off, either. My vocabulary isn't that large."

Beth turned to look at his face. "Oh please. If that were true, you would never understand what I'm saying and it's quite apparent that you always do, even when other people don't. Returning to my point, that was a horrible thing to do to poor Liz, and your readers will not be pleased."

"What do you suggest? Everybody lives happily ever after? It's not a romance novel, Beth."

"I'm not sure. I need to think about it. But I'm sure there has to be a way to rework the plot a bit so that Liz doesn't have to meet such a horrific end. Aside from making readers like me burst into tears, it also precludes any possibility of a follow-on book."

"Hey, our poor long-suffering hero Preston could meet another woman. It's not impossible, you know. Liz isn't the only fish in the aquarium. Although I guess now she's floating on the top of the tank."

Beth glared at him over the top of her glasses. "I believe you're the one who suggested that we not speak ill of the dead. And I continue to affirm that you need to resurrect her."

"Maybe I can turn it into a zombie novel. That might be fun."

Beth sat up in preparation for mobilizing Arlo again. "Well, I haven't finished the book yet. But if I find any zombies, I will think less of you as an author."

"Duly noted."

As they slowly walked back along the trail, Beth was overwhelmed with a sense of déjà vu. In just a few days, she was going to return to Tucson. This was just like the summer before she went to college. As time started running out, she and Drew had spent more and more time together, going for hikes on trails like this one. Drew had spun long, complicated tales about his weird family, and woven throughout Beth's memories of that time were many moments of laughter and an overall sense of well-being. It was notable, because she'd never felt that way since then. Well, until recently.

They stopped to wait for Arlo. Again. Beth squeezed Drew's hand. "I probably should have asked you this quite a while ago, but how long are you going to be house-sitting for Mrs. Oliphant?"

He shrugged. "I'm not really sure. She seems to think she may be in that assisted-living place for a while."

"Where were you living before I saw you at the reunion? Don't you have to get back somewhere?"

"Not really. I was renting a cabin in Tahoe. But dang, you think it's cold here? I was going to move in the fall, but then the book took longer than I thought and I almost froze to death in that place."

"Is all your stuff still there?"

"Nope. I don't have that much stuff. Like I said, I move around a lot. There are some things in storage in North Carolina. A lot of it is my Dad's though."

"What are you going to do next?"

He smiled at her. "Hey, what's with all the questions all of a sudden? You're one to talk. What are *you* going to do next?"

"Go back to Tucson and try to find another job, I suppose." She looked up at the darkening sky. "Perhaps just lie in the sun for a few weeks and attempt to thaw out."

Drew laughed and put his arm around her shoulder. "Do you think you can get that animal in motion again? I think our sun is leaving."

After they got back to the house, Beth started on dinner. Drew checked his e-mail and then joined her in the kitchen. He came up behind her and kissed Beth's neck, causing thrilling tingles to shoot down her spine. She turned around and put her arms around him. "Thank you. What was that for?"

"Just being social." He gestured toward the pan on the stove. "That looks promising."

Beth could no longer deny the obvious, and it was beyond time to say something. Years beyond. There was no way she was going to panic and screw this up again. She had to let him know how she felt.

Looking into his eyes, she tried to figure out what to say. "Drew. I…don't…I mean I want to. I would like…it's…been so. I don't know how to say…I thought it was all just…well, you know. But it's not."

His eyes widened in curiosity. "No, I don't know. What are you trying to say, Beth?"

"Drew. I…I love you. I think I always did, but couldn't admit it before. I was too scared. But I am positive now that I have fallen in love with you all over again."

His kiss was slow and tender. "Me too, Bethie. I love you too."

Beth ran her fingers though the hair at the back of his neck. "How do you feel about the desert? If you are truly as homeless as you sound, I'd be happy to share my home. It's warm."

Drew took her hand and looked down at it. "I'm not sure that's such a great idea right now."

"Why not? We have gone for days without me lashing out or you disappearing. We have proof of concept as far as cohabitation."

"True. And there are some other notable perks to living with you. But this is like that summer after our senior year. It's an unusual slice out of time. Here, you're basically on vacation. This isn't your real life, Beth. What happens when you get another demanding job at some huge tech company?"

"I go to work?"

"Where?"

"I don't know."

"That's my point. Right now, there's no stress. For these two weeks, everything has been mapped out for you. All you have to do is go to the bookstore during the day and read my crummy novel at night. It's all pretty low-key. You're kind of like Arlo in that you don't necessarily do well with the stress of major life-changes. It tends to freak you out."

She grinned. "I promise I will not defecate in your shoes."

"Thanks, Beth. I'm touched." He bent to kiss her neck again. "I just think we should take it really slowly, that's all."

Beth stepped back. "Wait. Is there something you're not telling me? I mean, you know all about Graham. I know you said you're not married, but is there someone?"

"Nope. Not lately. I wouldn't be here cohabitating with you if there were."

Beth tilted her head slightly. "I am happy to hear that, but perhaps a bit surprised."

"Recently, I've been too busy writing. And as noted, I'm not the easiest person to live with, so my few attempts at something more long-term didn't end well. When I was doing a lot of traveling, I was never in one place long, and I never met anyone special." He raised his eyebrows. "You don't really want me to go into a whole lot of detail here, do you?"

"I suppose not." Beth sighed. "So are you still worried about what happened with me ten years ago?"

"Maybe. I prefer to think of it as being cautious. We both have a lot of changes happening right now. Let's just take it day by day and see what happens."

Beth took both his hands in hers. "Okay. But I'm going to leave in a few days, and I'm going to miss you. I don't want to think about how much."

"I know. So we need to do our best to enjoy the next week as much as possible." He grinned. "We can't run off to

LA and see the Dead, but maybe I can come up with other ideas."

"You *are* a very creative person."

~

The next week passed far too quickly. During the day Beth sorted books with Linda and then returned to the house to find out what Drew had plotted for the evening. One night he declared it was drive-in-movie night, so they needed to make popcorn, watch one of Mom's old Hitchcock movies, and make out. Beth didn't watch much of the movie, but it was okay, since she'd seen *Psycho* before anyway.

Another night he brought tiramisu from the Italian place, which Cindy had told him was "to die for" on one of their not-so-accidental dog-walk meetings. Beth said, "Cindy still has the hots for you, doesn't she?"

"She just thinks Dixie is cute. And I prefer brunettes anyway. So here's the deal. To get any tiramisu, you have to speak Italian."

Beth raised her palms toward the ceiling. "I don't speak Italian."

"Well then wow me with fake Italian." He grinned and waved the box in front of her. "It's the language of love. If what you say sounds sexy, I'll give you a bite."

"Si."

"Really? That's the best you can do?"

"Ragu."

He picked up a spoon. "Fine. I'll start because this looks really good. *Tu sei il sole del mio giorno.*"

"What does that mean?"

"You are the sunshine of my day, which, given the rain we're having, is notable. I could turn into a mushroom if this weather keeps up." He picked up the spoon and took a bite of the tiramisu and rolled his eyes in melodramatic ecstasy. "Cindy was right—this stuff is incredible."

"Oh please. You're not going to hog it all, are you?"

"Italian."

Beth waved her hands and said in a singsong voice, "*O sole mio.*"

"You kind of cheated, but thanks. Here you go."

Saturday evening, after closing the store, Beth walked slowly back to the house. It was hard to believe she was leaving Alpine Grove the next morning. It was going to be difficult returning to her regular life without Drew. She would miss their nightly conversations and all the tales of his travels. She smiled at the memory of his Oktoberfest saga. Then there was his description of seeing the Taj Mahal at sunrise. He said the iconic white marble building lived up to all the hype and that there was a reason it was one of the wonders of the world. Maybe Beth would get to see it someday too.

She kicked an antique chunk of ice off the sidewalk. What were the odds that a long-distance thing would work? Probably not good. But Drew had made no mention of visiting or even seeing her again. He waved it off, saying that he wanted to wait and see where they ended up. It all sounded logical and responsible. Beth hated it. She was supposed to be the responsible one, not him.

She opened the door to the house and Arlo and Dixie ran toward her, barking enthusiastically. The new medication the vet had prescribed for Arlo seemed to be helping, and the exercise and a regular routine seemed to have evened out his digestion. It didn't hurt that he liked Drew and Dixie, but Beth knew the dog would be thrilled to have Margaret back, since he absolutely adored her mother.

Drew had turned on the radio and Mom's favorite oldies station was playing. He came up to her, grabbed her around the waist, leaned her back, and gave her a passionate kiss. He grinned. "Goodness gracious, great balls of fire!"

Beth straightened, readjusted her glasses, and said breathlessly, "I'm glad to see you too, Jerry Lee."

"A little rock-and-roll can make cooking more fun."

"What are we having?"

"Pizza. They delivered it a couple minutes ago. I thought Arlo was gonna have a coronary, he was barking so hard. I think he stressed-out the delivery guy."

Beth giggled. "Sounds good."

The strains of "In the Mood" by the Glenn Miller Orchestra filled the room and Drew took Beth in his arms, whirling her around. "So, do you remember how?"

"You tried to teach me swing-dancing at the prom, but I am not sure I was the most apt pupil."

He pulled her closer to him, "You did fine."

The song ended and Beth leaned her head on his shoulder. "That was such a magical night. I still can't believe you asked me."

He touched her chin, encouraging her to look at him. "You looked beautiful in that green dress. And there were a lot of magical nights afterward too."

Beth smiled. "Yes. I've always been glad my first time was with you. It was terribly awkward and nerve-wracking, and when I look back on it, the whole thing was actually somewhat humorous. But you were so sweet and kind. It was one of the most wonderful experiences I've ever had."

Drew kissed her. "Hey, you may have gotten an A in biology, but the only way you can really learn about sex is to try it out."

"The next day, I kept thinking, well, so that's what all the fuss is about. And I felt like everyone knew and they were looking at me."

"Maybe they were. You looked pretty happy."

"I was. Sneaking off to the beach was so much fun." She touched her necklace at the base of her throat. "That was when I found my silver heart pendant just sitting there in the sand at the edge of the water. The waves were splashing around me, and picking it up felt like some kind of sign."

He touched the heart with his fingertip. "Do you ever take it off?"

"No, I always wear it. I don't think my mom ever found out about our illicit trip either. She still refers to you as that nice boy I went with to the prom."

"Hey, I can be nice."

"I know. Are you sure you don't want to visit the desert? I can't stand thinking about how much I'm going to miss you."

"Beth, we talked about this. I am gonna have to do the revisions on the horrible novel. This week has just been a reprieve, since my editor stopped e-mailing me. At this point I'm just waiting for the other shoe to drop. It sounds like she's having some crisis with another author who is dealing with even more writerly angst than I am. She tells me that creative people can be very annoying. I can't imagine why."

Beth giggled. "Perhaps because they can be a wee bit temperamental."

"Plus, I told Mrs. O that I'll be here until I get the revisions done. If this dismal weather keeps up, I sure won't be distracted by any outdoor activities."

The next morning, Beth and Drew packed up their things and loaded them into their respective vehicles. Beth put Arlo in the kitchen and locked the gate. She bent to stroke his head. "Be good, buddy. Cindy will be by in a few hours. And then Mom will be back. I promise I won't tell her about the rug if you won't." Having completed his goodbyes, Arlo wagged a few times and strolled over to his bed for a morning nap.

Beth locked the house behind her and stood in front of Drew, not knowing quite what to say. The sky was gray and the air was heavy with an almost imperceptible drizzle. "I'll call you as soon as I get to Tucson."

"I'll be here." He gave her a lingering gentle kiss and touched his fingertips to her cheek. "Choose to be happy, Bethie."

Chapter 9

Drama & A Dare

As she drove home from the airport through the desert landscape, Beth opened the sunroof on the Acura and enjoyed the feel of the sun on her skin. She finally felt like her bones might thaw out again. After arriving home, the first thing Beth did was change her clothes, since it was a balmy seventy-three degrees. Time for a return to t-shirts and flip-flops.

After not checking her e-mail for two weeks, Beth was both curious and afraid to see what lurked in her inbox. For years she had been obsessed about being as connected as possible for work, and it had been somewhat freeing to be rid of the digital tether while she was in Alpine Grove. But now it was time to buckle down and find a job. There had to be something out there somewhere.

She fired up her computer and tried not to be too disappointed when she discovered there were no e-mails from *TheRealAJEmerson* waiting for her. Oh well. She'd told Drew she'd call today anyway.

There were a few e-mails from the Amazon web site advertising books she didn't want and one from an RTP colleague commiserating about being laid off. Two more e-mails were from people she'd asked about employment reporting back to say they didn't have any job leads. There was a lukewarm e-mail from her former boss Joan that said she "might" be able to pass Beth's name on to someone she knew at a company in Seattle. Overall it was a demoralizing series of missives. The only bright spot was an e-mail from her doctoral dissertation adviser at the university, wondering what she was planning to do next semester.

That was a good question. If she was going to be in Tucson, maybe she could return to her studies. But not every employer was as supportive of higher education as RTP had been. She couldn't keep signing up for classes and dropping them. And eventually, she'd get so far behind that she wouldn't be able to catch up.

Technology wasn't going to wait around for her to figure out what she was doing. It was going to march on without her, whether she liked it or not. The dissertation was about process improvements in product usability testing. Methods of testing and correcting usability problems would change as products changed, and this fact was undoubtedly not lost on her adviser Deborah Hartson. She sent a reply to Deb requesting a meeting, since she hadn't had a chance to talk to her before she went to Alpine Grove. It might help to discuss the situation she was in as far as her employment options, or lack thereof.

That evening Beth tried calling Drew. The phone just rang and rang. Apparently, he still had not acquired an answering machine. She'd been thinking about his book and had a couple of ideas on how it could be rewritten so Liz could survive the end of the series. Maybe he was out walking Dixie. Beth was tired from the trip, so she went back to her computer and sent a quick e-mail to him and went to bed. Tracking down Drew by phone seemed to be problematic.

The next morning Beth slept late, enjoying indolently drowsing in the late-morning sun that was streaming through her bedroom window. Being a lazy underachiever wasn't all bad. Resuming her neglected exercise program could wait until tomorrow.

Later, Beth made some breakfast and turned on her computer, willing herself to muster some enthusiasm for the job search. It was Monday and she had no more excuses. But first, she needed to call her eye doctor to make an appointment for new contacts. Maybe new glasses too. She pushed the horrid things back up to the bridge of her nose, trying not to think about the huge red marks that undoubtedly were blooming on her skin because of the thick, heavy lenses. The ruddy mottled look was definitely not attractive. When she checked her e-mail, she found Drew had sent a short reply.

Hey Liz,

Sorry I missed your call. I was outside standing in an icy-cold rain watching my small brown puppy run in circles like some kind of crazed drenched rodent. I'll try giving you a call tomorrow.

- A.J.

It was a relief to hear from Drew, but she desperately wanted to speak to him. Once he heard from his editor, Beth had a bad feeling he might take the criticisms poorly and vanish into his cavern of despair again.

Today's plan needed to include calling her mother to find out how her vacation had been. Beth had left a long note explaining all the options she'd researched for getting the sofa repaired, but it would probably be a good idea to talk to Mom and apologize verbally. She sighed at the prices she'd received. Upholstery-repair options in Alpine Grove were limited and expensive. Sorry Mom.

After a depressing foray through both the online and paper job ads, Beth felt a strong desire to get out of the house. Sitting and stewing about being unemployed wasn't going to help anything. There was no reason to panic because she had the severance package, but eventually she was going to have to work again doing something. The jury was still out as to what that something might be.

Looking at a map, she settled on the Sabino Canyon Recreation Area, which was yet another place in Tucson she'd never been that everyone said was beautiful. She hopped in the Acura and headed in the direction of the Santa Catalina Mountains, navigating toward the north side of town. After winding her way through the opulent neighborhoods in the foothills, she arrived at the Visitor Center. She spent some time reading about the plants and animals of the Sonoran Desert before walking up the main road. Feeling virtuous for opting not to wimp out and ride the tram, Beth strolled along, taking in the mountain views as she traversed the stone bridges that crossed Sabino Creek. It was a beautiful day and after two weeks of cold, snow, and rain, the sun felt wonderful. Walking also seemed to help her think. Whatever she did next needed to include getting off the management track. Supervising employees was too stressful for her and not going to daily meetings anymore had been utter bliss. Figuring out what she didn't want to do felt like a good first step anyway.

She returned home and checked her messages. Naturally, Drew had called when she was out, but she smiled at his slow drawl. Just the sound of his voice made her feel less anxious. She tried calling back and listened to the phone ring seventeen times before giving up.

With a sigh, she turned on her computer. Time to send A.J. a little reminder e-mail to buy an answering machine, for heaven's sake. This was getting absurd. She checked her e-mails and found that her adviser Deb had replied. She'd had a cancellation and could talk to Beth the next day. Talking to her adviser was always enjoyable because Deb had an irreverent sense of humor that often included jibes related to being one of the only women in a male-dominated field.

Beth clicked on the next e-mail in the list, which was from an address she didn't recognize. Her mouth dropped open at the contents of the e-mail. Apparently the person Joan had contacted wanted to talk to Beth. A Seattle firm had an opening for a job managing a user-interface design team for a company that created enterprise database software. Beth was quite familiar with the company, Prophecy, because a number of its products competed with some of RTP's software lines.

Beth leaned back in her chair, mentally composing a reply. Joan had given the hiring manager Beth's name and some information about what she did at RTP. Now he wanted to talk to her as soon as possible. Because of new Internet requirements, the company was growing at an astronomical rate.

Beth knew that in the technology realm, the Seattle area was up and coming. It was in the middle of an economic boom, thanks to the growth of companies related to the personal computer and Internet industries, so Seattle was becoming the Silicon Valley of the Northwest. She had read that both wages and job opportunities were at an all-time high. It would be exciting to be in the middle of all that innovation. Working for a software company instead of a defense contractor had a lot to recommend it too.

Beth couldn't wait to tell Drew. Maybe all her worrying would be for nothing and this job would just fall into place like it had with RTP. She stretched her arms out in front of her and then settled into composing a reply that would impress the entire Prophecy human-resources staff.

~

The next day Beth went to her eye doctor and ordered new contact lenses. It would be such a relief to have peripheral vision again. Since she had a glimmer of hope that she might become a member of the workforce soon, she also ordered new glasses that weren't so uncomfortable. They still had thick lenses, but the manufacturing technology had improved and the eye doctor assured her they would not be as heavy as her old ones.

The next stop was the University of Arizona for her meeting with Deb. She walked along the familiar grassy area past the student union and the library, working her way toward the computer science buildings. She knocked on the open door of Deb's office and smiled.

Deb was on the phone, but waved Beth into the office, indicating that she should take the chair across the desk from her. Beth sat down and looked around the familiar office as her adviser finished up the conversation. The walls were like a computer museum, with a decor that included a flower made of old punch-cards and a clock created using a platter from a huge mainframe hard disk. Deb liked to tell stories about how, when those big disks crashed, you could tell because there was a peculiar burning smell. According to the now-legendary tale, the clock platter had contained important data before it went out in a particularly inopportune and noxious way.

Deb ran her fingers through her short, pixie haircut and stuck her tongue out at the phone. Beth giggled. Her adviser had been teaching at the university for a long time and had more than once expressed her contempt for some of the infantile behavior of her fellow professors. Deb finally hung up the phone and raised her eyebrows at Beth. "Sorry about that. More departmental wrangling. But welcome to my humble abode. How is my number-one usability geek? I have missed receiving your impassioned rants about functional user-interface design in my e-mail inbox."

"Is this a bad time?"

"No. You probably know all about it already, since your favorite professor is in the middle of it."

Beth shook her head. "That's unlikely. Since I'm no longer involved with Graham, I'm gloriously unaware of current university intrigue and hearsay."

Deb leaned forward and folded her hands on the desk. "That's a surprise."

"Recently, I came to the conclusion that my relationship choices have not been what you might call ideal. It became evident that he wasn't the person I thought he was. And that he'd never change. I only wish I'd acknowledged that sooner. *Much* sooner."

"You were awfully young, Beth. And he's quite a charmer."

"That's kind of you to say. I'm just glad those years are behind me now. I feel a little foolish for willfully ignoring the problem for so long, but it's time for me to move forward."

Deb raised her eyebrows. "On that note, I assume you're here because you want to talk about your PhD."

"I do. I'm sorry I had to drop my classes. As I explained in my e-mail, RTP laid me off and then I went to visit my mother in my hometown. Then I went back to take care of her bookstore while she was on a trip. It was all a bit complicated."

"You've sure been busy since you left RTP. How can I help?"

Beth shook her head. "I'm not sure what to do."

Deb unfolded her hands and turned her palms up. "Well Beth, what do you *want* to do?"

"I don't know. What good will a PhD do me outside of RTP? Technology changes so quickly that an advanced degree in computer science seems pointless. And I might have a lead on a job in Seattle." Beth shrugged. "It's unlikely, but my supervisor at RTP told someone at Prophesy about my qualifications. They might be interested."

Deb grinned. "That's wonderful, Beth. They'd be fools not to hire you!"

"I think it could be a great professional opportunity. But it's in management. And I'd have to move and probably sell my house. That's upsetting too. I love my house. And then I'd undoubtedly never finish my PhD, which is also distressing. I'm *so* close to being done." Beth slumped in the chair and gazed down at her sandals. "I'm just extremely confused."

"Only you can decide what you want, Beth. How are you doing on your dissertation?"

Beth grimaced. "I finished the research, so at this point it is mostly the writing aspect, which I had difficulties getting to because of work. The long hours at RTP were exhausting.

But all my research data is on my computer. I just need to write the dissertation, and of course take those last couple of classes. Then do the oral defense of the dissertation. All of that would be challenging if I were in a different state. Thus, my conundrum."

"Beth, it seems like you have a lot to think about. If you want me to take a look at what you have so far on your dissertation, I can. Or if you want to drop out of the program, you should let me know that too."

"I know. I'm sorry I'm in such an unsettled state. This isn't like me at all."

Deb stood up and started gathering up her notebooks. "That's for sure. But maybe it's a good thing in the long run. You might love working at Prophesy just as much as you did at RTP. In any case, I'm sure you'll figure it out. Right now, I've got to run to a meeting. Let me know what you decide to do."

Beth left the office and walked slowly down the hall. It was silly to think that her adviser would have all the answers, and that Beth would suddenly magically know what to do. But she still felt unaccountably let down by the conversation. She'd always told everyone how much she loved her job at RTP. But now she found that she was enjoying *not* being there a lot more than she'd expected. Maybe talking to Drew would help. It always did. She missed him terribly—the constant dull ache of his absence was distracting and the struggles to reach him were vexing.

Beth was torn from her ruminations by the sound of angry male voices in front of her in the hallway. Graham and Gerald Hearst, the head of the department, were speaking loudly, and given the body language, it looked like they might actually come to blows. Beth wanted to crawl into a hole and disappear. Nothing good could come from meeting Graham here. She slowed her pace. Should she turn around and pretend she didn't see them?

Graham glanced quickly in her direction and pointed at her. He shouted, "This is all your fault!"

Beth took a few steps backward, shaking her head. "Graham, I have no idea what you are talking about."

Dismissing his prior conversation with a backward wave, he strode purposefully toward Beth until he was uncomfortably close. Leaning toward her, he said in an angry whisper, "You hacked into my computer didn't you? Only you have the skills to do that. No one else who has been in my house could have possibly done it."

For a moment, Beth couldn't decide if she was embarrassed or angry. Anger won out, and she scowled at him. "Graham, I have never touched your computer. Given your recreational activities, I certainly don't want to know what visual data you might have stored on it."

He shook his finger at her. "Aha! You wouldn't say that if you hadn't done what I know you did."

Beth pushed her glasses up to the bridge of her nose. "I have no idea what you are talking about. I've been out of town for two weeks. And in point of fact, the last time I saw you, we were at my house, not yours."

"It could have been a while ago. And then you just got around to e-mailing the pictures, you vindictive, malicious little shrew. You waited until now, since you knew I was up for tenure again."

Beth waved her hands in front of her face. "Get away from me, Graham. I have nothing to do with any of this. Consider

interrogating a few of your vast array of female companions."
She turned, stepped around him, and went down the hall,
passing Gerald and averting her eyes so he wouldn't see the
angry tears welling in her eyes. Whatever Graham had done,
it was certainly his own fault. Maybe moving to Seattle
wouldn't be so bad. There was far too much drama here and
she just wanted to be done with it.

~

Beth was fuming as she walked across the campus toward the
parking garage. She got into the Acura and took a roundabout
way home, going north, then east, shooting down the windy
curves of River Road through the Catalina foothills. She
opened the sunroof and let the relaxing warmth soothe her
frazzled nerves. Yes she had a temper, but being accused of
something she'd never even consider doing was utterly unfair.
Just because she knew about technology, it didn't mean she
was a hacker. He had a lot of nerve.

When she got home she checked her messages and found
that Drew had not called. Maybe he'd sent an e-mail. And
Deb was right—Beth needed to take a serious look at her
dissertation research again. After she turned on her computer,
she found an e-mail from the HR department at Prophesy.
They wanted to set up a phone interview with her the next
day. Her heart pounded in her chest. This job could really
happen. Maybe this opportunity would be the next step in
her new life.

The phone rang and Beth jumped to answer it. Drew
must be calling back. Finally! She picked up the phone and a
deep male voice said, "Hello Beth. It's your father."

Beth paused for a moment, attempting to reorient her mind to this information. She hadn't talked to him in months. "Dad. This is a surprise. How are you?"

"I'm just calling to see how you are doing. I had a nice chat with your mother the other day and she said you helped with the store when she went on her cruise. That was very kind of you, dear."

"Um. Thanks. It wasn't a big deal. She probably told you I lost my job."

"Yes. I'm sorry about that. But I know you'll find another. You're smart and a hard worker. Any company would be lucky to have you."

"Thanks, Dad."

Her father cleared his throat. "So, ah, well, I am going to be attending a conference in Phoenix next month. And I was hoping that I might be able to see you."

Beth twisted her necklace. "Really? Oh. I guess I'll be here. Well, um. Okay, yes, sure, that would be fine. I could drive up there. Or...or you could come here. Whatever you think is best. You have never seen my house. It's not much, but it's mine."

"You mother has told me about it. It sounds great, dear. Maybe I can buy you lunch or something. You decide what you feel comfortable with and let me know, okay?"

"Sure, Dad."

Her father gave her some details about his trip to Phoenix and they ended the call. Beth gazed at the phone as if it were an oracle that might reveal powerful insights. Her parents had gotten over their issues with one another years ago. Maybe Jill was right and she should too.

Beth tried calling Drew, who was either out or in the process of disappearing again. She had a bad feeling about the lack of communication from him. She sent him an e-mail and then replied to the Prophesy people, letting them know that she'd be delighted to talk to them about the position.

Unable to face the idea of looking at her dissertation, Beth shut down the computer. It had been a long and disturbing day. Tonight was going to be all about bad TV and junk food. Then exercise class tomorrow to make up for it.

The next morning, Beth returned from the class sweaty and exhausted. She heard the phone ringing as she opened the front door and ran to answer it. Out of breath, she gasped a feeble hello and smiled when she heard Drew say, "Dang, what happened to you?"

"Exercise class. I think the instructor was in the military. There's a possibility I may expire right here in my living room."

Drew chuckled. "I'm glad to hear that you are keeping your body in good shape. I'm pretty fond of it."

"I'm so glad you called. I was starting to get worried. And I have so much I want to talk to you about. How are you?"

"I'm okay. Been better, but like they say, this too shall pass, and all that. And if it would ever stop raining, I'd be happier than a June bug. It's gotta stop raining by June, right?"

Beth wiped the sweat off her forehead with her hand. "I hope so. I am not sure how happy a June bug is, but I'll take your word for it. Ugh. I need to sit down."

"You sure you're okay?"

"Yes. I wish I could just take a nap, but I can't talk long. I need to take a shower and then I have a phone interview."

"That's great. What's the job?"

"It's with Prophecy, a company that is a competitor of RTP's in the database arena."

There was a pause and Drew said, "Yeah, I've heard of them. Aren't they in Seattle?"

"Yes! There are a countless technology businesses springing up there, but Prophesy has been around for many years. It's an established company, but they are growing rapidly because of the Internet."

"Sounds great."

"I don't know yet, but it could be an exciting opportunity. I also talked to my adviser about my PhD."

"Are you gonna go for it, after all?"

"Oh, I don't know, Drew." Beth waved her hand in exasperation. "I'm so confused. I thought talking to my adviser would help. But it didn't. And then Graham was in the hall and he yelled at me. It was just awful. He called me a shrew and accused me of doing something horrible. I was so upset."

"Did you get angry?"

"Well, yes, I guess. But he was so nasty today. And I didn't *do* anything. I would never touch his stupid computer. There are thirty-thousand people wandering around the University of Arizona—why did I have to run into him?"

"Just lucky, I suppose."

"It's like meeting you at the reunion. I never dreamed you'd come. But I'm so glad you did. It was like a miracle. Like when you asked me to the prom. What were the odds?"

"Well, yeah, I suppose."

Beth giggled "In that case, statistically the odds were in your favor, since it's not like dozens of people were clamoring for my attention."

"I got that impression."

The tone of Drew's voice was oddly subdued, and suddenly Beth had to know. "So I have always been afraid to ask, but why *did* you ask me? Me, of all people?"

"That was all a long time ago, Beth."

"I know. So what? Tell me."

He sighed. "All right. I was standing around waiting in the lunch line and John and Tony were razzing me about how I had all these ladies after me and still wasn't going to the senior prom. It was a stupid conversation and I wanted to get away from them, if you want to know the truth. Anyway, they said some kind of harsh, uh, stuff about you. I said they were wrong and then they dared me to ask you."

Beth twisted the phone cord around her hand and clenched it in her palm. "You asked me on a *dare*? And you never bothered to mention this before? That's like a movie or some abominable after-school special. How could you not tell me this?" Did everyone in high school know this, except her? How humiliating.

"It's not a big deal. And it was way more fun than I ever thought it would be. You know that."

"I'm just sort of stunned. And whatever the opposite of flattered is."

"You don't know?"

She jerked at the phone cord coils. "I can't think of anything right at the moment."

"Belittled?"

"Thanks, Drew. I've always said you have a much larger vocabulary than you let on. I really should go take a shower, so I'll be ready for this interview."

"Are you mad? Don't let what I said get to you. That's all ancient history. It doesn't change anything. You know what happened later. It worked out. Well, sort of. Until it didn't, I guess."

Beth sighed. "I know. I'm sorry. It's just another blow to my already tattered ego. This hasn't been a good day. And I miss you. It tears at my heart. I hate being so far away from you."

"I know Bethie, me too. Let me know how the interview goes."

They said their goodbyes and Beth hung up the phone. A dare? Really? Throwing her arms up in exasperation, Beth turned and walked down the hall toward the bathroom. Trying to sound like a confident professional after reliving yet another ghastly high-school indignity was going to be a challenge.

~

Despite Beth's concerns, the interview went extremely well. The hiring manager was starting to speak as if she'd already been offered the job, which was disconcerting. Using terms like "when you're here" implied that they were optimistic about her prospects. Beth was getting excited, but she knew almost nothing about Seattle, except that it had a temperate climate. It rained, but it didn't get bitterly cold and it almost never snowed. Decent weather was certainly a drawing card. Given her experience in Alpine Grove, if the job were in Minnesota, she wouldn't be even slightly interested. She'd be perfectly happy to live out the rest of her days without seeing the thermometer drop below freezing.

The next day, Beth went to her first stained-glass class. It was unlike anything she'd ever done before, and on the way home she stopped at an art-supply store to get the recommended tools and materials. The design she had selected for her first project was so pretty that she couldn't wait to get started.

After she got home, Beth tried calling Drew and discovered he had finally purchased an answering machine. At last! She left a message about her art class and the interview and asked him to call her.

Later he returned her call, and after Beth had blathered on about her interview for a while, she realized he'd said almost nothing. She grasped the pendant on her necklace. What was going on with him? "Drew, is everything all right with you?"

"I'm fine. It's just been a long day for me and Dixie, that's all. That little pup is crashed out like a light."

Beth smiled at the mental image of the brown puppy flat on the floor snoring away. "What did you do?"

"We went to see Mrs. O. I guess she's not feeling well. She said she wanted some puppy cuddle time."

"Oh, that's so sweet. I'm sure Dixie was happy to oblige."

"Yeah, she's a sucker for love. I'm kinda behind on my revisions, though. There was one other thing she mentioned."

"What's that?"

"She's gonna sell her house."

"What? She's lived there forever. Is she okay? I thought she had gout. She's not really sick, is she?"

"I think she's okay, but the house is just too much work for her. She wants to give me first-dibs on it. Assuming I can fix this fool manuscript, after I submit my revisions and get the final advance check for the book, I'm going to buy it."

Beth dropped her hand from her necklace. "What? You mean you are going to live in Alpine Grove *permanently*? Have you lost your mind? What happened to the wimpy southerner who bundles up when the temperature drops below sixty?"

"I can always get away in the winter to someplace warm. But I started thinking back on all the places I've lived and I've had some of the best times of my life here. If I'm gonna settle anywhere, why *not* here? And I like the house a lot."

"I don't know what to say."

"How about 'congratulations on becoming a homeowner'?"

"I suppose." Beth gazed out the window at the large ocotillo that stood like a sentinel in the yard. "I guess I was hoping you'd want to spend time with me."

"Your mom lives here. It's not like you never come to Alpine Grove. You even said you get homesick for the trees."

"But I can't *live* there again. Freezing my toes off at my mother's house reminded me why I never ever want to live any place that has a lot of snow again. I hate snow and ice."

"Well, you just told me you're going to move to Seattle, anyway."

"No, I didn't. I haven't even been offered a job. Even if I were, it hardly ever snows there. What if you lived there too?"

"Have you ever spent any time in the Northwest, Beth?"

"Not really. I've seen pictures. It's very green and pretty."

"That's because as you probably know, it doesn't snow much, but it does rain. It rains *a lot*. Alpine Grove in the spring is nothing by comparison. We're talking months of drizzle—it's the kind of gray weather that makes me want to take to my bed, pull the covers over my head, and never leave."

"Well, what about Tucson? You could visit here. It's warm and very sunny." She looked down at her legs and grinned. "I'm wearing shorts right now."

"Sure, Beth, if you stay there, which from what you said doesn't sound particularly likely. You know, I've really got to get to work on these revisions now."

"Drew, it feels like something is wrong. I can tell by your voice. Is the book going okay? Are you sure you don't want to visit? Maybe I could help. Communicating by telephone is so difficult, and we don't seem to be terribly proficient at it."

"I'm fine. It sounds like you have a lot of stuff going on anyway. Maybe you can get that PhD stuff done before you move. Have you started writing the dissertation?"

"No. And I told you, I'm not moving. Nothing has changed. I don't have a job. Plus, I need to take two more classes for my degree."

"I'm sure you'll figure it out. Hey, Dixie is awake. I gotta go."

Beth clutched her necklace. "Drew, I love you."

He said softly, "I love you too, Bethie. Talk atcha later."

Beth hung up the phone. She could tell from the particular tone in Drew's voice that he was retreating again. She was willing to bet that the revisions on the book were not going well. Pulling off her glasses, she wiped her eyes, trying not to cry. There was no way this would ever work, because even after everything that had happened, he obviously still didn't trust her. And buying a house in the one location she was positive she didn't *ever* want to live pretty much quashed the idea of them being together on any type of long-term basis. Maybe it was stupid to believe they could get over everything that had happened in the past.

Over the next few days, Beth made an effort to stop thinking about Drew. She went to her exercise classes and began digging into her dissertation research, since she didn't have much else to do after her routine perusal of employment ads. Going over her dissertation reminded Beth why she had enjoyed her university classes so much. It was fascinating to delve into technology and how people interact with it. There were good reasons why certain software interfaces led to user frustration and others did not.

While she had been at RTP, she had been so busy dealing with day-to-day managerial work that she had lost touch with some of the aspects of technology that she found the most intriguing. Days full of meetings and trying to reach some sort of consensus among recalcitrant people about trivial minutia were not exactly intellectually stimulating. As a manager, many of the problems she had to deal with were people problems. Interpersonal communication was not exactly something she excelled at, yet she had been responsible for keeping everyone on track and content. No wonder she had been so stressed for so long. In fact, she was finding that she missed RTP and her job as a manager less and less all the time. It was like a great burden had been lifted and she could think more freely again.

Beth tried calling and e-mailing Drew, which was a futile effort. It seemed he was done communicating. She'd left a number of messages in an effort to cajole him into picking up the phone, all to no avail. Beth knew what he was doing. After stewing about it, she decided to leave one final message.

After the machine beeped, Beth said, "Drew, I know you're there and you're probably listening to me right now. You've made it clear that you don't want to communicate. Fine. Don't call. Don't e-mail. I can't force you to, and I promise this is my last message. But I want you to know that I know exactly what you're doing. You've retreated into Gollum's lair again and I want you to stop it. You are a brilliant writer and I love you. And if you have spent all day in bed, which I know you have, I want you to take a shower and get dressed right now. Furthermore, I am guessing that you are berating yourself instead of writing. You have a deadline and I want you to stop dwelling on what your editor said and figure out how to fix the book. If you need help, I am here, and I would give anything to help you. No one knows those characters better than I do, except you. If you agree, get on a plane. You have my address."

Beth hung up the phone. She'd said her piece. If Drew wanted to wallow in creative despondency, he was on his own.

∿

A few days later, Beth returned from her exercise class and went into the kitchen for a drink of water. This time there might have been a few endorphins and she even had a tiny bit of hope that her body wouldn't collapse from overexertion. Getting into any type of decent shape was going to take a while.

It was another sunny day and she opened the sliding-glass door out to the backyard so the warm breeze could flow into the house. Out of the corner of her eye, Beth noticed movement in the shade under her pergola. A person's foot was dangling off the lounge chair. Beth covered her mouth with her hand, trying not to scream. Someone was in her backyard! Maybe she could quietly tiptoe back to the living room and call the police. Drew leaned out around the back of the chair, turning his head to look at her. He grinned. "Dang, it's nice out here. All I need is a margarita."

Beth dropped her hand from her mouth and ran to him. "Drew! I'm so glad to see you. I can't believe you're here. How did you get into my backyard?"

He got up and stretched out his arms, enveloping her in his embrace. "The airport shuttle dumped me at your front door. When you weren't home, I just climbed over the block wall so your neighbors didn't start to wonder about the creepy guy loitering on your front stoop." He kissed her and looked into her eyes. "I missed you, Bethie. I got your message. The last one."

She put her arms around his neck. "I was right, wasn't I?"

"Yeah. I hate admitting it, but you were. I kept thinking about all the criticism so much that I couldn't even see the story anymore. I could use some objectivity here. You've always been good at pulling me out of these nasty mud bogs my brain gets into."

"I've been thinking about the story and I have a few ideas." Beth kissed him again, took his hand, and led him inside the house. "I was working on my dissertation, but I kept having thoughts about your book, so I typed everything into a memo so I wouldn't forget."

"How corporate of you."

She nudged him. "The memo format can be useful."

"I'll take your word for it. Beggars can't be choosers. Lay it on me."

"Well, since the case revolves around serial arson, I do understand why you killed Liz in that way. But it's just too awful. What a horrible way to die. Burning to death? How *could* you? Every time I think about what you wrote, I just start to cry."

He shrugged. "Yeah, okay. I got that."

"Well, we all know about the first suspect. But what if the clue caused Preston himself to be the second suspect?"

Drew raised his eyebrows. "Okay, you have my attention. So wait, you want me to toast Preston instead? You thought killing off Liz was a problem? Taking out the hero is worse—doing that definitely ends the series in a very permanent way."

Beth shook her head. "No, no, not that. Preston has to survive too. I think you can do something more circuitous that leads to a more satisfying ending. I created a flowchart."

"A flow chart? You turned my creative work into a flowchart? Ugh."

"Flowcharts can be helpful for visualization." Beth turned on the computer. "Sit down and let me show you. Your story was so intricate, I didn't want to lose that. I just made a few little tweaks in the storyline." She clicked a few times and brought up a diagram on the screen. "See. Like this."

Drew put his elbow on the desk and rested his chin on his palm. "Hmm. Okay, that's interesting."

"Interesting? Oh, please. What are you actually thinking?"

"I like it. Well, sort of." He pointed at the screen. "But what if you move that thingie over there?"

Beth leaned over him to use the mouse. Grasping her around the waist, Drew dragged her into his lap and nuzzled her neck. "I like the scantily clad you. It's like summertime again. And hey, someone has been working out."

Moving away from him, Beth said, "I really need to take a shower."

He kissed her and murmured, "Want company?"

Later, Beth copied the flowchart onto Drew's laptop and set up a makeshift office for him in her guest bedroom. She worked on her dissertation while Drew holed up with his novel rewrites. He had only a few days left to meet the deadline to submit his revisions.

Looking up from her data analysis as Drew emerged from the bedroom, she smiled. "Hi. How is it going?"

"Better. I need to get away for a little while, though. It feels like my brain is melting. Wanna go somewhere? I could stand to absorb some sun."

"Yes." She clapped her hands together. "You can experience the Silver Bird!"

"I saw it in the driveway. It's cute. Can I drive? Sometimes driving helps clear my head."

Beth narrowed her eyes. "I assume that with years of practice, you are a better driver than you used to be."

He gestured an X across his chest. "No speeding tickets in years. Cross my heart."

"All right. Let me get the keys. I know just where to go. You'll love it."

Beth directed Drew to the north side of town, so he could take the route up the Catalina Highway to Mount Lemmon that she'd driven a few weeks ago right after she bought the car. If he wanted to drive, that was the place to do it, away from the city traffic and up toward the trees.

Drew glanced at her and grinned as he shifted gears. "I like the Silver Bird. Thanks for letting me drive."

"You remain a serious lead-foot."

"Hey, I'm just seeing how she handles. The sun feels good after being cold for so long."

Beth put her hand on his leg. "I'm glad you're enjoying yourself."

He smiled. "I am. You know, except for the whole desert thing, this is kinda like the road up the hill to Alpine Grove."

"Yes. I noticed that too. It's significantly shorter, though. Windy Point is up ahead on the left. We should stop and look at the view."

Drew pulled off the road and into the parking area. They got out, walked over to the long stone wall, and looked out over the valley below. The warm breeze swirled around them and Beth took Drew's hand. "It feels like a long time since I came up here, but it's only been a few weeks."

"Yeah, considering you lost your job, you've been kinda busy."

Beth turned and looked up into Drew's face. "Something has been bothering me."

"Uh-oh, that's never a good way to start a conversation."

"I'm serious. It's about what you told me about the prom. The fact that you went with me on a dare."

"Beth, I told you that's ancient history. It doesn't matter."

"I know. But there's something I don't understand." She squeezed his hand. "After a decade, I now finally know why you asked, given that in high school, we had never even talked to each other before. But I don't know why you kept seeing me afterward."

"Well, the short answer is because I wanted to."

Beth smiled. "How about the long answer? I have no idea why. You've said more than once that I am rather high-maintenance, as you like to put it."

"Well, that night…the way it was for me…I don't know." Drew bent his head and kissed her quickly. "Okay, so we get to the prom and we're there in that dim room. The endless eighties music is playing and we're sitting there all uncomfortable, not knowing what to say to each other. I'm thinking, 'Dang, this is gonna be one long evening.'"

"Well, this is all quite flattering, so far."

He kissed her knuckles. "I'm not done yet. So I figure, I should at least ask you to dance, since hey, that's what you're supposed to do, right?"

"And you did."

"Yeah, I did. So I took you in my arms and it felt all awkward and weird. But then I looked down into your eyes. You have the most beautiful expressive eyes, you know. And I guess I really saw you for the first time. I realized you weren't the stuck-up brainy snob everyone said you were. When I looked in your eyes, I could see that you were just scared."

Beth nodded. "Utterly petrified, actually."

"I thought to myself that every girl remembers her senior prom. I had the chance to help make the memory of that night fun or miserable for you." He shrugged slightly. "I opted for fun."

Beth hugged him. "I'm so glad you did. Even if I still can't swing-dance very well."

"It's okay. You have lots of other talents. And once we finally relaxed and started talking, I don't know—things just kind of clicked. You were just so easy to talk to and you didn't treat me like I was some dumb Carolina hick."

"Well, of course not. You're one of the brightest people I've ever met. And you're brilliant in wonderfully creative ways that I am not."

"Too bad you didn't tell that to my teachers in North Carolina. That's half the reason my Dad dragged me out to Alpine Grove. It was either move to Alpine Grove with him or get shipped off to military school."

"From what you've said before, I think you may have had some bad influences back East."

Drew grinned. "If you mean my burn-out so-called friends, yeah—I think they would count as bad."

"Well, given your Cedar County High School transcript, and your later accomplishments as an author, I think your father did the right thing. Plus, if he hadn't dragged you out West, I never would have met you, so I'm very glad he did."

"Yeah, I know. Me too." He smoothed her windblown hair from her face and looked out at the view. "Thanks, Dad, wherever you are."

Chapter 10

Ventilation & Conversation

Kat came upstairs into the living room, where Joel was sitting on the sofa with Dixie, the small brown puppy, curled up in his lap. She sat down next to them. "Are you ready to relinquish puppy-sitting duty?"

He looked up from his book. "Oh sure, wake her up, why don't you? This was the easy part. Earlier, I pulled the remote control for the stereo and several books out of her mouth. She may be small, but she is a chewing machine."

"Do you suppose the library will notice the tiny teeth marks in that romance novel?"

Joel nodded and put his hand on Dixie's back as the puppy stood up and yawned. "I think you may need to give up on that one."

Kat gathered the puppy in her arms and leaned back so she could snuggle Dixie to her chest. "But she's so cute. Who could resist this face?"

"You're such a softie."

"Apparently, so is Drew. The poor guy looked pretty tired when he dropped her off." Kat held the wagging puppy up in front of her. "You're running your Dad a little ragged, aren't you?"

"When is Drew coming back?"

Kat stroked Dixie's head. "About a week, I think. He said he has to deal with a deadline."

"A deadline for what?"

"I have no idea. He didn't say." Kat put the puppy on the floor and handed her a chew toy. "Speaking as someone with my own deadlines I don't want to discuss, I didn't want to ask."

"How's the article going?"

"Not too well. I don't know why I put myself through this stupidity every time I get a new article assignment. If I would just sit down and write, it would help. I have this whole internal war going on. It's a miracle I finished the one that was due while you were gone."

"It didn't sound like fun."

Kat leaned forward and put her elbows on her knees, observing the puppy's enthusiastic chewing. "Writing at three in the morning does not result in my finest prose."

Joel rubbed her back. "And you didn't have your free proofreader around."

"I know. You always find stuff. The editor even made a comment about a word I misused. It was one of those things a spell-checker doesn't find, and it was embarrassing. I'm amazed they gave me another article to do." Kat shook her head. "I'm not sure I'm cut out for this type of work."

"You're a good writer."

"But the whole uncertainty of it makes me nuts. It's a miracle I managed to get this writing job, and if I screw it up I have nothing."

"You can find something else."

"According to the freelance-writing books, I should be doing that now. Every week I should be sending out ten or twenty stirring query letters that make editors swoon so that I will have a steady income."

"Well, you could do that, right?"

"But I don't *want* to." Kat sat up and crossed her arms in front of her chest. "I hate writing query letters. The whole process is dumb and largely a waste of time. You do endless research, write up all these ideas, and just throw them out there into the wind, hoping some random editor might be interested. The editor at the magazine I'm writing these articles for now said they get hundreds of queries every week. And they never even look at them, because they set up an editorial calendar and assign writers to the articles. Right after I got my computer, I sent out a bunch of query letters that led to nothing. I got this writing job from a classified ad looking for writers, not from a query letter."

"Well, in a few months you can start boarding more than one or two dogs at a time. That will help the income stream."

Kat turned to look at him. "Every time I look at the construction estimates I have a mini heart attack. What if I blow my entire inheritance on this and it doesn't work?"

Joel put his hand on her arm. "Starting any business has costs and risks. We've talked about this a lot. What's wrong?"

"I'm not sure. Cold feet? It's just that as we get closer to actually building the kennel, the whole thing gets more real, I guess. Seeing the plans the architect drew up made it even more real. Not to mention writing the check."

"Well, one thing is that you've already been running the business in a small way and found out you're good at it." He grinned. "You even have repeat customers."

"That's true. I have seen quite a few of these dogs more than once. But some of the experiences were, uh, difficult. Or messy. Or both."

"Well, if you're talking about Arlo, it should be easier once you have a kennel that's easier to clean."

Kat leaned back on the sofa and stared at the ceiling. "I'm not sure the rug can be saved. I think Arlo pushed it over the edge."

"That stain is kind of gross."

She turned her head to look at Joel. "But what if I'm making a huge mistake? All of this affects you too, since you live here. That means you get to do things like remove critters from walls, baby-sit puppies, and walk dogs."

"I know. Usually when you start to have doubts like this, it helps to remember why you want to start the business in the first place."

"Well, every time I think about returning to working in a cubicle I want to throw up."

"Let avoidance of nausea be your guide."

Kat nudged him in the ribs. "Very funny. I'm serious. This is going to be a lot of work."

"I know." He leaned back on the sofa and reached out to caress her cheek. "But honestly, what's the worst thing that happens? The business fails, and then we'll do something else. The house is paid for, so it's not like you won't have a roof over your head. We'll figure something out."

"You're right. I think I just needed to do some recreational whining."

Joel cocked his head. "I don't hear chewing." He sat up and looked down at the floor in front of the sofa. "Dixie has made a break for it."

Kat looked around the room. "Again? What a sneak. That little thing is seriously stealthy."

The small puppy ran out of the bedroom with a pair of underwear dangling from her mouth. Kat and Joel both leaped off the sofa and ran after her. Kat said, "Dixie, come back here!"

Joel got to the puppy first, picked her up, and extracted the panties from her mouth. He held them out to Kat with a grin. "I believe these are yours."

Kat examined the torn fabric. "That's a little too much ventilation. I think these need to go with the rug on the next dump run."

"Well, you said Maria wanted to go shopping."

"She's gonna be disappointed when she finds out about the lingerie-shopping options in Alpine Grove. The KMart out on the highway is not exactly Victoria's Secret."

Joel stroked the puppy's fur thoughtfully. "I suppose not. Their ads certainly aren't as much fun."

～

Over the next few days Beth worked on her dissertation and read over Drew's changes on his book after he revised various sections. Having him around was encouraging her to write because he mentioned techniques like target daily word counts. As a result, she had made significant progress on her own gigantic writing project. Having a file full of actual text for her dissertation was somewhat startling after not getting anywhere on the written portion for so long.

Drew emerged from the guest room and flipped a floppy disk onto Beth's desk. "That's it. I'm done."

"Really?" Beth grabbed the disk and put it into the drive of her computer. "I can't wait to read it. The changes you've made so far have worked out so well. I know your editor is going to love it."

"You can read it later. We need to get outta here." He took her hand, pulled her up from the desk, and gave her a hungry kiss. "Where are the car keys?"

Gasping for breath, Beth pushed him away and pointed at the kitchen. "Wow. Over there. In the drawer."

Drew released her and ran to the kitchen. Grabbing the keys from the drawer, he raised his arms over his head and yelled, "Road trip!"

Beth giggled, grabbed her purse and followed him outside, locking the door behind her. As they got into the car, she said, "Where are we going?"

"You'll see."

After navigating south, they got onto Interstate 10 heading east. Beth looked at the on-ramp sign and then at Drew. "I really don't want to go to El Paso, if that's what you're thinking."

"Neither do I, but I don't want to leave the great state of Arizona without seeing the town too tough to die."

"What?"

"Tombstone! Come on, Beth. Wyatt Earp? Doc Holliday? The O.K. Corral? It's the Old West at its finest. I can't miss out on that."

It was the first mention Drew had made of leaving and Beth wasn't sure what to say. Obviously, he was setting up a life in Alpine Grove and he couldn't board Dixie forever. But she had enjoyed the last few days so much, she didn't want him to go. "It's a bit of a drive. I've never been there before."

Drew glanced at her. "That does not surprise me."

"I think you just want to get on the freeway so you'll have an excuse to drive fast."

"Well, there is that. But I'm done with my revisions, so it's time to celebrate. And where better to do that than at an authentic Old West saloon?"

Beth touched his forearm. "I had no doubt you'd finish it."

"Well hey, at least one of us was optimistic."

Later, Beth and Drew walked hand in hand down the shaded wooden boardwalks of Tombstone's Allen Street, gazing at the window displays and chatting about the various souvenirs, artwork, and Old West memorabilia. They arrived at a building with a sign that said the establishment served 'good whiskey and tolerable water.' Drew grinned at Beth, "Looks like an authentic saloon to me."

They entered the dimly lit eatery, which had a long dark wooden bar running along one side of the room. Behind the bar was an immense mirror and cabinets full of hundreds of bottles of liquor, including many selections of whiskey. It seemed that the sign out front didn't lie.

Beth sat down at a table. "This place looks like something out of a movie set."

Drew picked up a menu and peered over it at Beth. "I'll let you know if I see Wyatt Earp or Big Nose Kate."

"You won't see Kate. Her establishment is across the street."

"Maybe we can go there next."

After lunch Beth reached across the table to take Drew's hand. "Congratulations on finishing your book. Do you feel this has been a suitable celebration?"

"I don't know what counts as suitable. But it has been fun. Lunch was great. And now I can say I've seen the Boot Hill Graveyard and the O.K. Corral. And you can too. You can't complain about not seeing anything around Tucson any more. Maybe it will take you less than ten years to get around to visiting the Space Needle in Seattle."

"Drew, I'm not moving to Seattle."

"Yeah, I know. You haven't gotten the job yet. But you will. Unless they are incredibly stupid, in which case you don't want to work there anyway. But don't worry, some other company will come knocking before you know it."

Beth squeezed his hand. "I don't want to work at a place like that or live in Seattle. After the interview, I sent them an e-mail and told them I wasn't interested. It was before you arrived. I thought about it and realized that I am enjoying myself too much here. I don't want to take another management job or move."

"What are you going to do?"

"I don't know. Take my stained-glass class. Go hiking. Work on my PhD. I've been relishing the process of evaluating my research and writing my dissertation."

Drew leaned back in his chair. "You're having a good time writing? Really?"

Beth grinned. "Well it's been more fun since you've been here agonizing over your own words in the next room. But yes. I did a tremendous amount of research and it's been enjoyable delving back into it and actually writing up my conclusions."

"Interesting."

Beth folded her hands in front of her on the table. "That word never means anything tangible when you say it. What are you really thinking?"

"It's just not like you to not be going places, as you like to say."

"I just want to be happy. I have a severance package, so I don't have to map out the rest of my career right now. My mortgage is tiny and my car is paid for. This is the first time I've had the financial freedom to just do whatever I want. You got to do that, and maybe I'm a little jealous. So I'm going to take advantage of this opportunity. First I want to finish my PhD." She took a sip of water. "I may also create some potentially homely stained-glass artwork. Perhaps my ability to cut glass without breaking it into tiny shards will improve by the end of the class."

"What about the future and everything being perfect?"

"Nothing is ever perfect. I shouldn't wait for some illusory determination of perfection to begin enjoying my life."

Drew grinned. "You won't get any argument from the lazy underachiever over here."

Beth took off her glasses and rubbed her eyes. "How many times do I have to apologize for that?"

"Maybe once more. I think one more time would be good."

"I'm sorry, Drew. Please believe me." Beth put her glasses back on. "And one more thing. I know you don't trust me, but I am not going to give up on us, even though you've opted to move to Alpine Grove. I love you and I want to be with you. If that means I have to visit the frozen tundra or coax you out here to the desert again, I will. I don't want to lose you a second time."

Drew took one of her hands in both of his. "I think that's the nicest thing you've ever said to me, Beth."

"Good. Because I am not making this up. I mean it."

~

Drew was quiet on the drive back to Tucson, holding Beth's hand for most of the trip as they cruised along the freeway, letting go only to shift gears. They went back into the house and Beth went to her desk, flipped on her computer, and sat down. She smiled at him. "You can't distract me from reading the end of your book now. I have to know what happened."

He leaned over to give her a kiss. "Okay. I'm gonna try to clean up the disaster area that used to be your guest bedroom."

Later, Beth looked up from the screen as Drew walked back into the living room. He glanced at her face and his eyes widened. "Oh jeez, not again. It's horrible, isn't it?"

Beth smiled at him and wiped a tear off her cheek. "No. It's not what you think."

He walked over and crouched next to the chair. "Bethie, why are you crying?"

"Oh Drew, that was the best ending ever. You did it. These are happy tears." She took his hand. "When Preston finally kisses Liz, my heart just melted into a little puddle of goo. Your readers are going to love this!"

He grinned. "Well, first it has to get past the cast-iron editor, so we'll see."

"You have nothing to worry about. I'm sure of it." She put her hand on her chest. "And you dedicated it to the Real Liz Logan. I can't believe it."

"Well it wouldn't be done if it weren't for you, Liz."

"I found a couple little typos that I marked in the file." Beth pulled the disk out of the drive. "Here you go. I know it's not a romance, but after six books, it was about time our hero and heroine got a break. They have the most amazing connection and they deserve it after all they've been through. I'm so happy. Well done."

Drew stood up, took the disk from her, and put it on the desk. "Thanks." He took her hand, encouraging her to leave the desk. "Hey, can you come over here for a minute? I need to talk to you."

Beth followed him to the sofa. "I know you have to leave. I've been trying not to think about it."

"Yeah, I do. I need to collect my small hungry puppy before she chews her way through Kat's entire house."

Beth giggled. "Between Arlo and Dixie, that place is never going to be the same."

"I know. I told Kat I'd pay for any damage. For such a tiny thing, that animal sure is expensive."

"My mom said she got the sofa fixed. I called for a number of repair estimates and left her a check to cover it."

"Thanks Beth. I'll pay you back. There's something else I've been thinking about."

"You have been rather quiet."

"What you said in Tombstone…that I don't trust you. You're right." He looked away from her, out the window. "I want to trust you. I really do. But there's a part of me that thinks the moment you get a job offer from some huge company or I do something to piss you off, that will be the end of it again."

"No, Drew, I told you, I'm not going to…"

He turned back to her. "Beth, no. I know what you're going to say and there's no way you can promise you won't get angry again, just like I can't promise I won't take to my bed like some type of Southern belle with the vapors. No one can predict the future. But what I do know is that we are way better when we're together than when we're apart. Did I ever tell you how I started writing novels?"

Beth shook her head. "I did wonder how that came about."

"Well, you know that I used to sketch people. On my travels I had notebooks filled with doodles and scribbles. After a while, I started adding words, since a lot of times I didn't speak the language, so I just made up stuff to amuse myself." He grinned. "Putting words in people's mouths was fun. Basically, I ended up with kind of crappy comic books. But then I started writing more words than drawing and I ended up with notebooks full of impressions of people. Character sketches, you might say."

"You must have learned a lot from doing that."

He shrugged. "Mostly I learned that people are the same everywhere. I kept thinking I'd find deep answers if I traveled enough. But when it comes to life, it seems like everyone's just kinda making it up as they go along."

Beth laughed. "That's good to know. What did you do with all the notebooks?"

"That's some of the junk in storage in North Carolina. But I had one story that I couldn't get out of my head. And all that time, I kept dreaming about you, too. It all got muddled in my mind and finally I got a laptop so I could try to type it up, and maybe stop thinking about it."

"Is that when you wrote *True Alibis*?"

"Yup. I did this massive brain dump over the course of a month. Thank goodness I took that horrible typing class with Ms. Hightower in high school. My fingers could barely keep up with what I was thinking."

"That's remarkable. You just sat down and wrote it?"

"Pretty much. So then I had a hundred-thousand words that I didn't know what to do with. I got a book from the library on how to get a book published. I figured if I could get someone to publish it, that would be great, or if it was garbage, I could just chuck the whole stupid mess in a drawer and forget about it. So I called a few places and found an agent who was willing to take a look. The woman flipped for the thing, shopped the manuscript around, and a couple of publishing houses were interested. There was a bidding war and it was auctioned for, well, a lot of money."

"That was the six-book deal?"

"Yup. So then little ol' slacker me had to start coughing up more words. I kinda freaked out, if you want to know the truth. But I went back to the notebooks. And thought a lot about you, obviously."

Beth smiled. "Yes, I got that impression. I dreamed and thought about you too."

"Writing can be cathartic. Anyway, by the time I got to book six, I was figuring, okay I finally had you out of my system. But as you know, I had a little trouble ending the series."

"I think it was more than a little."

"Okay, yeah, I was stuck in a horrendous way. The stories and dreams in my head...they just all evaporated. That's when another one of those cheerleaders called me about the high-school reunion for the ninety-fifth time. And she said she'd seen you at the bookstore. That's when I decided to go. I had to find out what it would feel like to see you again. I thought it might help."

"You found out."

"Yes. So I met my deadline. I finally killed off Liz in the book and I figured that would finally get you out of my head." Drew looked into her eyes. "Except it didn't work. I might have gotten you out of my head, but not out of my heart. It seemed to have other ideas."

"I see."

"I tried to blame it on too much naked Monopoly, but it's not just that."

Beth raised her eyebrows. "You seemed to enjoy yourself."

"Don't get me wrong—I'm all for nudity and board games. But then I figured that even though we love each other, we just couldn't stand to live together. And then we found out that wasn't really true either. Being with you is easy. You're so smart and sexy, and you even put up with my off-the-wall impulsive ideas and moody behavior. After what you said earlier, I realized I'm just afraid to take a risk."

"You? I am the one who tends to be risk-averse. I'm scared of uncertainty, not to mention people I don't know and public speaking."

"That may be true. But I was afraid to actually trust that you could actually love me." He gestured toward the windows. "I was afraid you'll decide I'm really the lazy underachiever you said I was, and bail again. After what happened before, I didn't want to take the chance. But then I'd miss out on what could be the best thing that ever happened to me."

Beth touched his arm. "What are you saying?"

"That if you're serious about making a commitment to being together, I am too. Whatever it takes."

"Really? So you'll spend time with me here?"

"Yes. I was thinking that depending on what happens, we could spend the winters here and the summers in Alpine Grove, since you won't be in school then." He grinned. "You might have to miss some of that 110-degree heat though."

Beth threw her arms around him. "Oh Drew, I'd love that. I miss Alpine Grove so much in the summer with the lake and the trees. We could go hiking again. By then I should be in better shape."

"Yeah, I plan to move the boat down from Lake Tahoe too."

"You still have it?"

"Of course. I was living on it for a while when I was writing one of the books. Until it got too cold. It's in dry-dock storage at the moment."

"It's been so long since I've been sailing." She kissed him. "We had so much fun on the *Carpe Diem*."

"Don't worry, sailing will come back to you." He pulled her arms away gently and looked into her eyes. "There's just one thing. You have to promise to talk to me if you are interested in another job. We're definitely not good at a long-distance thing. That means we'll have to figure something out together."

"I will. I promise. I made a horrible mistake before and missed you for ten years. I won't do that again. I know I want to spend the rest of my life with you. Wherever that might be."

Drew gave her a long look. "Me too. We've known each other for a long time, Bethie. I don't think anyone knows me better than you do."

Beth smiled. "I'm positive no one understands me like you do either. As the Grateful Dead would say, it has been a rather long, strange trip."

"You're right. And we should take the rest of it together." Drew moved and knelt on the floor in front of her, taking both of her hands in his and looking up into her face. "Will you marry me, Beth?"

A tear slipped out of the corner of her eye as Beth nodded vigorously. "Oh Drew…yes. Absolutely. Yes, I love you."

He moved up next to her and enveloped her in his arms. "I love you too. I never stopped."

Beth took off her glasses, wiped her eyes, and grinned. "I guess you'll have to change the dedication in the book to L.L. Emerson."

Drew hugged her again and looked into her eyes. "All right, but one last question. How about coming back to Alpine Grove with me? Just for a week or so? Then we can drive back here to Tucson with Dixie." He grinned. "I'm talking major road trip. With a puppy for added excitement and rest stops."

"That sounds wonderful. I can't wait to see little Dixie again."

Chapter 11

Epilogue

Drew navigated his old Ford Bronco around the mud holes and ice patches in Kat's driveway. He looked at Beth. "Spring break-up is gonna be bad this year."

"I think you're right. It's only a matter of time before this driveway turns into a morass of sucking mud. I hope Kat is aware of that fact."

"Well, she's gonna find out pretty soon now."

They got out and as she looked up at the trees, Beth took a deep breath and said, "It smells wonderful here. And it's starting to have that clean, light feeling in the air like spring might actually arrive soon."

Drew walked around the vehicle, took her in his arms, and kissed her. "Yeah, but it's still cold. This wimpy Southerner is glad we're heading south again for a while."

"I am too. Spring in the desert is pretty in its own way. The desert in bloom is striking."

"Not to mention the fact that spring arrives a whole lot sooner there."

Kat opened the door and walked down the steps carrying Dixie. Joel followed with the puppy's crate. At the bottom of the steps, Kat put the puppy down and Dixie ran toward Drew until she was halted by the end of her leash. "Easy there, Dixie."

Drew grinned and ran over to Dixie, crouching down. "Hey there, Dix! I missed you." The puppy wagged frantically and yipped, practically levitating at the sight of her favorite person.

Kat handed Drew the leash. "Here you go."

Drew collected Dixie in his arms and stood up. He looked at Joel. "You must be Cindy's brother. She told me a lot about you on our walks through the neighborhood."

Joel smiled. "I'll try not to think about what she probably said, but it's nice to meet you."

Beth walked up to the group, and Kat said, "Hi Beth. How's Arlo?"

"He's fine." Beth waved in the general direction of town. "We just came from my mother's house. She took him to the vet for a follow-up visit to discuss the new medication. I'm pleased to say that Mom got to experience the fat-dog lecture too, so she knows I wasn't kidding."

"I've heard that's one of Dr. Cassidy's favorites." Kat looked at Drew. "So it's kind of difficult to sneak up on this place, given the level of barking. I, uh, looked out the window when I heard the dog-alarm. I guess you two know each other…um…really well."

Joel looked down at Kat and arched an eyebrow.

Kat glanced at Joel and turned to Beth. "I'm sorry if I'm being nosy. I just didn't know you had met."

Drew grinned. "We met in high school. Actually we're getting married this summer. And you're officially invited."

Beth held out her left hand to show Kat her new ring. "Yes, we're engaged. I just told my mother and she is very excited. Although perhaps a bit surprised."

Kat shook her head. "Well, I sure had no idea. Congratulations!"

Drew readjusted Dixie in his arms. "Thanks. We're taking Dixie on a road trip back to Tucson now, but we'll be back later this spring after it warms up."

Beth said, "Drew is buying a house here, so we'll be migratory."

"Migratory?" Kat gestured toward the sky. "You mean like birds?"

Beth nodded. "We'll spend summers here and winters in Tucson. I'm finishing up my PhD and then it looks like I may be working for the University of Arizona. I'd just be an adjunct professor to start, but there is an assistant professor position that will be opening up in the computer science department. Someone was just let go because of a...well... a departmental personnel matter I suppose you might say. My dissertation adviser is putting in a good word for me."

Joel said, "Beth, that's great. With your experience, you'll be an excellent teacher."

Beth shrugged. "I am a bit nervous, since I am not used to speaking in front of people. But I definitely know the subject and my adviser is very supportive. So is Drew."

Drew smiled. "Once Beth sets her mind to something, she tends to figure it out. Anyone who can give a speech at graduation in front of half of Alpine Grove can deal with a few nerdy undergrads."

Beth said, "This summer my mother wants Drew to do a book-signing at her store."

Drew glanced at Beth. "I'm not sure that's a great idea."

Beth put her hand on his arm. "You realize that now that my mother knows, in this town, there is no secret anymore.

Virtually every resident of Alpine Grove will know within approximately thirty-six hours."

Kat said, "Know what?"

Beth said, "Drew writes novels. Are you familiar with the works of A.J. Emerson?"

Kat nodded vigorously. "I love those!" She turned to Drew. "Wait, you're A.J. Emerson? When is the next book coming out? I am dying to know what happened with Preston and Liz."

Drew smiled. "Yeah, I am. But I swear on my great-granddaddy's dear departed soul that if I tell you what happens, my editor would kill me and yank my new contract from my cold dead hands."

Beth looked at him and grinned. "It's true. He's not making that up."

They said their goodbyes and Drew and Beth loaded up Dixie and her crate into the Bronco. As they bumped down the driveway, Beth said, "People seem a bit surprised that we're getting married."

"I don't see why. If you know someone really well and being with that person makes you happy, why *wouldn't* you get married?"

"I don't know. There might be good reasons. All I know is that I'm glad I'm choosing to be happy with you."

"Me too, Bethie. Me too."

Thanks for Reading

Thank you for dedicating some of your reading time to *Bark to the Future*. I hope you enjoyed Beth and Drew's adventures and I wanted you to know that I'll be writing more books that will feature Kat, Joel and various other residents of Alpine Grove who bring dogs to the new boarding kennel. The sixth book, *Howl at the Loon*, is available along with ten other books in the series.

If you would like to be notified by e-mail when I release a new book, you can sign up for my New Releases e-mail list at SusanDaffron.com.

I know that not everyone likes to write book reviews, but if you are willing write a sentence or two about what you thought of *Bark to the Future*, I encourage you to post a review at your favorite book vendor site or share a message with your social networking friends.

If you would like to share your thoughts about the book with me privately, you can reach me through the contact page on the SusanDaffron.com web site.

I look forward to hearing from you!

~ Susan C. Daffron

Acknowledgements

Writing a novel is never easy and I'd like to thank my husband James Byrd for his support and encouragement throughout the writing and publishing process.

I'd also like to thank my alpha and beta readers for their eagle-eyed reading and great feedback:

- James Byrd
- Cynthia Daffron
- Dian Chapman
- Sheila at Frostbite Publishing

About the Author

S usan Daffron is the author of the Jennings & O'Shea series and the Alpine Grove romantic comedies, a series of novels that feature residents of the small town of Alpine Grove and their various quirky dogs and cats. She is also an award-winning author of many nonfiction books, including several about pets and animal rescue. She lives in a small town in northern Idaho and shares her life with her husband and three really cute dogs.

www.ingramcontent.com/pod-product-compliance
Lightning Source LLC
Chambersburg PA
CBHW020350120726
47904CB00002B/534